disc

This book shou ... or before
the due date.

NA1 9/19

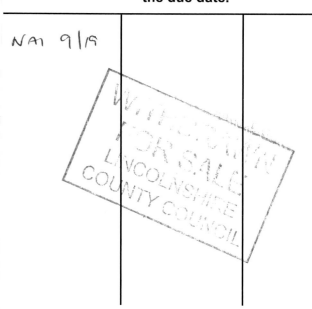

05252040

Acknowledgements

I wish to thank Dave and Jenni once again for their constant encouragement, help with editing and for their belief in me as an author.

I should also like to thank Jim Palmer, editor of 'Writer's Muse' magazine for his encouragement and support

BLACK VELVET

Sheila Adams

BB

First published in 2013 by Bredbury Books
Stockport, Cheshire

Typesetting by Dave Uttley.
Cover design by Sheila Adams and Dave Uttley

Printed and bound in Great Britain by Deanprint Ltd,
Stockport, Cheshire

ISBN 978-0-9564183-1-9

www.bredburybooks.co.uk

For Dave, Jenni and David with much love

1

I came to with a headache that thudded like a teenager's stereo. How long had I been unconscious? I hadn't a clue and it was too dark to see my watch. Where was I? Somewhere dark and dank, indoors, maybe a garage or a cellar. How had I got there? A chill penetrated my bones as I dredged that evening's events from my memory.

I cursed silently. I was in trouble, real trouble, and surprise, surprise - once again no-one knew where I was. My boyfriend Steve says I'll never learn and he's usually right. He was at work when I went out. I tried to remember if the case file was on the table, because as usual I hadn't left a note. But how was I to know I'd end up in danger when I set out?

My few functioning brain cells puzzled over why the routine surveillance of an errant husband could have gone so badly wrong, and I was forced to the conclusion that Howard Banks was probably a crook rather than an adulterer. To attack - and imprison - a skinny female private detective over an alleged affair would be excessive, even for one of my clients' spouses, and I did get some weird ones.

One minute I'd been keeping watch on the house Banks had entered. The next, I'd been grabbed from behind and silenced with a heavy glove across my mouth. I'd fought back, but my reward was a blow to the head.

It had started out as one of those cold nights you get in Hull when a chill wind blows in from the Baltic and lowers the temperature to Arctic depths. Despite wearing as many layers of clothing as possible, I'd begun to shiver not long after arriving in the street where Sue and Howard Banks lived. The heater's warmth had about as much impact as a candle in a sports hall. Hard to believe Easter had come and gone, and summer was supposed to be starting. I hate to say it, but I think Gran's right - the weather isn't what it used to be.

A glimmer of light from the front door meant Banks was on the move, just like his wife had said. A few moments later, his car glided past me. A top model Lexus. No problems for Howard defrosting and scraping. It probably had heated seats along with everything else. Was I jealous? Of course I was. I certainly wouldn't scoff next time Mum suggested I take along a hot water bottle on night surveillance.

When he'd reached the end of the road, I'd set off. There'd still been a few cars around, so I'd been able to slip behind a red saloon. Banks had driven faster once he'd reached the ring road, but I'd managed to follow him to a small industrial site off Sutton Road.

It seemed an unlikely spot for a romantic rendezvous, but there are no set rules for that sort of thing, as I well knew after four years of private detective work. I once tailed a man to the local, less-than-fragrant, council tip. A woman turned up on a motorbike and they climbed into a paper-recycling skip. The noises they made left little to the imagination. But I digress.

The Lexus had stopped at the end of a cul-de-sac. I'd just turned round past the entrance and killed the lights, when it sped off, back to the ring road. I'd not been able to see if he'd picked up anyone up.

When he'd headed towards Cottingham, a pleasant suburb of Hull, it'd seemed more like it. He'd stopped outside a house in a leafy avenue and gone up the path. I'd driven about fifty metres further on and jotted down the address. After about ten minutes, I'd got out to stretch my legs. It was bitterly cold. A brisk walk and a bit of clandestine snooping and I'd have called it a night. I'd easily be able to find out the name of the occupant and ask Sue Banks if she wanted me to do more. And that was when it'd all gone pear-shaped.

I guessed Banks must've noticed me following him earlier and pulled into the cul-de-sac to see if he was right, then he led me into a trap. The house in Cottingham was probably nothing to do with him. He must've gone up the path, climbed over into another garden and doubled back behind me. Although a small man, he'd proved to be stocky and strong. I'd been unable to move my arms to claw at his face, nor my legs to kick at his balls.

He might not be very tall, but Banks was turning into a 'Mr Big' in my mind. Before tonight I'd just had him down as a small, well-dressed bloke who told his wife he had to work a lot in the evenings. She didn't believe him, but I was beginning to. I knew for a fact he had his fingers in a lot of pies. He had a large garage consisting of a showroom selling upmarket cars, a workshop, and a small engineering works, but I'd checked them out and they shut at six. It looked as if his night-time activities were of the shady variety. Manufacturing of an illegal nature or tinkering with stolen cars perhaps.

I jerked back to the present. My hands were bound behind my back to some sort of post or solid object. I was lying on the floor, but my legs were tied together too. I couldn't move, but I could hear. And someone was coming.

I went from chill to boil in a matter of seconds. Panic caused a wave of heat to spread through my body and my stomach cramped with fear. I felt sick, and concussion wasn't the only reason. My battered head jumped to the inevitable conclusion. I was going to die.

There was a loud clanging as a roller shutter door opened. In the dim light I could tell I was in a garage workshop. A figure dressed in black entered. I heard a sharp intake of breath and then a familiar voice.

'What the… Rach, is that you? Are you alright?'

I nearly wept with relief, but that changed rapidly to panic as I realised Steve might be in danger too. 'Watch out for Banks, Steve. He - he's dangerous.'

'Well I think it's safe to say I knew that before you did, Rach. We've been after him for months. But how did you get yourself involved?'

'I just …'

'No, on second thoughts, don't answer that now. Let's get you out of here and home under a hot shower. There's no need to worry about Banks. He's on his way to a cell I've earmarked for him, and I'm going to find sending him to jail a whole lot sweeter after what he's done to you.'

'You mean you didn't look for my file when I didn't come home, go to Banks' house, find out the business properties he owns, and come rescue me?'

'I didn't know I needed to. I haven't been home yet tonight, love. Like I said, we've been watching Banks and his gang for a couple of months now. It was just your luck that we raided this garage of his tonight. It seems like you got caught up in something much bigger than you thought.' As he spoke, Steve was slicing through the plastic ties with his penknife.

'Ouch!'

'These plastic ties are really tight round your ankles, Rach. You're going to have some really colourful bruises when you wake up tomorrow. Come on, let's get you home.'

I sank gratefully into the passenger seat of Steve's car. As a police inspector, Steve was able to take the decision to drive me home, rather than take me to the police station. Banks was already in custody, so my written statement could wait until the next morning, but Steve wanted to know all the details then and there. As I explained how I had come to be following Banks, he groaned. 'Rach, I do wish you'd give up this job and find something safer to do.'

I hadn't the strength to answer and didn't feel this was the time to renew our long-standing argument over whether I should be a private detective. Steve didn't push it, but led me into his flat on Dagger Lane and undressed me. He helped me shower and tucked me up in bed. 'You've got skin as soft as velvet, Rach. I just wish you didn't insist on turning it black. Much as I'd love to stay, I have to go back to the station. Will you be okay on your own?'

I nodded.

'I'll get someone to pick your car up from Cottingham and I'll drive it back when I leave. Now get some sleep, love. I'll be careful not to wake you when I get back.'

When I woke up the next morning, Steve must have already left for work. I felt like I'd been hit by a truck – oh, and several hammers, and maybe even a pickaxe. There didn't seem to be a square inch of my body left unscathed. I tried to get up, but could only roll gingerly onto my side, feeling new pains as I unearthed new bruises. I knew without looking they would be dark red, purple, yellow and black, but not blue. I don't know why they say 'black and blue'. I'm the world's greatest expert on bruises. I bruise so easily, my mum could have been falsely accused of mistreating me when I was a child, if anyone had noticed. It's a wonder she didn't drag me to the doctors, worried I had leukaemia, but thankfully Mum didn't know the symptoms.

I lowered my legs over the side of the bed and stood up. What had happened to my feet? My ankles were a solid mass of pain. It was much, much worse than being hit by a hockey stick. Premiership footballers would be out of the game for six months if they had one ankle in this state, but I had to get up. I had to walk somehow. There was only one way I was going to feel better, and that was by making a statement to get Howard Banks a longer sentence than Steve's charges would bring on their own.

After a leisurely breakfast and the application of some ointment and some heavy supporting socks, I felt capable of walking the short distance to the police station. Even if I didn't run into Steve, I knew he'd be pleased with me for going and making a statement, and that would go some way towards deflecting his anger that my job had got me into trouble again. Our life had just about got back to normal and I wanted it to stay that way.

A fortnight previously, things had been a bit frosty, or at least on the cool side, between me and Steve, after he'd heard Pete refer to 'that cosmic kiss' when I was playing back my phone messages. After the initial stony silence, I'd managed to convince Steve that Pete had a vivid imagination and was just teasing me. At least I think I'd convinced him. Pete's an old school friend who I met up with again almost a year ago, after he'd moved back into the area. He gets me information from computers loath to part with private details, such as who owns a certain car. Girls queued up to go out with him in the sixth form, and things don't seem to have changed much since then, but for some reason he wanted to add me to his list of conquests.

However, there was a slight exaggeration in what I told Steve. Pete and I had actually kissed. I couldn't tell you if it was cosmic or not, because I'd had a couple of glasses of wine, and I'm usually tipsy after just the one, but I do remember it taking place. I just didn't think Steve needed to know.

As a result I was steering well clear of Pete since that phone call. My relationship with Steve had been going through an uncertain patch at the time Pete kissed me. Steve had been working all hours and I'd been having doubts about his commitment, so I was flattered by Pete's attentions and went out with him a few times, but I was really just lonely. Steve and I had since managed a mini-break to Bruges. Our romantic few days had made it easier to persuade him that he had nothing to worry about in the way of competition.

With Steve a busy police inspector, it was amazing we'd managed to get away. Now my social life was back to the very occasional trip to the cinema, rather than the wine bars and fancy restaurants that Pete had taken me to over the preceding few months, whilst Steve had been one hundred percent occupied in trying to track down a serial killer. In the end I was the one who found the killer, and I'd been lucky to escape with my life.

Towards the end of the investigation, I'd moved into Steve's flat for protection and we've been pretty close ever since. When he got home from work late that night I was quick to tell him I'd been to the station to make a statement. Then, before he could say anything, I jumped straight in with, 'Steve, I'm so sorry about last night. I should have let you know where I was going.'

'Are you sure you can't find an ordinary job?'

'You know most of my cases are dull as ditchwater.'

Steve nearly choked on his coffee. 'You've discovered two bodies and been abducted by a serial killer, all within the last six months. I wouldn't describe your life as dull. On second thoughts, make that abducted twice, after last night.'

'Alright, sometimes things have turned out a bit complicated...' Steve snorted. 'But the things that happened to me could have happened to anyone.'

'Only to you, love. Don't I always say: calamity follows you around?'

'Well, it wouldn't matter what job I did then, would it? Look, I promise to let you know where I'm going in future, and not to take any risks.'

Hard to believe when I look back, but that day I really did believe I'd just gone through an unusually dangerous patch in my work, and all would be plain sailing from then on.

3

A couple of days later Steve came home to his flat, the flat I'd moved into without the preliminary wedding, much to my mum's disappointment, and announced, 'I've got to go to Amsterdam.'

'Why?'

'The body of a Dutch bloke turned up in the marina overnight, and we've just found an absolute fortune in diamonds in the safe in his hotel room.'

'When are you going? Can I come?'

'No, sorry. There'll be no time for sightseeing. It's just a quick trip to see the Amsterdam police, interview his wife and business partners, and see we can trace the origin of the diamonds. I'm flying tomorrow. I'd have gone tonight but I've just discovered my passport ran out last week. I've brought the forms home. Do you think you could do me an enormous favour and drive over to Liverpool and get it renewed for me please, love?'

'Don't you have to turn up in person?'

'The boss has faxed through some sort of high security approval. If you take my old passport and the forms and new photos, they'll hand it to you. You did say you hadn't any new cases after the Banks fiasco.'

'Do I get one of the diamonds?'

'No, there may be thousands of pounds' worth, but they're evidence. I'll bring you something back, though, I promise.'

'Okay. Just give me the details.' For a second or two I did wish he'd at least joked about getting me a diamond set in a ring, but then I put it from my mind. He'd mentioned marriage out of the blue to prevent me moving out of his flat when we were chasing the serial killer. He'd not actually proposed, but the thought was already out there in the open between us, waiting for the right time.

I put the forms behind the clock where I'd see them easily and told Steve about my day.

The next morning I just nipped out for a pint of milk and called round to Mum's to tell her not to expect me for lunch as planned. I got back, thinking I'd have a quick coffee and then make tracks for Liverpool and the Passport Office.

'My keys, where are they?!' I scrabbled through my handbag but there was no sign of them, including the one to Steve's flat. I looked again, thinking I'd slipped them into a different part of my bag, willing them to appear this time, but came up with nothing. 'Damn!' I got back in the car, looked in the foot wells at the front and back, looked on the back seat and the little compartment below the gearstick where I sometimes toss things. I looked through my handbag again. I got out and walked to the door of the flat, scanning the path. I fished out my mobile and rang Mum. No reply. She must have gone out.

'Shit!'

I really had lost them. I keep my car keys separate from my house keys. I can't stand a big bunch hanging from the steering column and rattling. I tried Mum's mobile number. She cut me off. She can't get the hang of taking a call. I rang again and this time she answered. She was in the car with Dad. They were almost in York. She offered to come back to look if I'd left the keys at her house, but I said I'd ring Steve. I couldn't spoil her day out. She said she'd be back at about five, if I was still stuck, but that would be way too late. I needed to get in the flat to get those forms. There was nothing for it, I thought, after searching my bag yet again. I'd have to ring Steve.

The duty sergeant said he was in a meeting. He was going to be mad, and we'd have a major discussion about security and changing the locks. I decided I'd have to go to the police station and borrow his keys. I rang again and spoke to Matt, Steve's sergeant, asking if Steve's keys were in his drawer, and if so, could he bring them down to the front desk. No luck. This was getting worse. Steve'd kill me if I didn't get his new passport in time.

I knew he wouldn't have his mobile on in a meeting, but I left a message on Steve's voicemail to say I'd rush over straightaway as soon as he was free. I'd wait in the café in the marketplace.

I sat around, nursing a cup of tea, getting more and more worried the passport office would be closed by the time I got there. It was an hour later when I got a text from Steve saying curtly, "go home now". No 'love', nothing else. I was almost at the door when a squad car screeched to a halt, and a constable jumped out with the keys. 'I've got orders to drive you to Liverpool or you might not make it.' I grabbed the forms and we were off at ninety miles an hour with blue lights flashing and sirens blaring. Weaving in and out of traffic at that speed was scary, and I was almost sick a couple of times, but we got there twenty minutes before the office closed. People stared as I was escorted to the counter by a policeman, but I was so glad we'd made it, I couldn't care less. We drove back at a mere seventy miles an hour. All my efforts at starting a conversation were met by monosyllabic answers. I was never more pleased to get back and put my feet up with a cup of tea.

When I heard a knock on the front door at around half past seven, I was scared of what Steve would say. He was going to be hopping mad, but at least I'd got him his new passport.

As it was, he looked quite sheepish as he strolled in and kissed me on the cheek. 'It seems the Dutch police are sending someone over here, so I didn't need the passport for tomorrow after all. Jan Petersen, the man fished out of the marina, is known to them as a small-time crook. Sorry, love.'

'No, it's me who should be saying sorry. I messed up. Here's your keys.'

'Did you find your set or do we have to change the locks?'

'Can't find them. You can search my bag if you want, but I've looked everywhere.' Steve emptied it out on the coffee table while I warmed up his dinner in the microwave. After all the stress, I'd been starving when I got back from Liverpool, and had already eaten. I could see his bewildered look when he found a small stone (picked up when we walked on the beach together), a collection of car park tickets (I kept meaning to put them in the shoebox where I keep business receipts for my accountant), tampons, two sorts of lip gloss, a packet of paracetemol, plasters, a Swiss army knife, a birthday card I'd forgotten to post, my mobile, a sewing kit, a twist of string, assorted scraps of paper with directions, shopping lists and other notes on them, a condom, a piece of material I was hoping to match up, some toffees, a comb, a key ring with no keys (one of those pretend coins you put in a supermarket trolley), a brolly, a small magnifying glass, some Boots vouchers, a carrier bag, tissues, sunglasses in a case, a half-empty bottle of water and a DVD I'd copied for Mum with no title, along with the more usual items like a purse, chequebook and pen, but he drew a blank too.

He got my car keys off the hall table and went out to search the car, returning five minutes later holding my set of house keys triumphantly aloft.

'I knew you wouldn't have lost them, just mislaid them.'

'Where were they? I looked in the car. Everywhere.'

'There's a tiny little tray, maybe supposed to be an ashtray, at the side of the back seat, just below the seat. It's a bit out-of-sight.'

'That's a stupid place for a tray. I've never seen it. And how did my keys get there?'

'Same way your phone got right under the passenger seat the other week, love. Fell out of your bag. Like I said, I knew you'd have only mislaid them.' Sometimes I hate it when he's right, but I have to admit it saved me getting new keys, and probably new locks too.

4

The next morning I called round at my flat to see if there'd been any calls on the answer phone in my office (or spare bedroom, to be more exact). I was going to have to get it moved over to Steve's one day, but the logistics were beyond me. I suspected Steve could tell me what to do, but we never seemed to have that sort of conversation. And he might use the opportunity to tell me I should give up the flat, which I wasn't quite ready for yet. I needed a bolt hole just in case. In case of what, I wasn't sure, but I couldn't shake off the niggling worry he'd move on again, like he did after we'd finished university.

He'd moved down to London to the Met to climb up the police career ladder. He'd intended to keep seeing me and return to Hull after a couple of years, but somehow the days between contact lengthened to weeks and then months, and I'd thought he'd gone to London forever. Then he got promoted and came back up north as he'd always intended, and the rest is history, as they say.

I still had the odd day when I wasn't sure whether we had a long-term future. After all, so many police marriages fail, what with the long unsocial hours, and the natural desire not to talk about work, because of its often unsavoury nature. He was never around when I needed him for emergencies, like the day my car was involved in a hit-and-run. I had few, if any, single friends so my life was occasionally lonely. We hardly ever booked holidays, either, as Steve never knew when he might be called in to work.

However, I had my family and best friend Sarah for company when Steve was working under pressure. His working hours fit perfectly with the irregular nature of my job, we get on really well together and our sex life is great. And when we do manage to get away, we have a great time, like we did in Bruges. The weather was a little chilly, but every day of our four night break was sunny with blue skies. We'd wandered the streets and along the canals, taking photos and browsing the shops. Whenever we wanted to remind ourselves of our trip, I could wear the white cotton apron with a bib and lace frill, which Steve had bought for me. It was very demure. Not me, you might think, but worn with nothing underneath, the effect was the total opposite.

There were a couple of calls. One was from the council. I rang the number that'd been left and spoke to a Bob Hatcher of the Parks department. He wanted to know if I was able to investigate who might have been upsetting the wallabies in East Park. He'd had a report of a couple of lads hanging around and some cries from the wallabies, and when he'd gone out to look, there were lots of rubber bands in the enclosure. They must have been using them as catapults. Not exactly a major crime, but unpleasant enough. It was a bit too minor for the police, and Bob said I'd been recommended by his brother's neighbour, a Mr Phillips. I knew I'd done a good job for him, unmasking a pilferer at his factory, not to mention sorting out a disgruntled ex-employee, so I wasn't too surprised.

'What sort of age are we talking about, here? The lads, not the wallabies, I mean.'

'No more than eleven or twelve. They should have been in school.'

'Okay. I'll see what I can do.' I told him my rates and we agreed on a mix of investigation and observation over the next two weeks. He couldn't pay for more than that out of his budget. I took the name and address of the woman who'd reported seeing the lads. Who knows, maybe just my hanging around would scare them off.

At least the weather was finally beginning to show signs of warming up properly. It had been a long cold winter even by Hull standards. We'd had the usual warm week in early spring that had sent people scurrying to buy new barbecues and patio furniture, then it'd reverted to cool cloudy days and chilly nights. Typical English weather.

As I was putting the phone down, it occurred to me that if I spoke to the secretary at the local high school on the edge of the park, she might be able to tell me if they'd had any young truants - kids who couldn't settle to secondary school, perhaps. It's a wonder Bob Hatcher hadn't thought of that, but I wasn't going to tell him and lose myself a job.

The second call was from an Elaine Nicholson. She had adopted her daughter Chloe sixteen years ago, and now Chloe was ill. It was serious - her only hope for survival was a bone marrow transplant. There were no near matches on the donor register, and Elaine and her husband felt powerless because they didn't match either. She'd tried to track down Chloe's natural parents but was getting nowhere. I took her details and said I'd call her back by the weekend. I'd have to call on Pete, but if anyone could track someone down by trawling records and databases, then he was the man for the job.

I drove out to the high school before lunch. The secretary was a bit wary of admitting that truancy existed in their school, but these days there are statistics on everything to do with education, so it was no point her pretending she didn't know of any. So, when I went on to say I could probably clear it up before it got in the papers, she became amazingly helpful.

'Stuart Leggett and Ricky Leigh. First years. I bet it's them. I'll give you their addresses if you like.'

I didn't think she should give them to me, seeing as how I had no official status, but as Steve says, I look harmless enough and it's other people's hard luck if they don't know better. I told her I'd let her know what transpired. I thought I'd use my secret weapon, if he was amenable. There's nothing Steve likes better than a bit of community policing, or setting kids on the straight and narrow before it's too late, as Gran would say.

I was starving, and speaking of Gran, I'd promised to call round and see her. I couldn't face her on an empty stomach. Her idea of a snack wouldn't fill my little finger and her cake of choice is a slice of cheap Swiss roll, so I went to Morrison's and did a bit of a shop, then called back at my own flat to eat. I could have gone round to Mum's, but I knew she was going to Meadowhall with Auntie Lesley, because when I'd been round last time, Mum had told me so. Dad had rolled his eyes in mock horror at the thought of all the temptations to spend money in the massive out-of-Sheffield shopping centre. The only thing worse in his view, would have been going with her himself, to try to curb the spending.

I got to Gran's about half past two. I was outside a lot earlier but this large black dog emerged from nowhere and started barking at the car. I thought it might take my leg off if I got out, so I had to sit there till it sidled off. I can't help it. I'm scared of dogs. I get that from Mum. She was once riding her bike and this big dog ran alongside barking and jumping up. She was terrified she was going to fall off or that it would nip her foot or chew her skirt. She's never forgotten, and she reminded us whenever we saw a dog. It's no surprise I've turned out like I have.

Gran had a letter on the table. 'It's from The X Factor. I'm definitely going to be on the telly, our Rachel. Just wait till I tell your Mam. It'll be such a surprise.'

If I'd been eating, I'd have choked. 'I'm sure it will be, Gran. Do they say when?'

'No. Just that I've been selected for an appearance as one of the unlucky ones who didn't get through to the second stage.'

I stirred my tea and wondered if the Meadowhall trip would leave Mum in high enough spirits to cope with the revelation that Gran would be on TV, singing a Tina Turner song, dressed in scraps of red satin. She can't sing and she'd look ludicrous – I should know, I got shanghaied into driving her over to Leeds for the auditions - and they'd obviously only picked her because she was really bad, not because she'd almost made it through. I felt sure Mum must've put it out of her mind. I know I had. I could picture her face now. She'd be mortified and dreading the neighbours seeing.

'Well that's really exciting, Gran. Good for you.' I knew Gran was really chuffed. I couldn't begrudge her the thrill of being on TV, and anyway, I didn't live just round the corner, unlike Mum. The only consolation for Mum was that Gran is Mum's mother, not Dad's, so her surname is Maudsley, not Hodges.

'Have you any news? Has Steve popped the question yet?'

'No, Gran, but I think he's working up to it.' I could have told her instead about the other questions he'd asked the previous night as we lay in bed, but I kept them to myself. She thinks I'm saving myself for my wedding night. She told me all her other news. Mavis's budgie had died and she'd asked Gran to help bury it. Typical Gran, she'd told Mavis to flush it down the toilet, as it was nothing but skin

22

and bone. I told her about my latest cases. She hoped I'd find a relative for the transplant and said the lads from the park needed a clip round the ear and she'd sort them out if I wanted.

Before I knew it, it was nearly five. Steve wasn't going to be too busy until the Dutch police inspector turned up. That meant he wouldn't be more than an hour late, which was good as I needed his help. On the way home, I called round to show the witness the photos I'd somehow got from the school secretary. You might think I'd been lazing around half the day visiting Gran, but I was waiting for my witness to get home from work. She'd spotted them on her day off, but wasn't normally around during the day. She recognised them from the photos straightaway. Now all I needed was a handy policeman who was feeling full of his favourite food, and that would be one case solved and I could submit the bill when I liked.

And bless him, Steve agreed, after he'd had gammon with a mound of mashed potato and cauliflower cheese. They do a nice frozen mixture in Sainsbury's – cooking isn't my strong point. We drove round to each of their houses and by the time Steve had finished with them, they'd apologised and seemed genuinely sorry for what they'd done. Not content with that, Steve made them agree to go down and help the park warden muck out the wallaby shelters. Then he said he'd be keeping a personal eye on them, and they'd end up with a police record if they missed school or got up to anything else. It helped that their parents supported Steve. Some don't care, or openly defend their kids when they're caught up to no good. Steve said he'd have hauled them down to the station, if he'd thought the message hadn't got across. Job done, we went home and had a couple of glasses of wine and one of our infrequent early nights.

5

The next day Steve went to work with a skip in his step and I felt able to contact Pete without being swept along by his flattery.

'Hi Pete. How's things? I've got a job for you, if you've time to help me out.'

'Who's that?'

'It's me. Rach.'

'I know. I'd recognise your voice anywhere, Rach, but it's been a while. When I last rang, I seem to remember Steve answered and made it clear my call wasn't welcome.'

Oops. I'd forgotten that call, and also that I'd not actually spoken to Pete since catching the serial killer.

'Sorry, Pete, I really am. I should have called you and let you know how things turned out. Things were a bit manic at the time and then Steve and I took a holiday in Bruges to get over it all. I've not been back that long'.

'That's okay; I won't hold it against you. I've been out of town myself for a week or so. Bahamas. Next time I go, you should come along. It's a bit warmer than Belgium. I'd be glad of your company,

25

and that trip to Bruges is probably the only trip Steve will take you on this year.'

'You're probably right, but no offence, I don't want to go away with another bloke. Steve and I are really close now. We're living together.'

'Oh, right. I didn't realise. I'm pleased for you, Rach, I really am!'

There was an awkward pause. I didn't know what to say. I thought of the times he'd been there for me when I'd needed help, when Steve was too busy working. I did like Pete. He was exciting and very attractive, but I thought back to the last time I'd seen him, the time when I'd embarrassed him in the most exclusive restaurant in Hull, first by spilling red wine over the pristine white tablecloth and then by catching my heel in my skirt as I stood to leave, exposing stockings and suspenders to the other diners. Pete hadn't been pleased, whereas Steve would've thought it hilarious.

Pete was still talking. 'Anyway, you know where I am if Steve lets you down, and we can still be friends, can't we?'

'Course we can.' He always had so many glamorous girls in tow, I was a little taken aback at his reaction, but really glad he didn't seem to bear a grudge. I wouldn't like to lose him as a friend, and not just because I'd still need his help every so often. I went on to give him the details I had for Chloe Nicholson and he promised to get on with trying to trace her natural parents or any other close relatives.

I called round at Mum's on the way home.

'It's just not fair.'

'What isn't, Mum?' I presumed she meant Gran's future appearance on TV but that wasn't all.

'I'm fed up of sport on the telly, Rachel. There's golf on all day and they're already on about the football World Cup. It's driving me crazy. Your dad says I won't let him have Sky Sports so I shouldn't mind putting up with it when it's on ordinary telly, but it's on all the time at the moment. I know we have the recorder, but I never get chance to watch what I've taped.'

'So, Mum, does that mean you wish summer was over already and the X Factor was back on again?'

'You know I'm dreading that this year now Gran's had that letter and she's likely to be on it. I'm just a bit fed up, that's all. I've not been sleeping very well either with hot flushes and that. Your dad doesn't seem to understand.'

'I can't help with those, Mum, but I could try to explain to Dad how you feel. I'm sure he'd be more sympathetic if he realised what you're going through, and if there's something you're desperate to watch, you can come round to Steve's when he's working, if you want.'

'Well, you won't get anywhere with your Dad, but thanks for the offer to come round. Maybe next week one night.'

'Just give me a ring and I'll pick you up. Now let's get a drink and sit in the garden and you can tell me the latest.'

'I think Gran's got a bit of business for you. She bumped into Mrs Foster this morning – remember her? She used to live next door to Gran before she was moved into sheltered accommodation. Anyway, she wants you to check out the factory across the road from her bungalow.'

'I thought Mrs Foster was a bit loopy. Do you think she can afford to pay me anything, or will it be another of Gran's favours?'

'Why, are you short, Rachel? I can give you ten pounds if you are.'

'No, Mum. I'm fine. It's just that Gran keeps finding me cases that bring in no money and I get involved in them and then a paid case comes along and I'm rushing round like mad, because I'm trying to do both. As it happens, I'm free at the moment. I rang the council this morning after finding and sorting out the kids who were messing about in the park, and I only have to invoice them. Then I'm just waiting for information in connection with another case.'

'Oh, good. Gran asked if you could call round to Mrs Foster's this afternoon. If you pick Gran up, she'll interpret for you. I know Ida's hard to understand.'

Talk turned to family and I left around half past eleven.

The afternoon saw Gran and I being manhandled into Mrs Foster's bungalow just off Hedon Road. She shut the door behind us.

'Did anyone see you?'

'I couldn't see anyone, Mrs Foster.'

'Good. You've got to stop it happening. It's the factory over the road. They've murdered Henry and he's not the only one.' Her voice faltered, and she looked near to tears.

'Now, Ida. Stop carrying on, so. It's not that bad,' Gran snapped.

I looked at Gran. I couldn't believe what I was hearing. Since when was murder 'not that bad'?

'Ida,' I said as kindly as I could, 'perhaps you could tell me what happened and I'll make some notes.' I wanted to reassure her that someone would be taking her seriously.

'Don't waste your time, Rachel,' Gran interrupted. 'We're here to investigate the goings-on at the factory across the road, not Henry's death. It'll have been his own fault anyway, I expect.'

There she went again. Treating this Henry's killing as if it was nothing at all, with no thought for poor Ida.

'Well, I'm sure Ida would like it investigating, and that's what she asked me round for.' And less of the "we", I thought, but I didn't dare say it out loud to Gran. 'Have the police been called in?' I asked Ida.

Gran snorted. 'No need for them. He'll have just gone and got himself run over, I expect.'

My face paled, but then it suddenly dawned on me. I must have been having a slow day.

'Henry – was he, err, a flesh and blood relative?'

'He's my cat. Who did you think we were talking about?'

'It doesn't matter. So, Ida, what's the connection between Henry's death and the factory from over the road? Do you think a sudden noise frightened him and he ran under a car?'

Ida looked up. 'He wasn't run over. They killed him and sold his body. And it's not just him. Others have gone.'

'Which others?'

'Blackie from number twelve, Sooty from number fifty-seven and my Henry. They're all black cats and they'll be used for Black Magic, you mark my words.'

This conversation was beginning to turn surreal.

'Did Henry have a collar?'

'He's a cat not a dog. I don't take him for walks on a lead.'

'Well, forgive me for saying this, but if he was run over, the Council wouldn't know who owned him and they'd have taken his body away.' The same could apply to the other cats too, I thought, if they were all owned by little old ladies in sheltered accommodation who wouldn't think to buy a cat a collar, or wouldn't have the money for one.

'No. It's all a plot. They're killing them and selling their bodies. I need you to do something about it. They're there till real late at night. I can hear them.'

I decided it was time I was out of there, before I became as loopy as Ida.

'Alright, Ida, I'll investigate the noises at the factory, but I'll also ring the Council and see if they've collected any dead cats lately.' Ida crumpled again at the words 'dead cats', so Gran and I saw ourselves out.

'There must be something going on at that factory, Rachel. Ida wouldn't be making it up,' Gran said as we were leaving.

'I'm sure there's an innocent explanation but I will look into it, I promise, Gran.'

'Oh, I'd steer well away from it if I were you. I didn't realise till I saw the sign, but that caravan factory's owned by Simon Robinson.'

'So?'

'Wait till we get back. I'll tell you more over a cup of tea. I'm parched. That Ida didn't even offer us a drink.'

After we were settled with a cup of tea and a custard cream, Gran had kept me waiting long enough, so I asked her what she knew of Simon Robinson.

'I knew his father, James, a long time ago. He used to live next door to my friend Mary. A handsome man, and good too. He'd help anyone. He made a lot of money in the building trade. He wanted to set up both his sons, Luke and Simon, in the caravan business. You know there's a lot of call for them round here. But it wasn't for Luke. He went off to university and became a doctor. He moved down south somewhere.'

I nodded and waited for Gran to get to the point. She would eventually, but she generally went all round the houses first.

'Well, Luke might well be a nice lad, but Simon was a naughty kid, always in scrapes, and he didn't

31

improve, by all accounts. Seems he turned out to be a right nasty piece of work. You wonder where it comes from, don't you? Nice family like that. It can't have been his genes. Must've been the people he mixed with. I can't tell you much about him now. Mary's not mentioned him since she moved. Anyway, you want to steer clear of him, our Rachel. I doubt he'll have anything to do with the cats, but there may be something going on at the factory.'

'All the more reason to look into it.'

'You won't get paid for it. Just give Ida a report when you've checked with the Council. She'll not pay you for that either, but it'll get her off my back. I'd already thought of them but I didn't want to suggest anything in front of her, because you're supposed to be the detective.' I grinned at that. Gran obviously thought she was just as capable of doing my job. 'And anyway, she wouldn't take my word for it.'

'Yes, I see, but maybe the noise and lights at night mean something's really going on?'

'Rachel, don't even think about it. The last case you went out at night, you came out of it black and blue, and if Simon Robinson's involved in anything, it could end up turning out the same.'

I sighed. I should stop telling Gran about my work, but she'd wheedle it out of me somehow. I didn't want her worrying, but I thought it was worth investigating, so I changed the subject for both our sakes.

'I forgot to ask, Gran, how was the meal?'

'You mean the social club do? It was a disaster.' Gran's face lit up with the realisation that I was a new audience for her tale. 'The food was alright but that's about all that was. When we got there, they herded us into this big room and there was a long table right down one side. Betty and I got ourselves chairs with our backs to the middle of the room, but the ones who moved slower, those with Zimmer frames and sticks - they had to sit on the benches with their backs to the walls. It took them ages getting in, and of course when one of them wanted to go to the toilet it was a right carry-on, because they all had to get up to let whoever it was, out. Those organisers had no sense at all. Fancy having benches for old folks to sit on – and pushed against the wall, too!'

'Oh dear,' I said sympathetically, though Gran seemed to be relishing the memory.

'It gets worse. I had this old woman next to me. I had to cut up her food and wipe her chin because she dribbled when she ate. I hope I don't get like that when I get old.'

I laughed. 'No chance, Gran. You'll still be the one sorting the others out when you're a hundred.'

She grinned and went on, 'and then the coach didn't come to pick us up till four o'clock. Betty wanted me to call us a taxi so we could escape, but the coach could have turned up any minute and that was free. A taxi from Walkington back to Hull would have cost us a fortune. I thought as how I should write to the Hull Daily Mail, so they could do an article exposing the mistreatment of old people

33

but Betty said no-one'd be interested, and I should write a letter to a woman's magazine instead and I might win myself ten pound.'

'Maybe you should, Gran. It'd pay for your meal, at any rate. I'm afraid I've got to get off now though.'

'That's alright. I've got things to do as well, you know.'

I drove home, chuckling at the thought of regaling Steve with the tale of my afternoon with Gran. I just wouldn't mention the fact that I planned on visiting Simon Robinson's factory one night. What he didn't know wouldn't hurt him.

6

I got a text on the way home. It was from Steve to say an inspector from Holland had come and he had to entertain, so I should eat without him. I thought of that old Dutch TV detective show, Van der Valk, and wondered if the inspector was laid back and good-looking like him. Or maybe he'd be like the Swedish Wallander, not very talkative, and tired-looking. It'd be interesting to find out from Steve when he got in, though he's not the best at gossip. Of course, Steve could have asked me along as well, but they were probably talking shop and I'd be a spare part.

There were a few things I'd taped that Steve didn't like. Normally I'm all up-to-date but with Steve getting home a bit earlier since he'd caught Banks, I'd built up a bit of a backlog. 'Sundi, how do you fancy a night of Desperate Housewives?' I asked my bear. His face didn't register any pleasure, but he didn't object either. 'I'll take that as a 'Yes' then.'

I waited up till nearly midnight, but Steve wasn't in. Maybe they'd gone back to the station. I gave up and went to bed. In the morning I woke alone. Where on earth had he got to?

When I turned my phone on, there was a text to say, sorry he hadn't got home, a few of them had made a night of it. I don't leave my phone on overnight. I like my sleep too much.

I rang the station but his sergeant said he was tied up in a meeting. I sent a text asking if he'd be home to eat and then put it out of my mind. Later I got to wondering if he'd had to pay for a hotel room. Surely a taxi home would have been cheaper?

I had some shopping to do and I needed to make a trip to the bank. The morning flew by. I rang Steve at lunchtime when I'd not heard from him, but he was 'out of the office'. I was beginning to think he was avoiding me. I asked the sergeant how long the Dutch inspector would be stopping. If he liked to spend his evenings in a foreign town carousing till the early hours, I'd like to know how long it'd be before he'd be on his way home. The answer stunned me. I finished the call quickly so I wouldn't make a scene on the phone. I was hopping mad. I dialled Sarah, my best friend. 'He's having an affair!'

'You what? Calm down, Rach, and tell me everything.'

'He stayed out all night with the Dutch inspector and she's a woman.'

'Just him? Are you sure none of the others were there?'

'No, I'm not sure, but I bet they weren't. He's not even spoken to me since the day before yesterday. It's just been the odd text. He's guilty as anything and he's avoiding me. What shall I do? Move out and back into my own flat?'

'Now don't get carried away. Why don't you dress in something decent and turn up at the station with some excuse? See if you can spot her and see what she's like first?'

'I'd end up having it out with him and I couldn't confront him there. No, I'll wait till he gets home.'

'Are you sure it's not completely innocent anyway? You know what you're like for getting the wrong end of the stick. She could be an old battleaxe. Even if she's the best looker in the world, he loves you, Rach. Just because he got the worse for wear and didn't come home. She might be staying at a hotel out of town, and it was easier to stay than get a taxi and then have to trail back for his car. You know what Steve's like about being separated from his Alfa.'

'Alright, I'll give you that, but why did he text instead of ring?'

'Maybe he thought you'd be asleep. Maybe he's focussing on trying to make a good impression and he's really busy. He probably thought you'd understand, Rach. And don't forget it's not five minutes since you gave him cause to doubt you with Pete. You're hardly whiter than white.'

'There was nothing for Steve to worry about. I was just going out with Pete because things were a bit on-off with Steve at the time and he was never home while he was on the serial killer case.'

'Exactly. Just a false impression you gave. It'll be the same with this inspector, I bet you. She'll be off back to Holland any day. Why would Steve play away when he's got you?'

'He could have been too drunk to turn her down.'

'Now you are being silly. Over the limit to drive maybe, but never too drunk to know what's going on. That's just not Steve's style.'

'Mmm... You're probably right. I was just so annoyed he didn't tell me it was a woman. It made it seem like he has something to hide. I'll try and put it out of my mind. Wait for him to tell me.'

'That'll be best. Now can I get back to the ironing while Josh is quiet?'

'Sorry, Sarah. I'm a right pest, I know I am.'

'Don't be daft, Rach. What are friends for? Will you have time for a cuppa tomorrow morning?'

'About eleven?'

'Okay. See you then – and don't worry!'

Sarah was right, as she usually was. When you start to get stressed about something it pays to talk it over with your best friend. Steve got home the usual time that night and told me all about Anna Rijkhart, the Dutch inspector.

'Anna had this young constable with her, Dirk. She went to bed early after ringing her family back home, so we got lumbered with the lad. He'd never been to England and wanted to see a real English pub. Matt came up with the bright idea of going out to Cherry Burton to an old-fashioned country pub then afterwards Dirk wanted to go clubbing and we went to this place in Beverley not far from Matt's flat. Around two o'clock we put Dirk in a taxi back to his hotel. I walked Matt back to his as he was the worse for wear and I fell asleep on his sofa. I'm sorry I didn't let you know, love, but I didn't want to wake you.'

'That's alright. I did wonder if I'd upset you or something when you didn't ring today, but I figured you only had time to send me a quick text.'

Steve put his arms around me and kissed me. Thank God for Sarah. I'd have been having a go at him as soon as he walked in the door otherwise.

'So does she know why the bloke with the diamonds was over here?'

'His name was Jan Petersen apparently, and Anna didn't go into detail, because it now seems his death was accidental. She'll be taking his body and the diamonds back to Holland tomorrow when the paperwork's finalised, and taking it from there. I somehow don't think we'll have heard the last of it, but she knows where we are, if she needs anything from this end.'

'Can you be sure it was an accident?'

'Definitely. Jan Petersen was seen drinking heavily in 'The Ship', bitter and whisky chasers. Barman said he'd refused to serve him any more at around ten, and he almost fell off his stool when he left. It was packed in there, so he admits he didn't actually see him leave, or call him a taxi. I think at the time he was glad to see the back of him, but now he's feeling guilty he didn't look after him, since his pub's right by the marina. Anyway, the post-mortem shows no external injuries of any sort, just lungs filled with salt water, and a large quantity of alcohol in his blood. In other words, it looks like he lost his bearings while under the influence, strayed too near to the edge, fell in and drowned. He would have been too drunk to haul himself out or swim.'

We watched TV but straight after the news Steve said, 'I'm knackered, I'm afraid. Matt's sofa was so uncomfortable, I didn't get a lot of sleep last night. I can hardly keep my eyes open.' So we went to bed.

It had been really quiet on the work front. I was still waiting to hear back from Pete on the tracing of Chloe Nicholson's natural parents but that was it, apart from the possibly imagined events at Simon Robinson's factory. So I didn't expect much when I played back the messages on my office answerphone the next morning. Three messages. Wow! I could do with the work, but it seemed like a famine would be followed by a feast again, and I'd be struggling to cope. Maybe I could take Steve's kid sister, Carly, up on her offer to help me out, if she'd still not found a holiday job. She'd be breaking up from university any day.

I looked around as I waited for the answerphone tape to start, mulling over whether I could let her stay in my flat, so she didn't cramp our style. She could hardly travel over from Leeds every day.

Should I hold onto the flat or let it go? I'd been living continuously with Steve for over a month now and I wondered if we should have a talk about making my move permanent after all. It seemed silly to have any doubts about him now.

My thoughts were interrupted by a pleasant female voice asking me to ring her regarding an insurance matter. Strangely, she said I'd been recommended by Humberside Police.

The second caller was a man. He said he was worried that his son had gone and got himself involved in bad company, maybe even drugs. Finally, I heard the dulcet tones of my favourite solicitor's clerk. He only called me about once a month but when he did, he provided me with a lot of bread-and-butter work, serving papers on people and tracking down beneficiaries of wills. He said he'd got ten lots of papers to serve and another couple of jobs that would take longer, and could I call him.

Phew! Not just three jobs then, but at least a dozen. I sent a text to Carly, asking if she was still interested in a week's work, maybe more, and if so, was now a good time to ring.

In the meantime I sorted through the post, mainly circulars, then went round the flat with the vacuum cleaner, dusting and tidying as I went. I didn't want to return calls and promise a timetable based on having an nineteen-year old sidekick, and then be unable to come up with the goods.

When I finished vacuuming, I found that Carly had sent me a text, saying work would be great and I could ring her anytime. I hadn't heard it come in. You can't hear anything above that cleaner. I made myself a cup of tea and dialled her mobile, settling down to catch up on news. A lot younger than Steve, Carly was coming to the end of her second year at York University, studying Archaeology. She came over every six weeks or so to see her big brother, only a lot of the time he was working, and I went

41

shopping with her or to the coast. As a result, we'd spent a lot of time chatting, and we got on well together.

After we'd caught up on general news, I asked her when she finished uni and if she'd like to work for me for a couple of weeks at least, maybe more.

'That'd be great, Rach. It's really hard to get work these days and I was worrying that I'd have no money. I can see myself as a private detective. I'm getting a dab hand at forensic archaeology. Who knows, maybe I'll enjoy it so much, I'll change my career plan.'

'I don't think that would go down well with Steve. You know what he thinks of my job. But if I promise him I won't give you anything that could turn serious, then I think he'll agree, particularly if it means he'll get to see more of you.'

'Yeah, Mum won't mind me working in Hull. It's not that far from home. The only problem is that I don't want to outstay my welcome in your flat, playing gooseberry to my brother.'

'Well, I've been thinking about that, and I was wondering if you'd like to stay in my old flat, if you wouldn't find it too lonely. That way, your mum could come over when she's not working and you could go to the coast together. Then I wouldn't feel guilty about taking you away from her, as you've been away since Easter.'

'That sounds a great idea. I'll speak to Mum and get back to you, but I should be able to start in the middle of next week.'

7

That conversation over, I rang back each of my callers in turn and arranged to meet up with them so I could decide what Carly could do, and schedule in a start date for each. First I rang Susie at the solicitor's office. After speaking to her, I knew that Carly could do all the work, and I'd give her the fees. The jobs serving papers nearly all had contact addresses at their workplace where no-one was likely to get aggressive, even if they were getting news they didn't want. The other jobs required a bit of digging around on the Internet, possibly asking Pete for help, but I'd try and keep her out of his clutches, and I was sure she was bound to be more computer-literate than I was, so she'd be able to do more herself.

Next I dialled the number of the father who'd left a message. He said he couldn't talk at that moment, and asked if I could I call later. From that I read that his son was within earshot. I said I had a lot of work on and asked if his job could wait a week or so, or did he want to try someone else? He said he could wait, as long as it wasn't too long, so I arranged to call in and see him the next morning, just to get the details.

Finally I rang the lady from the insurance company. I'd saved her till last because her call intrigued me. I wondered who'd recommended me, and if it was something new and exciting, or just run-of-the-mill and boring.

'Clare Brenner? Rachel Hodges here, private investigator. You left a message on my phone.'

'Rachel, I hope you don't mind my calling you by your first name, but I've heard a lot about you. Thanks for ringing me back. I work for Thompson and Brenner. We specialise in insuring artwork. I've got a job you may be able to help me with.'

'Rachel's fine. What can I do for you?'

'I'm looking into the theft of some rather expensive paintings. The police have done their bit, but they haven't come up with anything concrete, and I could do with someone local to make enquiries on our behalf. It'll cost us a fortune to pay out on the insurance so we tend to stick in there, long after the police have put such cases on the back burner because they have other work to pursue. No-one got hurt so it's low on their list of priorities.'

'But why are you ringing me? What can I do that you can't?'

'Well, the thefts all seem to follow the same pattern and are from private collectors in the North Yorkshire and Humberside area, and I'm based in the South near Basingstoke. I can't be everywhere and you came recommended as someone who was good at digging around and solving puzzles.'

'Who was it that recommended me, if you don't mind my asking?'

'DI Jordan, Humberside Police. I gather you helped him track down a murderer and he said to you at the time that you should consider a career in the police.'

I laughed as I remembered my confusion when Inspector Jordan had introduced me to the widow of the deceased. I'd had another woman in mind totally, one I'd seen holding hands with the victim, a few days before he'd been murdered.

'Right, what is it exactly that you want me to do?'

'Are you willing to work for us, then? If so, could we meet, please? I can manage to come up there on a flying visit, enough to hand over the information and photos I've got and tell you what we'd like you to do.'

I arranged to meet her the following Tuesday. I was looking forward to it. It seemed like an interesting job and a new departure from what I was used to doing.

It was almost time to go and meet Sarah, but I decided to call Pete first and see if he'd got anywhere with tracking down Chloe's natural parents. He was his usual charming self, just stopping short of all-out flirtation. After we'd got that out of the way, he gave me a couple of leads, so I added those to my increasing list of work.

Sarah was in a great mood. Little Josh had got most of his teeth, the weather was warmer and he didn't seem to be snuffling and having trouble breathing, so she and her husband John were finally getting some decent nights' sleep and they had a sex life again. I was glad for her as she'd been going through a low patch. We had a cuppa while Josh giggled as he watched some bright-coloured TV show, and I could see that motherhood might not be the total nightmare I'd envisaged, though it still wasn't for me.

'So what did you find out about your Dutch rival?'

'Not a lot. I thought over what you said and decided Steve wasn't the sort for a one-night stand, particularly after the nights we've been having together lately. I let him tell me before I flew off the handle for a change. Good job I did, as it turned out it was the woman's young male sidekick who'd kept them out in Beverley, and Steve had crashed at Matt's. They're off back to Holland tomorrow. '

'Very sensible, Rach, Totally unlike you, I must say, but very sensible. I'm impressed!'

'Well you're the one who calmed me down, you should take the credit.'

'I think it's like you say, you and Steve have got so much closer now, and you're starting to trust him. You may have had a bad moment at first, but that's just old habits. You soon settled down.'

'Yeah. I'd better be going now, though. I've got a lot of work on.'

I used the rest of the day to follow up the leads Pete had given me - addresses of two women called Susan Earnshaw. Someone of that name had given up Chloe for adoption, but Pete wasn't sure without ringing or calling round, and I wasn't paying him to do that. I rang the first number in Anlaby and a pleasant voice answered. She was sorry, but she'd never had a child, though she would have loved one. She sounded as if she was telling the truth, so I thought I'd try the other number. This one was further out from Hull, in Sproatley, a large village on the road to the coast.

Once again I explained my business and this time I knew I'd hit gold straightaway. There was a sharp intake of breath, so loud I could hear it, followed by a long silence. Luckily this Susan seemed to be on her own and could talk freely, and once she started, she didn't stop.

'I grew up on a farm and got pregnant when I was only thirteen. There was an older man who worked for my dad. He was always friendly, giving me a hug and a peck on the cheek when I passed him in the yard, but one day when I was in the farmhouse on my own, he came in to make a hot drink, and well... I was young for my age and I didn't really understand what was going on until it was too late and he was hurting me.'

'It's alright. You don't have to go into detail.' By the sounds of it, she'd been raped, and I didn't want to put her through re-living the experience.

'He said that if I told anyone he'd say it was my fault for encouraging him, and of course I remembered that I had let him hug me. I was so ashamed I didn't want to tell anyone anyway. It was awful seeing him every day, but before I realised I was pregnant, he died in a motorbike accident. Just as well really, or my dad would have likely enough beaten him up or even killed him, and that would have torn our family apart.'

'In a way, it was a relief then,' I said.

'Yes, but by the time I told my mum, there was nothing anyone could do about it. I was too far along for an abortion, and I don't think Mum would have approved of one anyway. She told me I hadn't been to blame but I was too young to be a proper mother. She arranged for the baby to be adopted, and said it would be all for the best if we forgot everything about it. Mum and Dad satisfied themselves that the baby was placed in a loving home where she would be well looked after by someone who couldn't have children herself. The baby was taken away before I saw her. I only knew she was a girl.'

Susan paused, before continuing. 'When I met my husband, Mike, seven years had passed. Just as Mum had suggested, I'd decided my only option was to put the whole thing out of my mind, and get on with my life. I told Mike when he asked me to marry him. He's a good man and he said he understood. We have two children, a boy and a girl, and we're happy.'

I was worried that the revelation could have broken up someone's marriage, but the phone call seemed to be a release rather than a threat. Susan was older now, and though my call was a tremendous shock, she said she'd always known in the back of her mind that one day her daughter would contact her. I gave her Elaine Nicholson's details and she said she would ring straightaway. If she could be a donor, then she could make up for giving her daughter away.

I was pleased to bits that it had worked out so well. I didn't doubt that Susan would ring Elaine as promised, and I was right. Elaine phoned an hour or so later and was full of thanks and more hopeful for Chloe's future now. I love it when I get a happy ending. I felt so pleased I almost didn't want to send a bill, but I told myself not to be so sentimental, and rattled it off before I changed my mind.

I called at Mum's on the way back to Steve's flat. When I told her the good news, she started to fill up with tears. 'Oh, Rachel, that's fantastic. I must admit sometimes your job does seem to be really worthwhile. That reminds me, though. Gran says Mrs Foster's driving her crazy about the noises in the warehouse. Gran told her to phone the police if she was that worried, but she said she thought you should check it out first because she didn't want to look a fool again. It makes you wonder if she's rung the police about before, doesn't it?'

'I'll go round later tonight, Mum, honest. I'd best be off now and get Steve's tea ready. Say hello to Dad for me, won't you.'

There was a frosty moment before she said, 'when I see him, I will. He went round next door to Geoff's when I told him I was sick of the golf on the telly all day.'

'Oh dear. I'm sure Dad'll be back after the weekend when the golf's over.'

'He'll be back by teatime, if I know your dad. Geoff can't cook. At least I've been able to catch up on a few things I wanted to watch on TV. I'm just annoyed, that's all, but don't you worry your head about it. Give my love to Steve.'

'I will. Bye, Mum.'

Well, her plan might have backfired, but I bet that once the golf was over, all would be well in the Hodges household again, at least till football fever broke out.

When Steve got home, I could see he was a bit low. 'All those months of observation and we could only charge Banks with handling one stolen car. The CPS said the evidence wasn't strong enough for anything else. Someone must have tipped him off about our raid. I wish I knew who it might have been.'

'I'm sorry, but it might have been me, Steve.'

'But you didn't know anything about what he was up to at the garage.'

'I know, Steve, but think about it. When he caught me following him, he hit me and tied me up, and that gave him time to get rid of the evidence. I doubt very much that he knew I was following him because his wife thought he was cheating on her. He must have thought I was connected with the police, and therefore you were on to him. Your raid came after I'd been there most of the night. That's how they'd cleared everything out but one stolen car by the time you turned up. I didn't know where I'd been held. They probably planned to dump me somewhere far away after they'd got rid of everything incriminating.'

'You're right, Rach. Although I wouldn't have wished it on you, I have to say it's a good job we got him for abduction and wrongful imprisonment as well as the odd stolen car. Surely he'll get a stretch in prison for that, at least.'

When I told him about Susan, he cheered up no end, though his reaction was rather different to Mum's. 'Well, credit where it's due, Pete did a good job for you,' he said somewhat condescendingly.

'Well, I could probably have got the information myself if I knew where to look and had the time, but using Pete saves so much time. I'm sure it's all perfectly legal.'

'I suppose you're right. Anyone can look at Births, Marriages and Death records, records at Companies House, the Land Registry, phone directories, the Electoral Roll, and even Crown Court verdicts, and then there are press cuttings and so much more available on Google. And then of course, there's a lot more information that people willingly share with anyone who cares to read their Facebook pages.'

He went to on to say that all those places are in the public domain, but tax records, bank statements, phone bills, ex-directory phone numbers, voicemail and emails aren't. He added that passport details, immigration records, social security numbers, payslips, medical records and criminal records are all private, and unauthorised access is illegal.

'People do get access, though, don't they? There've been a lot of incidences where computer disks or sticks go missing or are stolen, and we're all at risk of someone selling our information on to criminals. And what about the checks that councils carry out before they employ people to work with children? How do they get the information?'

'CRB, or Criminal Record Bureau checks are allowed if the individual gives his or her consent. That's the only exception.'

Encouraging him to air his legal knowledge successfully deflected him away from Pete and whatever suspicions he might still hold about Pete's intentions towards me. He might have been correct as far as Pete was concerned, but any wavering on my part was now well in the past, which was why I tried to keep Pete at arm's length.

Steve may still have wanted to reinforce his place in my affections or maybe he just knew when he was on a winner, but he suggested we had wine with our tea to celebrate and then took advantage of my being under the influence to suggest a very early night. I never got to Simon Robinson's factory after all.

8

The next morning I met up with Tony Fitzwilliam to discuss his son Rob. When we'd spoken on the phone, I'd thought he was a bit disgruntled because I couldn't start straightaway, but when we shook hands and he smiled at me somewhat apologetically, I realised that was far from the case.

'I'm sorry if I seemed abrupt yesterday. It's just that Rob was within earshot and I was trying not to let him catch on. I'm really worried about him, though, and I want to find out what's going on as soon as possible.'

'I can appreciate that. I'm really sorry I can't spare any time this week, but I'll have an assistant next week, probably around Rob's age – how old is he?'

'Seventeen.'

'Good. As I was saying, I'll have a nineteen-year old girl helping me next week. Not only will that mean an extra pair of eyes and feet, but also she'll be less obtrusive if Rob goes somewhere I might not fit in.'

'Oh, yes, that sounds good.' Tony was very heavily-built so I wasn't surprised when he said, 'I work on the docks. I know you might think I should follow him myself but I'd stand out like a sore thumb.' I envisaged him operating a crane, lifting containers on and off ships and moving them around the storage areas. That idea disintegrated when he said 'I work for Barlow's, the importers. It's an office job, not bad, but I'm hoping Rob will get a few more qualifications, have a career rather than a job, and I'm worried he's got in with the wrong crowd. We get along fine really, though he's not much interested in rugby. We watch athletics and snooker though. He's never been secretive but the last couple of months he keeps popping out a couple of nights a week and he implies it's not our business when we ask what he's been up to.'

'I see. Has his schoolwork suffered?'

'Not as far as we know.'

'Any physical changes? Weight loss, shadows under his eyes?'

'No, nothing like that. He seems tired sometimes but then he's full of energy the next day so it's hard to know what to think. His mum and me, we're just worried he might be getting mixed up in drugs, or at any rate with the wrong sort, if he can't bring himself to tell us who he's seeing.'

'Alright. It doesn't sound like anything much, other than his being of the age when he wants to keep something of his life apart from his parents, but I'll see if I can find out anything to set your mind at rest. Does he go out the same nights every week, or do they change?'

'Mondays and Thursdays, about a quarter past seven. He's back by eleven usually.'

'I should be able to follow him next Thursday evening and I'll take my assistant along.'

'That'll be great. Thanks very much. Oh, I nearly forgot. I brought you this photo, so you can recognise him.' With that, Tony hauled himself to his feet, shook my hand and left the café. I didn't like to tell him he was making a big fuss over not very much, as he knew Rob better than I did, but a couple of nights out till eleven wasn't like staying out till one or two in the morning or not coming home at all, and it was only a couple of times a week. I hoped Rob was as pleasant as his dad, and whatever he was getting up to was entirely innocent but something he wanted to keep private.

I had scrambled egg on toast for lunch. I could have gone home and made it there but I was in the café already and I was earning some money at the moment. Afterwards I drove round to the solicitors and picked up the papers they wanted me to serve, and details of the missing persons they wanted tracing. They were happy with the papers being served by the end of the week. Carly was arriving on Wednesday so that gave us enough time.

I was so glad it was Friday. It had been a busy week. Steve wasn't working over the weekend and on Wednesday, he'd suggested we go to York and stay over Saturday night. He didn't mention it, but it was my birthday on Sunday. I hoped he'd remembered. When I got back I fully intended to make good on my promise to Mrs Foster to visit the Robinson factory. On Tuesday Clare Brenner was coming to see me about the insurance matter. I hoped Carly would arrive mid-week in time to settle in and then start on the Fitzwilliam case. It was going to be all go, so I was really looking forward to a weekend off first.

Steve came home late that night. 'We've got another dead body. It came ashore on the Humber side of Spurn Point.'

'Oh, no! What about York?' I asked, trying to keep the despair out of my voice.

'Don't panic. The body's pretty mangled, and hasn't been identified yet, but they found a ticket for the Rotterdam ferry in his pocket, so it might be another accidental death. He might have fallen off the ship. So, the good news for us, sweetheart, is there's not much to go on at the moment, until my lot do a bit of legwork. As I'm not needed urgently, I told them I was off to celebrate my Rach's birthday and I wouldn't be in till Monday morning.'

'Fantastic. I'll go and finish packing.'

The temperature had risen rapidly during Friday. Probably we were going to have our usual early summer in May and that would be it, until maybe an Indian summer in September, but at least we were able to take advantage of it for once. After a leisurely start on Saturday morning we drove the forty-odd miles from Hull and checked in at a nice little hotel tucked away in the back streets not far from the river. We had lunch nearby and then strolled round the shops, watching acrobats and jugglers, and drank coffee outside just like on the continent. It was wonderful. We sat in the Museum Gardens for a while, but it got really hot and an ice cream wasn't enough to cool us down, so we went into the Yorkshire Museum. There's one really special thing in there – the Middleham Jewel. It's gorgeous; a huge fifteenth-century engraved diamond-shaped gold pendant with a large sapphire. A metal detector found it in 1985 near Middleham Castle. It's described as one of the most exquisite pieces of English Gothic jewellery and sold initially for £1.3 million at auction. A few years later the museum raised £2.5 million to keep it in this country. Someone must have thought a lot of their wife or girlfriend to give her that, I thought. My mind wandered to my birthday the next day and to Steve's present. Would it be jewellery?

We sat by the river and had a glass of wine, then walked back to the hotel giggling - well, I was giggling and Steve was putting up with me. After we'd tried out the bed, we shared a shower before going out to a nearby pizza restaurant. It was lovely to have time to talk, and I was able to fill him in on my many cases, and the fact that his little sister was coming to visit.

'It'll be good to see more of her, but just keep her away from trouble, Rach. I'll be relying on you.'

'I won't give her anything she can't handle, I promise.'

The wine was making me sleepy so we called it a night.

When I woke up I could hear a rustling noise. I opened my eyes and saw there was a parcel on the bed, on Steve's side, and instantly remembered it was my birthday. Steve was out of bed, making me a cup of tea, but looked up when he realised I was awake and came over to hug me.

'Happy Birthday, love!' The parcel was large and soft. Material?

'Mmm... This looks interesting. What can it be?' I mused out loud.

'Don't tease me. Open it. I do hope you like it.'

I undid the paper gently, savouring every moment. Inside a layer of tissue paper I caught sight of black velvet. 'Oh, it's gorgeous, whatever it is.'

'I'm sure it's your size. The girl behind the counter was just your shape and she said it would fit.'

'It's beautiful,' I said as I shook out an amazing strappy black dress. I hoped he'd struck lucky and got the right size. When I tried it on, amazingly, he had. 'Oh, Steve, thanks ever so much. It really is perfect.' I stroked the soft velvet and gave him a big hug and a kiss.

'Now all we need to do is to find somewhere really special to go where I can show off my sexy woman, and I think I know just the restaurant.'

'Oh, Steve. You're so good to me. I don't deserve it. Where are we going?'

'Course you deserve it. You're scrumptious. I've booked a table at The Lodge, back in Hull, for seven o'clock tonight. Now open up your cards and see what everyone else thinks of you.'

A quick flash of recognition passed over me, making me blush. The Lodge was where I'd totally embarrassed Pete. I had to hope the staff wouldn't remember me. I'd told Steve I'd been out for a meal with Pete, but not what had happened, nor what I'd been wearing, and I didn't want him to find out. That was all behind us now. I reminded myself firmly that I'd remained faithful to Steve so I had nothing to feel guilty about.

After breakfast we were standing in reception waiting to check out, when we heard a scream. A waitress ran in. 'Someone come quick! I think he's dead!' Now, Steve could just have taken no notice and walked away. He'd seen nothing at that point. I knew that, and he knew that, but as a police inspector, at the very least he couldn't leave a possible crime scene open to possible contamination of evidence. So I wasn't surprised to have my romantic break set aside and find myself holding the end of a roll of duct tape as Steve stretched it across a doorway to act as a temporary measure to block access.

The body was male and looked quite peaceful. There was a knife in his hand, but little spilled blood. Amazingly, I didn't feel sick at all. Maybe I was getting used to seeing dead bodies. I wondered if he'd killed himself, although it was a surprisingly public place to commit suicide. His body was in a small lounge, used for meetings and such like.

'I wonder why he killed himself?' I mused aloud.

'What makes you think it's suicide?' asked Steve.

'Well, there's no sign of a struggle, and he's holding the knife himself. Maybe he didn't mean to do it. There's lipstick on this second glass. Maybe his girlfriend said she wanted to break up with him, and he stabbed himself to get her to feel sorry for him and stay. Maybe she thought it was just a nick, and he was playing games. There isn't much blood. So she continued walking out and without knowing, left him to die.'

'That's a very interesting theory, Rach.'

'Well, what do you think?'

'I'll tell you later.'

I was wondering if there would be a later, or if I'd be shipped off home unceremoniously on the train, my birthday meal cancelled. I knew it was selfish of me, but I wished we'd checked out just ten minutes earlier. But not only was Steve getting better at reading my mind, it seemed I had underestimated him.

'We'll be on our way any minute now, Rach, as soon as the local police arrive. Don't worry, they won't want me to get involved. I'm not going to start questioning anyone. It's not like TV where policemen get seconded to work on a case when they find a body.'

And he was right. Five minutes later, Steve gave a brief report to the sergeant who arrived, to the effect that we had seen and heard nothing, other than the waitress's cry for help, and he had secured the area without touching anything. Whilst he was doing that, I checked us out and then we were on our way. What a relief!

We drove home at a leisurely pace, calling at Beverley for lunch and to browse in the antiques centre there. Mum and Dad had given me some cash for my birthday and I fancied buying something a bit different with it. I found a really pretty piece of glass, sparkling blue and green. The lady at the desk told me it was Murano, made on an island off the coast of Venice in the sixties. That sounded impressive. I'd never bought an antique before, but I really just bought it because it would look nice in the lounge.

That night I wore my new dress and put my hair up. I felt like a film star and managed to shrug off any doubts about the restaurant. It was such a sophisticated place – I knew they'd be ultra discreet, even if they did recognise me. By the time we got there I'd even managed to stop worrying that I might embarrass myself again. As the wine flowed, I relaxed and enjoyed myself. The highlight was when our desserts arrived and mine came complete with a candle to make my birthday wish.

When we got back to the flat, there was a phone message from Steve's mum to say she'd spoken to Carly and, as it was a while since she'd seen Steve and me, the idea for Carly to stay in my flat and for her to visit, was a great one. She was also grateful to me for offering to pay Carly, even if it was only for a couple of weeks. She would drive her over on Tuesday afternoon, as she had a half day off, but she wouldn't be able to stay. She hoped to come over that weekend or the following one for a visit.

I tried to make a mental note to buy some real food, but it was difficult to concentrate. Whilst we'd been listening to the message, Steve had somehow managed to remove all my clothes apart from stockings and suspender belt, and the touch of his hands drove all sensible thoughts from my brain.

'You looked so sexy tonight, Rach', he murmured as I unbuttoned his shirt and trousers and put the clothes situation on a more equal footing. It was pretty late before we finally fell asleep, but I'd enjoyed every minute of my birthday and felt truly loved.

9

After Steve left for work, I rang Mum and asked her
and Dad round for a cup of tea, so I could show off
the glass vase I'd bought with their birthday money.
Mum bustled in with, 'your dad's parking the car,
Rachel. He's in a right mood, so watch you don't
upset him when he comes in.'

'What's up with him?'

'Football. You might know. City lost.'

'But that's nothing new, surely?'

'They've been winning lately. Apparently they
could have gone top this weekend but they blew it.
Those were your dad's exact words.'

'Well they must be still in with a chance of
promotion then.'

'Try telling your dad that. He just wanted to
savour the moment as it may never come again, or so
he said.'

'Right, I'll tread carefully and just talk about the
garden instead. What's been happening besides
football?'

'Not a lot. What about you, Rachel? Did you
have a nice birthday?'

'Super, thanks. Look what I bought with your
birthday money.'

Dad arrived in time to hear about our trip to York and they both admired the vase. I could see they thought it showed I was actually becoming an adult at last, buying an antique for the flat. We drank tea and chatted a while about neighbours, relatives and the latest bulbs in Dad's garden, before Dad said, 'well, we'd better be going if you want to call in Debenhams, otherwise I'll have to move the car so I don't get a ticket. I don't want to get in trouble with Steve.'

'You know parking comes under the traffic wardens and not the police, Dad, but I know what you mean, and it'll be murder to get another space at this time of day.'

'You're right there.'

Mum got up to leave but then said, 'I nearly forgot to ask, Rachel, how's work?'

'Great, thanks. I've got a flood of new cases. So much that I've been able to ask Carly to come over to help me with the straightforward stuff.'

'Oh, you'd better keep an eye on her, then. Steve won't like it one little bit if she gets mixed up in anything risky.'

'Yes, Mum. I do try to avoid risks, even if you don't think so, and I'll be sure not to send her out alone, except to boring offices during daylight hours.'

'I'm sure you will, Rachel,' Dad said, taking charge. 'Now come on, Anne, we've got to move.' With that, they left and I remembered my fleeting mental note to go food shopping for my flat. I thought I might as well get on with it whilst I had time.

I wasn't sure what students ate these days – junk food or healthy, but with Carly, I was betting on salads, so I bought lettuce, tomatoes, bread and marg, milk, coffee and orange juice to drink, and tuna, sardines and a pizza for snacks. That should set her up until she shopped for herself. I expected she'd be coming round to us for meals mostly. I only hoped she wouldn't report back to Steve's mum that I was a failure in the cooking department.

After lunch I opened files for my new cases and prepared draft invoices that could have the details and precise amounts filled in later, while I did some washing. There was even time to do the ironing before it was time to cook tea. We'd eaten lavishly in York and on my birthday, so I did plain salmon in foil in the oven with boiled potatoes and broccoli.

Steve was home on time, which was a nice change, so his tea wasn't overcooked or re-heated. I asked him how his day had been, and if they'd missed him over the weekend.

'I've had an interesting day, to say the least. The dead body washed up near Spurn Point has turned into a murder case after all. Someone wanted it to look like natural causes, as if he'd fallen overboard from the North Sea ferry, stomach full of alcohol, and was sucked into the ship's propellers. Now, though, we're sure it's murder, because the sodden ticket in his wallet was for the Rotterdam ferry due to sail the night before he was found.'

'So how does that make it murder?'

'Well the ferry didn't actually sail that night. Due to engine trouble that occurred at last minute, it was delayed. All the passengers were still sleeping onboard in King George Dock at the time the body was found.'

'And I suppose he couldn't have died by accident before he got to the ferry terminal?'

'No, or at least highly unlikely unless he fell into the Humber off another boat. But he'd only be likely to get that battered if he'd been sucked under a massive ship like the ferry. Or beaten up very badly, which we now think to be the case.'

'And that couldn't have been the return part of the ticket in his pocket? I mean, he didn't fall off an earlier ferry coming into Hull?'

'Impossible, I'm afraid. I forgot to say, his wife's now identified him and he only left the house the afternoon before his body was found. He was going to catch that ferry to Rotterdam. And this is where it gets really interesting. His name was Phil Cuthbert and he was a jeweller. He has, or rather had, a small shop on Anlaby Road. He's never been in trouble with us, but with his proposed trip to Holland and the jewellery business, there's a possible connection to Jan Petersen, the dead Dutchman. I've been talking to Anna, the Dutch inspector, about it. She's still investigating why her petty crook should have diamonds in his possession, that have now been valued at over a million euros.'

'Wow! Are you still sure this Jan's death was an accident, or could it have been murder too?'

'We're still positive it was accidental. Everything's been looked at again, but it seems like he fell into the marina without any help from anyone else, whilst on a night out before he met his contact and before he could hand over the diamonds. As you know, we originally had to leave that line of inquiry to the Dutch police, as it'd be like looking for a needle in a haystack, trying to find out who he might be meeting in Hull and what the diamonds were payment for.'

'Did no-one claim them?'

'No. At our request the local paper ran a small story about a man from Holland accidentally drowning in the marina, but that's all. We never publicised the fact that diamonds had been found in his hotel room. That way, we hoped to cut out the people who had nothing to do with it but fancied getting their hands on a fortune, and instead, get a few enquiries from interested parties, so we'd have some information to help the Dutch police. As it was, nothing came of it, and presumably whoever was waiting for the money wasn't aware of Petersen's death and got impatient when his payment didn't turn up.'

'So where does Cuthbert fit in?'

'He was likely to have been the middle man, an upmarket 'fence', if you like. We think he was going to convert the diamonds into cash, by selling them or converting them into jewellery, using his trade connections. When Petersen didn't turn up, he wouldn't have known what had happened. I doubt he'd have connected the accidental death with his contact, even if he'd chanced to read the couple of lines in the paper. He must have given it some time but then decided his only option was to go to Holland. It looks like someone higher up got tired of waiting for the cash, and didn't believe Cuthbert when he said Petersen hadn't turned up. Cuthbert was most probably beaten up to get him to reveal what he'd done with the diamonds, the diamonds he'd never received.'

'So you're back on the case now. Will you get to go to Amsterdam after all?'

'Doubtful. We'll have enough to do this end. Our next job is to interview Cuthbert's contacts and associates, and check his recent movements. But that's for tomorrow. Tell me about your day.'

I filled him in on what I'd been up to, before adding that I just had to pop out for a while. It was getting late, about 9pm, but by a lucky coincidence, there was a snooker match he wanted to watch on TV, so he didn't moan or get worried. Mentioning Gran's name may have helped, even though I wasn't actually seeing her. There was a tenuous link, as I was going to Simon Robinson's factory, across the road from Gran's old neighbour, so I didn't think I was really fibbing.

I got my coat and was out the door, before Steve could ask me when I'd be back.

The caravan factory was in darkness when I pulled up. Gran's old neighbour, Ida Foster, had told me she'd heard the noise in the evenings, not that it had woken her at night. I wondered again if there was really something suspicious going on, or if they were merely indulging in overtime to get work done on schedule. Working late in the evenings is hardly a punishable offence. I knocked on Mrs Foster's door but there was no reply, even though there was a light on. I was worried about frightening her and thought it would be unlikely she would open up to an unexpected visitor after dark, so instead of knocking again, I shouted through the letter-box, 'Mrs Foster, it's Rachel, Mrs Maudsley's granddaughter. You know, the private detective who came round the other day. Can I come in a moment, please?'

The bungalow door opened on a chain, but she wasn't keen on opening the door. I went away with the information that she hadn't heard the banging or seen the lights for almost a week now, but she'd ring me when it happened again. I didn't know whether I'd hear from Ida again, to be honest, as she seemed reluctant to take my number, but it was the best I could do.

At any rate, Steve was glad to see me back early.

10

Tuesday morning dawned bright and sunny, and I set off eagerly to meet the insurer at her hotel, that nice one in Pearson Park. It was a glorious morning and I had high hopes of taking on something new.

As I walked into the lounge, Clare Brenner rose to meet me, and smiled. 'Hello, I'm Clare. You must be Rachel. I'm pleased to meet you. I've taken the liberty of ordering coffee, but I'll order you some tea, if you'd prefer it.' She was in her forties, I guessed, well-dressed without being showy, about my height with her hair in a sleek blonde bob.

'Coffee will be fine, thanks. Did you have a good journey north?'

'Yes, thanks, and the hotel's lovely. It doesn't seem like we're in the city here.'

The waiter brought coffee and Clare got down to business, pulling a folder with photos and paperwork from her briefcase. 'I know I could have emailed these, but I wanted to meet you and give you a feel for what's involved.'

She gave me a list of the paintings and the addresses of the private houses involved.

I skimmed through the paperwork. 'Gosh, there are a lot, and all in this part of the country. It says here seventeen robberies in the last six months. And the police have given up on the case?'

'Not exactly, but it's a very low priority for them. They interviewed the owners, anyone employed at the houses, and any suppliers or other callers to the house, but they couldn't come up with any leads, nor anything to link the break-ins, other than the fact that valuable artwork was stolen from each of the houses. There were no fingerprints or other evidence left behind, and the paintings seem to have disappeared without trace.'

'I presume the police looked into the security companies involved.'

'Yes, it was one of their first priorities, but the alarm systems were supplied by various companies, so it doesn't seem likely that someone was passing inside information to the thieves.'

'How did the gang get access?'

'They disabled the security systems, usually by cutting wires or bypassing them, and then forced open or cut holes in windows, or picked locks to gain access. They cut the paintings from their frames and left, closing doors or windows as they went. The jobs were all very professional.'

'But wouldn't something alert the security companies to a break in the wiring or whatever?'

'Well, it seems that someone with wireless and computer know-how hacked into the systems at the security companies and prevented the burglaries from registering. The burglaries took place in the evening or overnight. Either way, it wasn't till the next morning at the earliest that anyone noticed the paintings were missing. The technical details are beyond me, to be honest. The police interviewed people known to them with suitable technical skills, but drew a blank. They came to the reluctant conclusion that the person they were looking for was unknown to them.'

'Possibly an IT student who needed the money?'

'Maybe. And they drew a similar blank when interviewing people who'd been involved in burglary on a large scale in the past. They think it was a gang from outside the area. Like I said on the phone, the police investigated thoroughly, but ran out of leads and in the meantime, other crime doesn't stop. They hadn't the manpower to keep investigating in an active manner, but they've kept the case open in the hope that a painting turns up, someone gets careless and talks, someone tries to export the paintings to a private collector abroad, or there's another theft, and this time they're caught in the act.'

'And what are you hoping I can do, that the police haven't been able to?'

'They haven't got time to re-visit all the houses. When the first burglaries occurred, they weren't in possession of knowledge they might have picked up from later burglaries. There may be someone who wasn't interviewed, who can come up with some detail. Having met you in person, I agree with DI Jordan, when he suggested that people might open up to you more easily. While you're chatting, they may remember something. For instance, we still think someone must have visited the houses to see where the paintings were hung. The police think the robbers would have had enough time to search the smaller houses if they were empty and the alarm disabled, but they wouldn't have wanted to spend more time than necessary, in my opinion.'

'Seems reasonable.'

'Also, as far as we know, there's no way the paintings have left the country, so we're also hoping you might find a way to visit the houses of some really serious private collectors in the area who weren't targeted. I have a list for you here. It's a long shot, but they may have bought the stolen paintings, or even ordered the thefts themselves.'

Clare paused to sip her coffee. 'But surely they wouldn't have the paintings hanging where any visitor can see them?' I asked.

'That's true. We know they won't have the paintings on open display, and if guilty, they would suspect any approach from someone unknown to them, but you may be able to gain the confidence of someone who works for them. They may be aware of a sudden increase in the number of new paintings that their employer has recently acquired. They may even have seen some and be able to identify them from the photos.'

'Well, I think I can do the job for you. What would you pay?' I hated asking, but it sounded quite a substantial job, and I was dying to know.

'Five thousand for four weeks' work, plus expenses.' Perhaps she mistook my glazed expression for misunderstanding, because she continued, 'obviously, if we feel that the period's worth extending, we would pay for any extra weeks on a pro-rata basis.'

'I should think that would be acceptable. Do you want me to send you weekly reports or update you whenever I find out anything that might be useful?' I was struggling to sound professional as the flashing pound signs were reverberating in my brain.

'I think a minimum of weekly reports, unless you find out anything of immediate importance, in which case you can ring me.' She fished around in her handbag and gave me an envelope with ten twenty pound notes, a total of two hundred. 'That should do for your immediate expenses. If you give me your bank details, I'll transfer a further twelve hundred into your account when I get back to the office. I'll make three further payments of twelve hundred pounds on a weekly basis, and if you fax over a list of your expenses with copy receipts, they will be settled weekly also. I think that's all, unless you have any questions?'

'I can't think of anything at the moment.'

'Well, you're welcome to ring me at any time, Rachel, if you find there's any information missing from that file - although I'm sure Humberside Police will be happy to help you out as well. Please don't take any risks. I'm not paying you danger money. If you find any suspects, I'm confident you'll inform me and the police, rather than getting involved.'

'I will, Clare, don't worry.' I smiled broadly, glad that my reputation for being rather too actively involved on past occasions, hadn't apparently made its way to Clare's ears.

She continued. 'One last thing. If we recover a painting as a result of your investigations, then you will be given the appropriate proportion of the reward for your part, and if you should come across a painting yourself, then you would get the full reward for that painting. Both reward amounts would be less the fee already paid to you, of course, but I think you will agree that's only fair.'

I nodded. I didn't dare ask how much the rewards might be. I just gave her my account details, gathered up the file and shook hands. On the way out, I congratulated myself in employing Carly. This case was going to need my full attention for four weeks, so I either needed to finish off my other cases first, or do some easy work on this one, until I could close the others. I couldn't wait to get home to open a file, and plan my course of action, before Carly arrived with Steve's mum. And I was so looking forward to telling Steve that for once I would be earning some real money.

I was bursting to tell someone. If I didn't, I might explode, or at the very least come across to Carly's mum as over-excitable or even manic. I might not be able to ring Steve at work but I could ring Mum. 'Mum, it's me. You'll never guess! I've got two hundred pounds in my purse and I'll be getting five thousand for four weeks' work.' I was aware I was almost shrieking down the phone, but who cared?

'Did you say five thousand pounds, Rach? Whatever for? That's amazing! Tell me all about it.'

As I'd expected, when I filled her in on the details, Mum was just as excited as I was. She was particularly pleased that it was a safe and boring insurance case, and hoped, like I did, that there'd be more work to come in the future from the same company. I felt a lot calmer after I'd spoken to her, and was ready to behave like a normal human being by the time Carly and her mum arrived.

11

I was determined to be on my best behaviour with Steve's mum, Julie, and I think I got away with it. Thankfully she doesn't seem to have a clue what I'm really like. Steve's too busy to ring or see her that often, and because they have a lot to catch up on, my latest mishaps and catastrophes are fairly low down the agenda. I'm not even sure if he told her about the recent attempts on my life, never mind about the minor events such as a stalker setting fire to my flat and hitting my car. He can't have done, or else she would hardly have driven her only daughter over to work for me.

We had a pleasant afternoon chatting about my more mundane cases. It helped that I could tell her about finding a tissue match for Chloe Nicholson, as that put me in a good light. I also stressed that the jobs I had in mind for Carly to do were all entirely free of any danger. Carly unpacked her things at my flat, and then they both came back to Steve's to eat with us, before Julie drove home to Leeds. She arranged to come over on the Friday evening and have a meal with us all at the fish restaurant overlooking the pier, before spending the weekend with Carly, seeing the sights of Hull and the coast.

I let Steve and Carly talk over a glass of wine while I cleared up, before settling down to listen to them reminisce and learn more about Steve's childhood. Steve had offered to drive Carly back to my flat, so I could have a drink, but I had set myself the task of being a responsible adult while Carly was working for me, and in any case, Steve rarely had chance to relax with family.

When I got back from dropping Carly off, he put his arms round me. 'Do you want a glass of wine now, Rach? It was really good of you to drive her back and let me drink.'

'No, thanks. It's late and I've got to be up early tomorrow to show Carly what to do and make a start on my big new case.' I'd been holding myself back all evening and all the excitement finally burst out. 'I'm going to be paid thousands!' I filled him in on Clare Brenner's visit and bless him, he knew exactly how much it meant to me. As he held me in his arms and kissed me, I didn't need any wine to feel intoxicated and I had to turn my bear, Sundi, to the wall so he didn't see what we were getting up to.

The next morning we were both up early. As he was on his way out, Steve said, 'I almost forgot. You'll never guess whose name turned up when we were looking into Phil Cuthbert's background. Howard Banks.'

'Was Cuthbert the jeweller found in the Humber?'

'Yes, Banks is Cuthbert's brother-in-law. Small world, isn't it? We don't know if there's more to it than that, or just that crime runs in the family. Hopefully we'll find out more soon.'

'I didn't think Sue Banks was that sort of person. After all, she'd have hardly had me investigate her husband, if she thought he was up to anything illegal, surely?'

'Cuthbert isn't, or rather wasn't, Sue's brother. He was married to Banks' sister. The grieving widow doesn't strike me as having had a whiter than white upbringing. You should have heard the language she came out with, when she discovered the police were calling. She changed her tune when she heard we were calling with the sad news of her husband's death, but it was a bit late to change the impression she'd made. She obviously thought we were there to investigate something he'd been up to.'

'Mmm. Nice, I'm sure. Is Banks still on remand?'

'Yes, so I've got a captive audience to interview this morning. His case isn't due in court till next week. I doubt if I'll get anywhere asking him about Cuthbert, but you never know, he might slip up. I'm hoping he gets to stay inside for a while, after what he did to you.'

'Me too.' I was a bit scared in case he came after me when he was released, but didn't like to say so to Steve. When I'd signed my statement, I'd been assured that my name didn't need to be released in court, but Banks wanted to find out, I didn't think it would present a problem to someone with his criminal connections. 'Anyway, you'd best be off, and so had I. See you later.' We parted with a kiss and a hug. I got my papers together, texted Carly to say I was on my way, and walked the five hundred metres or so to where I parked my car.

When I got to my own flat, Carly was ready. 'Hiya, Carly. Did you sleep okay?'

'Fine thanks. I'm raring to go.'

'Great. When I dropped you off last night, I did wonder if you'd rather be staying with us than on your own, but with only one bedroom, and Steve not keeping office hours, I thought my flat would be better than the sofa...'

'Really, Rachel, your flat's lovely, and it's no problem for me, being on my own. And there's the added advantage that Mum can stay here this weekend.'

'Well, if you're sure, let's get down to business. The main job I want you to do involves serving papers on individuals. I'll explain in a moment. The other job involves a young lad called Rob Fitzwilliam whose dad is worried about him. I've agreed to follow him, but I could do with your help in case he goes somewhere where I'd stick out like a sore thumb, because of my age.'

'You could still be taken for twenty-one, Rach.'

'Thanks a lot. You could be right, but the lad's only seventeen. It would be stretching it a bit to say I look like a sixth former, but you can get away with it.'

'Okay, well, I'll be glad to help, however I can.'

I ran through the paperwork for the first set of papers we had to serve, and then we set off to carry out the task itself.

'The main problem for you is going to be getting to the offices and workplaces to serve the papers. Most are in the town centre, a few others on bus routes, but there's a couple that are hard to get to, so I thought we'd do those together, and at the same time, I can show you what to do. Then I can leave you to get on with the others. That should leave me to get on with my insurance case. We also need to follow Rob tomorrow night. When all the papers have been served, I'll fill you in on the people-tracing jobs. Is that alright with you?'

'Yeah, that's fine, Rachel. I'm glad of the work.'

I was so glad I'd be able to pay her the total fees I'd get from the solicitor, without needing to keep any back for overheads for myself. Clare Brennan and her five thousand pounds was a godsend for Carly as well as for me.

'Now remember. You just have to make certain that the person named on the paper currently works at the office, and then you can leave it with the receptionist or someone else. You don't have to place the document in the person's hands. If anyone causes trouble, you can just walk away without getting involved. If they refuse to accept the envelope, just put it on the table and walk out, but that's highly unlikely to happen.'

'These papers are usually issued in connection with debts - generally a bankruptcy petition, or an order to attend the court for questioning in respect of an unpaid debt or an order to an employer to apply an attachment of earnings order to someone's wages,' I continued. 'Sometimes they're notices to quit from a landlord to a tenant. If requested by the solicitor, we can sign an affidavit to say when and where the document was served. The thing to remember is that they relate to civil, not criminal matters, and as long as the papers are left at the address supplied to us by the solicitor, then we have carried out our function. It's then up to the court, with the use of bailiffs if necessary, to make sure the order is carried out.'

'Seems straightforward.'

We made our calls in the depths of two different industrial estates and served the papers, no problem. I dropped Carly off in front of an office to serve the third lot of papers.

'If there's any problem at all, just give me a ring. Oh, and take your time. They have to be served this week, but you have a few days to get them all done, and you'll be working tomorrow night. I'm not sure when I'll be back this evening. I'm going up to the Wolds to make some enquiries, so it'd probably be best if you arranged your own meal. I'll ring you this evening to see how it went and I'll pick you up to eat with us tomorrow night before we trail Rob.'

That said, I set off for the first house that was burgled, owned by a private collector who lived not far from Driffield.

It was a nice day for a drive, and as I climbed slowly through gently-sloping pastures dotted with sheep up to the Wolds I felt relaxed and happy with the world. I turned into the grounds of Saxilby Hall, owned by retired Major Ferris, and my only worry was that no-one would be at home. At the worst it would only mean a further ten miles' drive to another of the houses burgled, but I rather wanted to start at the beginning. I would ring to make appointments at the rest of the houses, but I hadn't known in advance when I could leave Carly to work on her own.

Unfortunately my good mood had totally left me after I'd spent about a quarter of an hour in Major Ferris's company, trying to dig a little deeper into the theft of his typically Newlyn School painting by Walter Langley. If you'd set out to describe an archetypal upper class ex-military man, he would have ticked all the boxes. He talked down to me, belittling my investigative experience because I was 'some young girl'. He would only insist that he had given the police the 'correct' version of events at the time, and say there was nothing to add. He complained that the insurers would have settled his claim several months' previously, if the case hadn't been handled by 'that slip of a woman'. The only thing I did learn was that he had bought the painting at an auction in London.

Inwardly fuming, but determined to stay professional to prove that I was worthy of the title 'private investigator', I took my leave of him. As I walked back to the car I could hear the sound of a lawnmower, so I removed my car from Major Ferris's premises, parked fifty yards up the road and cut back into his garden. A well-built man in his mid-forties introduced himself as Bob and proved much more amenable. He confided that not only was the alarm system not always switched on, but the back door was often left unlocked as well. The gardener told me he'd been able to make himself a cup of tea on many an occasion when the Major had been out. Other than that, he said he couldn't comment. When I pushed him a bit, he said that, as much as he disliked the Major personally, he didn't think he'd be the sort to leave the alarm unset on purpose in the aim of raising money from an insurance claim, but instead thought he was just becoming increasingly forgetful.

I thanked him, and left. I didn't see it as an insurance scam either. Maybe if his had been the only house burgled, but as it was, the idea was a non-starter. No, my goal was to get some link to the thieves, so that the insurers could recover the paintings, not to cast doubt on whether the house-owners had submitted justifiable insurance claims.

I hadn't exactly learnt anything and as I reversed into the gateway to a field to turn around, I was just wondering if I'd find out anything at all to justify the insurers' fee, when my day took a turn for the worse. There was a horrible sound of tearing metal, like nails down a blackboard, only much worse. I got out to inspect the damage and found I'd scraped the wheel-arch of my car. It was dented and in one place the paint had been scraped back to bare metal. I'd scraped it on a concrete post I hadn't seen. Even though it'd been hidden by grass, I knew I hadn't been paying proper attention, and not for the first time, I had to admit that I shouldn't try to mull over a case whilst driving.

'At least you can still drive it, and no-one's been hurt. It's just a piece of metal,' I told myself, as I did every time I had a bump in the car. There were more important things in life, but it would be a pain to manage without the car, while it was fixed. I decided to ask Dad if he could paint something on as a makeshift repair to stop it rusting, then I could wait till after the case was over before I had it mended properly. Maybe it wouldn't even need to go to a garage. Maybe Dad could knock the dent out and give it a couple of coats of primer and paint. I whipped my phone out of my bag and rang him.

After he'd established I wasn't hurt and no-one else was involved, he said he'd take a look at it, if I drove by on my way home. Dads are great, aren't they? Well, if you're as lucky as I am, they are.

I cut towards the coast to the next house on the list. Since I'd not spent much time at the Major's, I thought I could fit another in before I headed back to Hull. I stopped outside Garrowgate House and ate one of my emergency biscuits. It wasn't an emergency. I just wanted one.

Garrowgate was older than Saxilby and had beautiful twisted chimneys and towers dotted about the roof. It was the sort of house I'd dreamed of living in when I was a child, with secret passageways and mysteries to solve around every corner – but no ghosts. I didn't and still don't like ghost stories.

I turned into the drive and noticed a distinct lack of cars. A knock at the door confirmed that there was no-one home. I decided to call it a day, pushed a brief note with my mobile number through the door, and drove to Mum and Dad's.

While Dad was looking at the car and doing his best with a hammer for the dent and a sanding tool thingy and some paint, I had a cup of tea with Mum and told her some more about the insurance job.

'It's fantastic, Rachel. You know I'm so pleased for you. How's it going?'

'Well it would be fantastic, but I've only interviewed two people at one out of seventeen houses and got precisely nowhere. They won't want to pay me if I carry on like this. And I scraped the car.'

'Tomorrow's another day, Rachel, and they wouldn't have paid you if they didn't think you were worth it. You won't be satisfied unless you catch the thieves yourself, but the reason they've hired you is to be certain there's nothing more that can be done, before they pay out.'

'You're right, Mum. Thanks. I didn't see it like that. I suppose I've just had a few cases lately where I've put people in jail.'

'Yes, well I think I'd prefer it if you don't do that again.'

I decided to change the subject and asked how my sister and her boys were. My sister's the capable one who never gets into scrapes. Her life is perfect, though I would find it dull, particularly if I had her husband. He's the most boring person I know, and so embarrassing. Can you imagine, at their own wedding reception he tried selling double glazing to me and the rest of the guests?

Still, when Mum told me about the footballing achievements of my nephews, John and Michael, there was such pride in her voice, it almost made me envious. I say 'almost'. I really don't think I'm the maternal type.

'What about Gran?'

'Well, she's not heard any more about when they'll be showing her exploits on the X Factor.'

'It won't start till the autumn, Mum. They have so many weeks of the auditions and then about twelve weeks of the real competition and that ends about mid-December, I think, so they can get the winner's single in the shops in time for Christmas.'

'Anyway, I don't need to wait till then for her to show me up. She's talking about organising a grey protest, whatever that might be, about the wheelie bins. She says she'll get her picture in the papers and get interviewed for local radio. She said she fell in her bin on Saturday while trying to get the paper out to look for table top sales. She'd thrown it away by accident. She says the bins are far too high for pensioners. She had to rock it backwards and forwards until it fell on its side so she could crawl out, and even then she nearly got stuck.'

A mind-boggling picture appeared in my head and I started to laugh.

'It's not funny. She was just being silly, because she could easily have called your dad, and I'm sure it doesn't happen to sensible pensioners. And they're not all so small that they can't reach. Just because she is. Everyone doesn't shrink when they get in their seventies, do they, Rachel?'

I ignored the rhetorical question. I know Mum doesn't like to think about getting old herself and plays down Gran's problems sometimes because of that.

'She's got far too much time on her hands, that's her trouble. I didn't think I'd ever say it, but she should find herself another man or she could get herself a job. She's fit as a fiddle. She could be a lollipop lady or something.'

I nearly choked on my tea. I could imagine the carnage if Gran had such a large metal weapon in her hands. No car would be safe from damage if she took against the driver for daring to look impatient, let alone not stopping immediately or in the right place. Mum must have realised what she was saying as well, because she said, 'She doesn't need to protest. Like I said, she only needs to ring your dad and he'd help her. She's just stubborn.'

At that point, Dad came in to say he'd finished his repairs and he thought I didn't need to take it in to a garage unless I wanted the paintwork back to showroom condition. In other words, it would last for a while. We both knew he was trying tactfully to avoid saying 'until you scrape it again', but we pretended otherwise. I drove home. Going round to Mum's always cheers me up. I didn't need to stop and buy chocolate to banish my earlier depression, which was now non-existent.

Steve wasn't too late and I told him about my day. Steve rarely talks about work, and I'm okay with that. After all, most of it's confidential until they make arrests, and I'd rather not know quite how much crime there is in Hull. Sometimes he tells me an amusing story, like the one about the thief who ran out of the house he was burgling and hid in the garden, when he heard the police arrive. When they went round the back of the house to the window he'd forced open, he made his escape. Unfortunately for him, he was so unfit that he couldn't carry his haul away quickly enough, so he pushed the stolen items under a car, intending to wait in a garden down the road until the police left. His big mistake was, the car he picked was the police car.

The only other time Steve talks about work is where there's a connection to my cases, and before he settled down in front of the Champions League match and football took over his brain, I thought I'd ask him how he got on with my old enemy, Howard Banks.

'As I thought, Rach, I got nowhere with him. I didn't want to offer him a deal, because he deserves everything he gets, but I need to solve this murder and there's more to that than meets the eye, if it's linked in any way to the diamonds. I wasn't happy about it, but I suggested we might be able to do some sort of deal, if he could help me with information about his brother-in-law's murder. I could tell it was news to him and he nearly clammed up completely. He just reminded me that Cuthbert was his sister's husband, not his blood relative, so he knew nothing about his dealings. If I didn't know better, I'd think the big bruiser was scared.'

'Maybe he's got involved in something out of his league, and he's scared he'll be the next body fished out of the Humber?'

'My feeling exactly. Anyway, I was glad in a way that he didn't give me anything, for your sake. I didn't want him getting off with a shorter sentence. So it's back to delving into paperwork and knocking on doors, to see if we get any other leads. It's slow and time-consuming, but the lads are getting on with that and I've been catching up on paperwork.'

I buried my head in a good book till the footie finished. Steve put his arms around me as I was making a drink and when he started kissing my neck, I thought it was time for an early night.

12

Thursday dawned bright and we both got up early and raring to go. There was a text from the owner of Garrowgate House to suggest I call to see him that morning at ten, so I planned my route through East Yorkshire accordingly, making appointments to call at a couple of houses afterwards.

Chris Hornby couldn't have been more different from Major Ferris if he tried. He opened the door himself and apologised for his absence the previous day. He was surprisingly young, early thirties at the most, with one of those twinkling smiles that make me go weak at the knees.

'There's no need for you to apologise. You couldn't have known I was coming. I hope I haven't kept you from going to work,' I waffled, thrown by his charming apology.

As he showed me into a lounge dominated by a beautiful stucco fireplace, he said, 'I'm a freelance architect. I work from home. As you can imagine, I've been wracking my brain as to how the thieves knew when I was going to be away from home. But I'm forgetting my manners. Please sit down. Would you like a cup of tea?'

'Yes, please. White, one sugar.'

'I'll just be a moment.'

He returned after about five minutes with a tray bearing a couple of mugs and a packet of biscuits.

'Do you live here alone?'

'Yes, I'm afraid I do, at least during the week. I know it's a large house for one, but it's been in the family for years, and I can't bear to part with it. It's also a place to keep the family's art collection. I don't want to lock it up in a vault. Stella, my wife, hates being in the country whilst I'm tied up working so we have an apartment in Hull. I use the house in effect as my office during the week and Stella joins me at the weekends. So, you can see, it's hardly ever unoccupied.'

'Please remind me. Was it burgled during the week or at a weekend?'

'A Friday night. A weekend when we were away. It was a last minute decision to go away, though, as I'd originally organised a surprise party for my wife that night.'

'The party was cancelled at last minute? Can you tell me why?'

'It's a bit embarrassing, really, but my wife had booked us a weekend trip to Paris and it was cheaper to cancel the party than the flights and hotel. It was her birthday, and she wanted to go away rather than have the surprise party she found out I'd organised.' He seemed uncomfortable, as I would have been if it had happened to me, but as Gran says, 'you may think you know the state of people's relationships, but if you knew what went on between couples in the privacy of their own home, you'd usually be way off the mark.'

'It was either coincidence that the thieves picked that night, which is hard to believe, or we were targeted because the house was empty. Believe me, I've tried to pin down who knew we'd be away, but besides the obvious tradesmen, neighbours and friends, there's a raft of social acquaintances I'd invited to the party that night, as well as people at the travel company, the taxi firm and so on.'

'Did you give the police a list of the names of the people you've mentioned?'

'Yes, but as I said to them, it wouldn't have been exclusive. I'm sure we were the subject of gossip and who knows how far the ripples spread.'

'Well, I can try to contact people on the list and dig a bit deeper, unless that would make things worse....' I tailed off somewhat lamely. I knew the insurers would want me to follow this up further. They didn't want to pay out and I had to be sure I wasn't leaving any stone unturned, so why was I giving him a get-out? Because I felt sorry for him, that's why.

Luckily for me, he continued, 'you couldn't possibly make things worse, I'm afraid. Shall I get you a copy of the list?'

'Yes, please. It seems to be missing from the papers I have.'

'I do hope you find a lead on the stolen painting. Bizarrely I suppose, I'm not interested in the insurance money. I really want the painting back. It's a Hockney, and as I'm sure you know, he lives near

Bridlington, and paints local scenes. I bought it from an auction in York. The subject of the painting is a place I know well from my childhood here, so it means a lot to me.'

I took my leave soon after, promising to keep him in touch with any developments. There was just a chance that someone named a contact who was known to the police. It didn't look as if they'd followed these names up at the time, probably because the robbery would have taken some planning and the police doubted it could have been done at short notice. Instead they might have thought the break-in was scheduled for that evening anyway, when the occupants were fast asleep.

I confess that I was pondering all this as I headed south towards Brandsburton. What had I said about concentrating on driving and not on casework? I'd never learn.

It didn't take long to cross High Wolds House and The Manor off the list of those which might bear further investigation. The stolen paintings were a landscape by Utrillo and a winter scene by Avercamp, respectively. The occupants of both houses had been out on the night of the robberies and could add nothing to their police statements. Both owners told me that they'd gone together to an auction in Ilkley and had bought them there. There'd been a public meeting the evening of the robberies about a proposed new housing development, and anyone who was anyone was there. As it had been widely publicised, it was likely the thieves could have known, and for that reason they broke into both houses the same night.

I thought I'd head back and ring some of Mr Hornby's friends before making tea for Steve and Carly. It was the night I'd agreed to follow young Rob Fitzwilliam. I listened to various people either express their amazement that the surprise birthday party had been called off, or support Mrs Hornby's decision to go to Paris instead. I supposed their view depended on which one of the couple was their closest friend. I didn't really expect anyone to say they'd been gossiping to their cleaner or gardener or whoever about the last minute cancellation, and I was right. One woman went so far as to say, 'Good God, no. Whatever anyone might think privately, it would be terribly bad form to discuss such a thing outside our particular circle.'

And that, I thought, was that for the Garrowgate House robbery. I made tea and Carly arrived, followed by Steve. Good job he was early for once as we had to be out by six thirty. Thankfully Carly had managed to serve all the rest of the papers without a single hiccough, so I wasn't in his bad books for placing her in danger. I could tell Steve didn't want to discuss his murder case in front of Carly. He just said he'd had a reasonable day and some progress had been made, but not much.

It was a bit of a rush but Carly and I got out in time to be at the end of the road where the Fitzwilliams lived, before Rob was likely to appear. His dad had told me he went out at a quarter past seven. Right on time, we saw a lad who matched the photo Tony had given me. He walked down to the bus stop on the main road. Carly suggested she took the bus with him, in case we lost him in the car, and I agreed. I didn't see how she could get in any danger.

I fancied I could see them chatting as the bus arrived, and hoped she would find it easy to ask for the same ticket as Rob. It's hard tailing a bus when you're in a car, as there's no reason for the car to stop, and you have to shoot on ahead and hope you don't miss someone getting off, or turn down a side street and wait for the bus to go past. Just how difficult, was proved true when the bus arrived in the bus station and neither Carly nor Rob got off. I was so glad that Carly had been on the bus to keep an eye on Rob. Though I was a teeny bit worried, now that I didn't know where she was.

I wondered whether to phone her. It might be inconvenient, but would set my mind at rest. I drove back slowly through the town to see if I could spot them but no luck, so pulled in and rummaged through my bag for my phone. I emptied everything out on the passenger seat. Panic began to set in as I failed to find it. I forced myself to take a deep breath. I had it last in the car when I'd texted Carly to check everything was alright before I set off home from Brandesburton. Carly would be fine. She was only following a nice polite seventeen-year-old boy in the early evening – almost broad daylight still, in Hull. A town she didn't know, with the possibility he'd got mixed up in some drugs scene. 'Stop it!' I told myself sternly. She'll be fine and the phone has to be somewhere. If it wasn't, I'd have to drive back to

Steve's for it, or borrow his phone. His flat couldn't be more than a quarter of a mile away.

But relief was at hand. Very close at hand and I'd just not seen it because I was convinced it had to be in my bag. My mobile was on the floor by the handbrake. I probably threw it on the seat and it slid off. And I knew the battery was charged. I often forgot, but had made a point of charging it when Carly arrived. I rang her number and thought I detected a note of relief.

'Oh, Rach. I'm glad you rang. I was just about to ring you. I expect you missed us getting off the bus, as there's no sign of your car. Everything's fine. He's a really nice lad. We got talking and I told him I lived in Leeds but was staying at my brother's in Hull and going to visit an old school friend. He told me where he was going and I have no reason to doubt him, but to do a thorough job, I suppose we'd better check it out.'

I have to say, she sounded very professional, and I hardly dare say it, even more than me.

'I don't think Rob realised I was following him, because I crossed the road and stood at another bus stop. He's gone into a building on Jarrett Street. There's no board outside or anything. He didn't knock, so either it's a private house and he has a key, or maybe there's some sort of entrance hall inside with different doors – maybe with signs. I thought I could pop in and look but wanted to check with you first, and I didn't want to bump into him again and blow my cover.'

Relief flooded through my veins. Carly was so much more sensible than I was. 'I'll be right there. Just hang on two minutes.' It took me about five minutes, because I had to push everything back into my handbag again first. 'So, what did he tell you?'

'He goes to a dance class. It's free expression, some jazz and jive too. Sounded cool. He actually told me he felt guilty, but he hadn't told his parents where he was going. He said he reckoned his dad wouldn't be pleased if he knew, because he hated "Strictly Come Dancing". I have to confess I told him to come clean. I said I reckoned it might be the skin-tight Lycra costumes the blokes wear that his dad didn't like, rather than the dancing. Rob said I could have a point. His dad said they looked like right idiots. Rob isn't planning to make a career of it, though. He's only interested in the dancing as a social thing. He'd gone along the first time with a girl in his year at school because he fancied her, but had enjoyed it more than he'd expected. He'd made some other really good friends there. There's something else I found out too but I'll tell you in a minute. You'd better nip in and check he was telling me the truth first.'

'Sounds like it to me, but we do need to do the job properly.' The door handle to the building opened easily and I stepped carefully into a large hallway. The doors downstairs were all shut but I could hear music upstairs, though it wasn't the sort of music I would listen to, rather discordant. Maybe it was some sort of modern jazz. Who was I kidding? Steve and I didn't go clubbing and I'd almost lost touch with the current music scene. I crept up the stairs and was rewarded by the view, through partially open double doors, of a class of young people. I crept back down the stairs, returned to the car and told Carly what I'd seen.

'Well, like I told Rob on the bus, I can understand him being concerned what his parents might think. I mean, maybe they're a little old-fashioned and might jump to the wrong conclusion. Not that there'd be anything awful about it, even if he was gay, which he obviously isn't.'

I looked across at her and she blushed a little. 'He's OK, that's all I'm saying. Only seventeen, I know, but he's fit and nice to talk to. If I was a couple of years younger I might've given him my phone number.'

'Well, I can see he might not want his parents to know and start asking questions. A lot of lads are very private at his age. Either way, I'm glad there's nothing sinister involved. I'm not sure what to tell his dad though. I think I might generalise and say he's taking an evening class. It's true, it'll set their minds at rest, but I'll have kept his secret.'

'That sounds like the perfect compromise to me, Rach, and who knows, he might take my advice and tell them soon anyway. He said he didn't like keeping things from them.'

'Okay. Job done and it's a good one, as my dad would say. Let's get you back to my flat. It's been a long day. Hang on though. I've just remembered. You said there was something else you'd found out.'

'Yes. I'm not sure whether you should tell Steve or not, but when Rob was talking about why he liked to go to the classes, he also said he hated the crowd who went to clubs, and wanted to keep away from the drug scene. I said that clubs should report any drug-dealing but he said he'd only been the one time to The Den and he'd been offered drugs by at least two people, and the staff seemed to turn a blind eye.'

'Thanks, Carly. I'll pass that snippet on to Steve.'

When I got in, Steve was glad to hear it had been a straightforward case and was solved. I didn't mention the fact that I'd lost Carly and she'd had to use her own initiative. He might have been impressed with Carly, but far from impressed with me for putting her in a possibly dangerous situation. When I mentioned The Den, he said he wasn't aware of open dealing in any of the clubs, so he'd mention it to the drug squad. They'd have an undercover officer check it out if necessary.

13

It was sunny when I woke on the Friday morning. Since I was up early, Steve and I had a leisurely breakfast together before he headed to the station and I drove round to my flat. My office was still there and I wanted to type up a report for Rob's dad, and an invoice. I'd ring him on his work number and arrange to meet him when it was convenient. Carly was in the kitchen, making breakfast.

'Hi Carly. You're up already, then?'

'Yes. It's a lovely day. Have you anything else for me to do?'

'Well, if you wouldn't mind typing up affidavits for the solicitors and signing them to confirm you delivered the papers, then that would be great. You could also type their invoice, and take everything round to their office. I have a sample invoice and affidavit from when I last did this sort of work for them. If they have any other work for me, then they'll give it to you. They did mention wanting some will beneficiaries tracking down. You could do a bit of preliminary work yourself, and if you get stuck, you can give Pete a ring. He helped me trace the natural mother of Chloe Nicholson, the girl I told you about, the one who needed a transplant.'

'Okay. That's great. By the way, I spoke to Mum last night and she's coming over early Saturday morning for the weekend, if that's alright with you. We thought we'd do a bit of shopping and some sight-seeing; go to the coast or whatever.'

'Sounds like a good idea. Unless you want the whole weekend to yourselves, maybe Steve and I could come along on Sunday and show you some of our favourite spots?'

'Great. If you don't have any more work for me, then I can always go back with Mum on Sunday night. I've enjoyed this week but I can't expect you to pay me for longer if there's nothing for me to do. I might be able to get something in Leeds.'

'We'll see what the solicitors come up with, Carly, but if you do get a chance of a longer spell of work in Leeds then I'd understand.' I was wondering how I would break it to her that she had been so efficient, I was running out of things for her to do. 'Right, I'm off then. I've got a lot more houses to visit today. If you need me, you have my mobile number. Oh, one last thing. I nearly forgot. Watch yourself with Pete. He's a really charming bloke, but he's a total flirt. He's had more women than you've had hot dinners, as my gran would say!'

The Old Mill was by the coast near Skipsea, and as I turned up the drive, I discovered that it was an old windmill that had been converted into a private home. It seemed on the small side to be filled with expensive art, but as I drew closer, I realised there was a modern extension to the rear. I had taken the precaution of ringing and arranging to meet the owner, Richard Staithes, and he opened the door within seconds of my using the ornate silver door knocker.

'Rachel Hodges? I'm Richard Staithes. Welcome to the Old Mill,' he beamed. 'I'm so pleased the insurance company haven't given up.'

'Good morning, and thanks for seeing me at such short notice.'

'No problem. Sadly, my wife died shortly after I retired, so I can organise my days to suit myself, and it's nice to have a visitor. Do let me show you around. I expect you'll want to see where the painting hung?'

I offered my condolences to him and followed him up the winding mill staircase. He paused on the second floor, and I got my breath back. The circular stairs had made me a little giddy, and I wondered who would choose to live in such a place when they had a modern annexe.

'I do hope you can track my painting down. Insurance money couldn't replace it. It was our favourite, a pre-Raphaelite painting by John William Waterhouse. I still have a reproduction of the companion piece, 'Psyche opening the door into Cupid's Garden'. The original is in the Preston Art Gallery and I knew it from visits when I was growing up. My aunt lived in Preston and thought the art gallery the only suitable place to take a teenage boy. As you might imagine, I liked the paintings of battles, but little else, except for the Waterhouse. Totally out-of-character to like such a romantic painting, but in some strange way, I fell in love with it. When I married, I bought a reproduction as a wedding gift for my wife, and she loved it just as much. When my business became successful, I started to visit auctions, and couldn't believe my luck when the original of 'Psyche opening the golden box' came up for sale. It had been in private ownership, but the estate it belonged to had fallen on hard times. I paid a fortune for it, but it was worth every penny. Just one more floor.'

As I stepped off the final staircase I realised why he lived in the mill. He'd had modern floor-to-ceiling windows installed, interspersed with exposed brick walls, and the views were breathtaking. Heaven knows how they'd designed them to fit with the curves of the walls. Wherever you stood, you could see out, with most of the views over the cliffs to the sea. On a day like today, with the sun sparkling on the deep blue sea and glittering like diamonds on the crests of the waves, it was sensational. Seagulls and gannets whirled overhead.

I thought for a moment that paintings would be superfluous, but then I saw the reproduction and I loved it too. I hadn't been able to get much of an impression of any of the stolen paintings from the small photographs, but as I tried to imagine the tiny picture of his stolen painting transposed into an enormous glowing oil painting like the one before me, I believed I could understand why he desperately wanted it back. My eye was drawn to the gap where it had hung, on the only other large section of exposed brickwork, directly opposite the reproduction.

'One thing puzzles me immediately, Richard. Why did they take the original and leave the copy? This looks like an original oil painting to me, as I'm sure it would to most people, thieves included.'

'As I told the police, the thieves must have stolen the painting to order. They must have somehow found out from auction records that I owned the painting, but didn't know about the reproduction. They were skilled burglars, not connoisseurs of art, and they just took what they were supposed to.'

'That's very interesting. Would you know if it's easy to discover who buys paintings at auction?'

'There's no list of buyers, if that's what you mean. I should think it's possible to find out, particularly if you attend the auction, and the bidding is done in person, but most people bid by phone, as I did, or even internet. I'm not sure if there's any knowledge circulated amongst art dealers, galleries or auction houses. It's possible that someone working at one of those places could have gathered information and used it or sold it on.'

'Thanks very much. I got the feeling the insurers thought the houses of known art collectors were visited and the stolen paintings identified as targets. You've given me food for thought, though. By the way, where was the auction house that you bought from?'

He told me the name of one of the large London auction houses. We chatted a little more over a cup of tea, and he tried to remember if he had missed anything from his police report, such as a stranger calling, but he didn't think so. As far as I was concerned, that didn't matter. The morning had been a huge success in opening up a new line of enquiry, and in introducing me to some beautiful artwork. I vowed to find out something about pre-Raphaelite paintings for myself. Maybe I could afford a small print of one for my wall. Or Steve's wall? Or a shared wall in a new house?

Back in the car, I allowed my mind to drift off to the house for sale on the Garden Village estate, which I had been looking at for prospective purchasers a few months ago. The houses all had established gardens and the estate was like a little green paradise inside the city. There was the small matter of the dead body I'd found in the house, but I'd played a major part in helping the police find the killer, and I was sure the area wasn't due for another murder. All I needed was another house to come up for sale there – and the small matter of Steve agreeing to buy it with me. I drove back to Steve's for lunch while my conversation with Richard Staithes was fresh in my mind. I wrote a report of my visit into the draft ready for Clare Brenner at the insurers. I'd only met her on Tuesday and agreed on weekly reports, but now I debated whether to send her what I'd learnt so far. However, I decided to stick to the agreement as there might be further discoveries to include by close of play the following Monday, and I didn't think the odd day would make much difference.

Next I rang Rob Fitzwilliam's dad, Tony. He was about to go into a meeting so I didn't go into any detail, though I did at least tell him that I had an answer for him already and he had nothing to worry about, and heard a gratifying sigh of relief on the other end of the phone. We arranged to meet outside his office at five o'clock, and I decided to go shopping. I'd achieved plenty for the day and only had a couple of hours free before I needed to set off for Mr Fitzwilliam's office. We needed food of every description, so I made a list and was about to head off, when my mobile rang.

It was the officious Major Ferris. I wondered what on earth he could want. Somewhat disconcertingly, he sounded totally unlike the person I'd met the other day at Saxilby Hall, turning on the charm and saying he had need of a discreet private investigator, and asking if I would be willing to investigate his granddaughter's fiancé. It had been a whirlwind romance, and now she wanted to marry as soon as possible. She was only nineteen, and in line for his fortune, as her parents – his only son and his wife – had died when she was seventeen, so the major was keen to know if the young man was 'honest and above board', as he put it. It struck me as a job that Carly could do, leaving me free for my insurance job, so we agreed terms, and I told him I'd call in with my reliable and very competent assistant on Monday morning to take down details and pick up a photograph. Good news, as I had promised Carly more than a week's work, and I wanted to keep to my word.

The supermarket was heaving, reminding me why I never shop on Fridays if I can help it. I only just made it to the office near the docks in time.

I gave Rob's dad the report to read later, but as it contained little, I summarised that Rob was merely attending a night class. Tony confessed himself puzzled as to why Rob couldn't tell them that himself, but I simply said that maybe there was a girl involved or else maybe he was studying a subject that they might think frivolous or which might distract him from his studies. I concluded that I felt sure he'd tell them soon enough if it suited him, and if it didn't, well, they knew he was only being private, and not up to anything he shouldn't be. That seemed to make sense to him. He paid my fee and I rushed home to unload the shopping and start cooking, feeling I'd dealt with the tricky situation rather well.

I'd decided on gammon and pineapple for tea. Carly turned up while I was unpacking and was thrilled to bits when I gave her the payment I'd just received. 'Are you sure? I didn't do much, Rach.'

'Positive. I couldn't have done it without you. You deserve it. I won't get the money from the solicitor for a couple of weeks, as they don't pay invoices promptly, but they are guaranteed to pay, so I'll draw out some cash to cover your earnings from them, as soon as I get chance. Good news, too, if you want more work. I've got another case you could do for me. It will take you into next week, and who knows what else might turn up? That is, unless you want to get back to Leeds? How did you get on today?'

As I spoke I was emptying bags and rummaging in the bottoms of those already empty. Before she had a chance to answer, I said, 'I can't find the tin of pineapple. I know I got one, because I nearly picked up a tin of pieces instead of rings.' After drawing a blank, I looked for, and eventually found, the bill. 'Oh, no. The pineapple's not on. I've done it again. I've left it at the end of the conveyor belt. I can't use pears instead, can I?' One look at Carly's face declared the answer to be a resounding 'no'. 'I could maybe do an egg each then?'

'Sounds good, Rach. Though, now I think of it, the pear might be interesting. Why don't you try it? You might invent a whole new dish.'

'You're humouring me, I can tell. You'd better carry on from where I interrupted you and tell me about your day.'

Carly summed up. She'd dealt with the paperwork and taken it to the solicitors and they'd given her details of will beneficiaries they wanted tracing. She'd traced one person, but had needed to phone Pete with the details she had for the other two. 'Pete was really kind, and he offered to show me how he works. I was going to go round on Monday.'

'Well, you can't', I said hastily, as I heard Steve's key in the lock. 'I'm sorry, but we have to run up to Saxilby Hall about your new case on Monday morning. Maybe another day. We'll talk about it later.' Steve would have kittens if he even

109

had a whiff of Carly talking to Pete, never mind going to his house.

Carly left at about half past nine to go back to my flat. She wanted to tidy up a bit as her mum was coming over the next morning. She was going to take her shopping in the morning and in the afternoon go to The Deep, the massive aquarium, which has marine creatures from the very depths of the ocean, as well as the usual exhibits and loads of interesting interactive displays. I went with my nephews once, as my sister had already been several times and although they never tire of it, she does. I have to admit, I'm not a great fan of museums, and I'd thought that once you'd seen one aquarium, you'd seen the lot, but I was impressed by the sheer depth of the tanks and found it more interesting than I'd thought I would.

Before Carly left, I suggested that while they were by the Humber waterfront at the Deep, she and her mum wander over the bridge to look at the statue on the other side of the river Hull. 'It's called "Voyage", and it's a bronze sculpture of a figure looking out in the direction Hull trawlers took to Iceland. It was stolen in 2011 but it was such a potent symbol of the Hull fishing industry, there was an outcry, and a copy was commissioned and unveiled in 2012. It has a twin, called "For", whatever that means in Icelandic, at a remote spot called Vik in Iceland, where the Hull trawlers visited and where trawlermen were sometimes rescued when ships ran aground. There was a big article in the local paper when the statues were originally unveiled by the Icelandic President and the Lord Mayor of Hull. It said that Iceland was established by Vikings from Denmark who 'stole women' from the north of England, many from the Hull region.'

'Oh, gosh. You could have been Icelandic, Rach, if you'd been around at the time.'

'Glad I'm not. I couldn't imagine living somewhere so cold. It's bad enough here when the wind blows down off the North Sea in winter. I bet my gran would have fitted in, though. She's a tough cookie.'

I waited to ask Steve about his murder case until Carly had left, but when I did, he still hadn't really anything new to report.

'The Dutch police finally got in touch with Petersen's next-of-kin. They didn't mention the diamonds, and when they handed over his personal effects, the relatives didn't act as if anything was missing. As they suspected the diamonds of being connected with a crime, they can withhold them, pending further investigation. So, either the relatives don't know what he was up to, or else they think he passed the diamonds onto his contact in Hull. Try as I might, I can't see Banks being involved in something worth a million euros, even though we were investigating him for stealing high value cars. Also, whatever my opinion of him for beating you up, I don't think even he is capable of torturing his own brother-in-law.'

'Torturing?'

'Yes, the post-mortem showed other injuries inflicted on Cuthbert before his death.'

'Don't tell me, please. I hate the gruesome details.'

'I know. Anyway, if it's not Banks behind this, then there must be another much bigger crook, either based in Hull, or operating out of the Hull area, but we're facing a dead end. We've had no sightings of anyone dumping a body along the estuary, and of course there's no CCTV to call on there. Also there are no reports that might suggest Cuthbert was snatched. So it looks like he met up with someone willingly at a remote place where he was tortured, killed and dumped in the river. At the moment, all we can do is keep our ears to the ground for any stray talk, and I've got men out and about searching around the small lanes near the Humber banks, in case there's been the slightest clue left of the murder, or even of a scuffle, but that's a really long shot. Even if we find anything, it might be totally unrelated.'

'What about his business records?'

'Our specialist team are looking at his finances, but it may take some time, particularly if they have to call Customs and Excise in to look at the VAT stuff. Unfortunately the Dutch police are currently having as little luck at their end, trying to track down who gave Petersen the diamonds and what they were buying.'

'Oh, dear, that's frustrating.'

'Yes it is, but it does mean I get another proper weekend without having to go into work.'

'Why didn't you say that first? Come here and let me give you a hug.'

14

The weather on Saturday morning was dull. Steve said he'd like to watch the FA Cup match on TV at lunchtime. I didn't mind as we'd be spending all day Sunday together with his family, but suggested he come with me to Mum and Dad's and watch the game there. He hadn't seen my family for ages and my sister was due to be there too.

We did a bit of tidying and cleaning together first, as his mum would probably be calling in the next day. We work well as a team. Steve's a very tidy, domesticated person, and he's happy to do his share if he's around. I admit I'm not the tidiest of people, but I can't live in a permanent mess and have regular cleaning fits when I attack the flat and restore order.

When we got to Mum's, the house was bursting at the seams. My big sister, Laura, and her boys had been there all morning, but said she'd go home when the match started. Not that my nephews weren't keen on football, but she knew they wouldn't sit still and that'd annoy Dad and spoil it for him, so they were going to watch it at home instead. So we took the chance to catch up with news while the boys let off steam in the garden under Dad's watchful eye. He's very proud of his plants, and didn't want them trampled under foot.

Bless him. He does like to educate them. When I took Dad a cup of tea, he had just rescued their football from a large thorny bush and was telling Mikey and Johnnie about the oldest ball in Britain, which had been found in Hull. I caught the end of the story. The ball was apparently found on the site of a timbered hall, on the corner of High Street and Blackfriargate in Hull, owned by the monks of Meaux Abbey. They had owned the port of Wyke, before it became Kingston upon Hull in 1299. He said the ball was made of wood and as it came from the thirteenth century, that made it medieval. It was used in a game like skittles but was banned because it led to gambling. I'm sure history was never full of interesting titbits like Dad's when I was at school.

After Sis and the kids left, Dad and Steve settled down to the match with a beer and a pile of sandwiches, while Mum and I sat putting the world to rights. I was telling her about my newly discovered interest in paintings, and Mum was confessing her ignorance and suggesting I get a book out of the library, when Gran arrived like a whirlwind.

'Hello, Rachel. Is that your young man's car outside? I haven't seen him in ages. I can have a word with him later if you like. It's time he put a ring on your finger. I don't want him taking away the best years of your life and then changing his mind and leaving you a spinster.'

114

Before I could answer, she was off again. 'Hello, Anne. I thought I'd get a bite to eat with you and save a bit of my pension. Shame you're only having sandwiches. I was sure you'd be having a roast.'

Mum defended herself. 'Sandwiches are better for in front of the telly. The men are watching football, and you're not to go embarrassing Rachel by talking to Steve about engagements.'

'Why ever not? You've changed your tune. You were only saying last week you were beginning to wonder if your Rachel would ever get married. I suppose I could stay to tea as well as have a sandwich now. You'll be having a proper meal when the football's over, won't you? I've just passed Maggie Longshaw down your road. Her youngest, Lucy, is expecting her second. I'll be dead before I'm a great-grandma. You should remember that, our Rachel.'

It's hard keeping up with Gran. She's like one of those wind-up toys when she gets going. At least if I couldn't get a word in edgeways, I could ignore her attempts to get me married off and pregnant.

'Did you read in the paper about those new bus shelters they're planning? The ones with the boards that are supposed to tell you when the next bus is coming? I can't see them lasting five minutes before the glass gets smashed and those electronic boards get stolen. How would they work anyway? They'll need a load of vans with men driving round adjusting the times of the next bus.'

'No-one needs to go out to them, Gran. They'll be computerised.'

'Well, they'll pinch the computers then. And even if they're welded or chained up or something, how much will fares go up to pay for computers all over town in the first place, that's what I want to know? My pension won't stretch any further as it is. Oh, this ham looks nice, Anne. Where did you get it from? Alice next door swears by Asda's, but I don't think you can beat Skelton's.'

'Shall I pour you a tea, Gran?' I hoped to stem the tide for a moment.

'Has it been mashing long enough? I don't like it too weak, you know.'

We did know. Luckily, at that point, Gran settled down to eat, and after lunch she got out her knitting while Mum and I washed up and made another drink. When we looked back in, she'd nodded off. 'Let's go in the garden a bit, Rachel and have a rest while we can.'

We watched the birds on the feeders and sat in the sun chatting till it started to get cool. When we went inside, Gran was with Steve and Dad, swearing like a trooper at the referee for giving Manchester United a penalty. 'He wouldn't have given one to Chelsea if the boot was on the other foot. The referees are scared of Ferguson. Either that or he bribes them.'

When we got in the car to go home, Steve couldn't stop laughing. 'Your Gran cracks me up, Rach. I never knew she was so keen on football. Good job she doesn't go to games or we'd be arresting her for racism and getting her barred. You should have heard what she said about the Scots and their kilts.'

'Nothing Gran says surprises me. She's a law unto herself. And she used to go to matches with Granddad years ago. How he ever got her home in one piece, I don't know. She even used to argue with our own fans. She didn't sing, did she?'

'No, she didn't.'

'I don't suppose she would in front of Dad. She knows all the filthiest songs and used to sing them to us till Dad caught her once.'

We picked up Carly and her mum at about seven, and drove to the exclusive fish restaurant opposite the pier. It's on the first floor, and from our table by the window we had a good view. They told us all about their day, but thankfully Steve restrained himself from talking much about Gran. I wouldn't like his mum to think I might turn out like her.

Carly enthused about the work I did. She said she could see herself as a private detective.

'You've only seen the nice bits, Carly,' I said quickly, aware of Steve starting to tense beside me.

Thankfully, talk turned to Carly's forthcoming birthday. She said she was thinking about learning to drive, and would be grateful for money towards lessons. I asked Steve if he thought it might be easier for her to learn in Hull than in Leeds.

'It depends on the test centre, although of course there are fewer hills.'

'Fewer hills? No hills at all, more like. They have to test your hill start on a slope leading to a bridge.'

'Funny. I'd never thought of that before. You must be right.'

We had a lovely meal. Steve and I don't dine out much, but this restaurant was one of our favourites when we did. After we'd made plans for the next day, we invited them back for a coffee, but they were both worn out after shopping and walking round The Deep, so they called it a night.

I'd stuck to one glass of wine, but Steve poured me another when we got in. 'You look pretty tonight, Rach.' I knew where he was heading, but I wasn't going to argue.

'You look like sex on legs in that suit, Mr Rose.'

'Not for long.'

'Oh, keep it on. I fancy being made love to by a well-dressed sexy man in a suit.'

The next morning we were up early for our day out with Steve's mum and Carly. Steve drove up past Beverley and Driffield to Sledmere. It's a lovely village centred around Sledmere House and estate. Most of the houses in the village belong to the estate and are very pretty. There's a large circular carved monument to those local men killed in the First World War, the so-called Wolds Waggoners, and another monument to one of the Sykes' ancestors, a well covered by a rotunda, as well as a handsome church.

The grounds of Sledmere spread some distance with deer in the parkland and woodlands, and elaborate gardens nearer the house. Strangely enough, I'd never been inside the house before, so I was looking forward to it. We all enjoyed wandering around. I loved the library, decorated in blue and lemon with twenty-two carat gold on the ceiling, but agreed with Steve that the best room of all was the Turkish Room, completely covered in stunning blue and white tiles, including the amazing fireplace.

We had lunch in the café and I wondered what it must be like to be part of the Sykes family, who had kept the house in the family for generations. Being surrounded by such treasures every day must have some effect on you when you're growing up. Not to mention the circle of friends you must move in. I didn't expect they would be sitting eating lunch, imagining living a life such as mine. They had some wonderful paintings, and that made me think of my insurance investigation. I wondered where all the ones that had been stolen ended up? Did they go to the States? They valued our history, and there probably weren't enough fine paintings from their history to go round all the collectors there.

After lunch Steve took us over the Wolds and down Staxton Hill to Scarborough. We parked near Peasholm Park by the North Bay and walked around the lake. It's one of my favourite parts of the town, but I have many. Then we drove right round the headland below the castle to the South Bay where the amusements, donkey rides and gift shops gather, before ending up above the Spa at the far end. We walked down the zigzag path through the sheltered gardens and had tea and a cake in the café just above the shore, before Steve took us up to the top of Oliver's Mount to take in the views of both bays, with the castle in the middle. A snapshot of Scarborough, no more, but everyone enjoyed it. Then he drove us back to Hull via the coast road, stopping for fish and chips in Filey where the fishing boats pull up at the start of Filey Brigg. When the weather's sunny, then there's no finer place in the world than the Yorkshire coast.

15

When I woke on Monday morning, for once I really felt like we'd had a weekend off, and felt all the better for it. Steve hadn't heard from work and he'd been able to relax and unwind as well.

'Bye, Steve. Hope you have a good day.'

'Thanks. I hope we hear something from the Dutch police today. Otherwise we've hit a brick wall. We put the word out round the area, but no-one seems to know a thing about who might have wanted to kill Phil Cuthbert and dump him in the Humber. I bet I'll have the Chief on my back today, wanting to know why there's been no progress.'

'Something'll break soon, Steve. I just know it will. See you tonight.'

'Will do. Hope your day goes well. Bye, Rach.'

I picked up Carly. She told me her mum had sent a text saying she'd got back alright, and asking her to thank me again for the lovely weekend. We headed out to see Major Ferris. I introduced Carly and we got down to business.

'I haven't spent forty years in the army, only to have some gold-digger run off with my hard-earned money.' I hadn't heard the word 'gold-digger' trip off anyone's lips in a long while, and had to restrain myself from reacting in a way the Major would have found inappropriate.

'My granddaughter Sally lived with her aunt at first, after her parents, my dear son and daughter-in-law, died. Now she's at the university and wants to be independent, but her inheritance was only held in trust until she was eighteen, as is the custom these days, so there's nothing to stop her blowing the lot. She's a quiet girl, and a sensible one, but at the age when her head might be turned by a good-looking chap. If that chap was unscrupulous, he might easily take advantage of her. I'm worried that she's got engaged to this John Munro not long after meeting him. If I die tomorrow, then any future husband of Sally's would have access to over a million pounds. What she does with her parents' money is her business. I expect she'll need it to pay her university fees, living expenses and bills for the house. But my money's a different matter.'

I was surprised when he suddenly softened. 'If it's a real and lasting love, then that's fair enough. I married my own dear wife when she was only eighteen and we were really happy. But I hope you can understand, I'd just like to be sure he isn't going to persuade her to spend or invest in something for him, and then clear off. I did float the idea of one of those pre-nuptial agreements, but Sally told me she loved and trusted John. It's just for my peace of mind…'

We took John's address and a photo. As he was a student at Hull University, I explained that Carly would be doing the majority of the investigation, because she would be able to mingle with his fellow students more easily, as well as looking into his home life and background. Major Ferris seemed content and we took our leave after agreeing a fee for one week's work, to be extended if anything suspicious was found which required further investigation.

As we drove off, I said to Carly, 'I have to admit I felt a little sorry for him. He came across all bluff and bluster to start with, and I thought he was only thinking of his money, but the more he spoke, I started to think differently. I think his concern is based on his love for Sally and her parents, and that he's genuinely trying to protect her, rather than keep his money safe.'

'Mmm… You could be right.'

'Either way, it shouldn't prove too difficult, and the money should help pay your own university fees.'

'Yeah, that's great, Rach. Thanks a lot.'

I dropped Carly off at the university, after giving her some ideas on how to make a start, and headed off to nearby Cottingham, to meet a Brian Mills, who had been robbed of a small but valuable cubist painting of horses by Franz Marc.

I didn't like Brian Mills from the start. He was - how can I put it? - ingratiating but shifty. In Hull we have our own name for men like him - smarmy. He was all smiles on the outside but I didn't trust him. He opened the door with a broad smile, but it was false. His hand lingered rather too long in mine. He was all agreement, anxious to please, but it all struck the wrong tone somehow. He wasn't concerned about his painting, or even about the insurance compensation. He just wanted to get rid of me as soon as possible, by saying he had nothing to add, but it was so good of me to call, and he'd be sure to get in touch if he heard anything and wasn't it a wonderful day, and I was on my way out, his hand on my elbow. I'd have loved to have picked it off with my finger and thumb but before I knew it, I was back on the driveway, door closed. Sixty seconds or thereabouts, and I didn't even get past the door.

I got back in the car and sat there, wondering. My intuition doesn't often let me down, and there was something fishy about Mr Mills. He claimed he'd bought the painting when on holiday in Berlin. I decided to speak to Steve about him and ask him to see if he had a record. Maybe his painting had been a fake, or he'd lost it, burnt it, or sold it, and he just wanted the insurance money. Except he hadn't pressed me for payment, had he? That could be part of the plan, though, to throw the insurers off the scent by seeming disinterested.

I sat in the car, writing a few notes, to make my point to the closed door, that I couldn't be got rid of that easily. I wished I could have sneaked round the back and looked in his windows, seen if he was hiding something - a stack of paintings under a tarpaulin perhaps, or a room filled with all the stolen paintings on the wall? He could have claimed his was stolen to cover up the theft of all the other masterpieces. But there was no easy way round the back. Tall iron railings separated the house from the garden, and on top of that, a couple of aggressive-looking dogs were roaming in the background. I would have to leave and make some more enquiries and then maybe make another unannounced visit when the shiny Jaguar was no longer parked in the drive.

I wondered whether to mention my suspicions in my report to Clare that night. I thought I probably would. Even if nothing came of any further enquiries I might make, it would do no harm.

With that call over more swiftly than I'd imagined, I decided to nip home and type up most of my report. I'd have done it over the weekend if Steve and his family had not been around. I had three main points of interest so far, and I hoped that something might lead somewhere. One was the aforementioned Brian Mills, although when I flicked through the copy purchase invoices Clare had been able to provide - the provenance to show the paintings were bought from a legitimate source - I found one for Brian Mills' painting, so it seemed he hadn't come by it by illegal means after all.

The second was the possibility raised by Richard Staithes, that someone at an auction house was leaking information to the thieves about where particular paintings only known as being 'in private hands' could be found, and subsequently stolen. Finally, I had a long shot idea. The wife who didn't want to live in the country, whatever her name was - oh yes, Stella Hornby - might have arranged the robberies to frighten her husband into moving back into the town. Mm... That did seem like a long shot, now I gave it voice, but better to include it, than regret it later.

I ate lunch, the report ready apart from notes on the coming afternoon appointments, and rang Carly.

'Hi Rach, how's it going?'

'Fine, thanks. What about you?'

'Well, I tracked down John Munro. He studies geography, lives in a university flat in the Lawns area of the university in Cottingham, but his department had a note on his file saying he's rarely there. Not surprisingly, he spends most of his time with his fiancée, Sally, at her family home. She moved back there when she started university, after living with her aunt initially. It was never sold. Presumably there was enough money left to her to enable her to keep it up, so she wouldn't have to pay student accommodation costs.'

'That's a good start, Carly.'

'I'm going to hang around the lecture hall this afternoon and try to follow John or his mates back to the union. Hopefully they'll go to the coffee bar and maybe I can engineer a meeting to try and get some opinions of him. Then tomorrow, I thought I could call in on some of his neighbours and some of Sally's, to see what other impressions people have.'

'Good idea. Are you eating with us tonight?'

'I'll say no, if you don't mind. I don't like being in the way and I want to wash a few things out, do a few jobs. I've got food in.'

'You're not in the way, but I'm not going to push you, because I'm sure you must want a bit of time to yourself, after having your mum and us around this weekend. I'll check in with you tomorrow then. Bye.'

I'd picked out two houses to visit that afternoon, one in Beverley near the Westwood, and the second near Cherry Burton, just a little further north. I loved the Westwood. Mum and Dad used to take us there when we were little, and I'd get filthy rolling down slopes and climbing the bottom branches of trees. That was in the small wooded part nearest to Beverley. The biggest part is open pasture where cows roam freely but cars can pull up off the road and you can picnic. There's a lovely view of Beverley Minster and across in the other direction, there's the racecourse.

Unfortunately, my visits didn't produce anything much in the way of new information. The first owner's wife had sacked their cleaning lady a short while before the robbery, but the police had investigated that line of enquiry and ruled her out.

The second owner had bought his painting from an auction in Frankfurt, bidding online from his home in the UK. Initially I'd toyed with the idea that all the paintings were bought from the same couple of auction houses, as all the owners lived in the same area. I hadn't realised so many auction houses were in existence, although I was aware from watching 'Bargain Hunt' and other antique programmes on the TV, that they take a huge commission from both buyer and seller, so there's big money in running an auction house. Unlike other 'small' businesses, it was no wonder none went out of business, even in a recession.

Although still possible, it seemed increasingly unlikely that one employee could have moved around between so many auction houses, picking up information. I wondered if an outsider could access auction house records. I went home, finished my report and emailed it to Clare Brenner. I only hoped she didn't decide I was wasting my time and her money. Maybe I'd be luckier in my visits to some of the collectors who'd not been targeted by the thieves.

I'd just finished when Carly rang. 'I thought I should let you know straightaway. Major Ferris might actually be worrying with good cause.'

'Oh, yes?'

'It seems that John Munro has a gambling habit. I saw him playing on a machine in the union bar after his lecture, though didn't register it as being significant, but I've since been to the flat where John officially lives, when he's not at Sally's house. I spoke to a lad on his corridor and he said John's addicted to those machines they have in pubs. He told me he was always trying to cadge a few pounds for food, because he'd spent up on the machines the night before. I'm not sure how much debt that would make, whether it would be tens, hundreds, or even more. Do you think I should follow him one evening?'

'If it's only to the union bar or a local pub, and you don't get into conversation with John, then it should be alright, but you don't need to do it alone. I could come along with you.'

'That'd be good. What about looking into his home life, though? I was thinking of ringing Pete and asking him what he could find out. I did say I'd be in touch anyway about the search for the will beneficiaries.'

I was torn. I wanted to keep Carly out of Pete's clutches, but I couldn't go everywhere with her or else I'd never get round all the houses with paintings. She could obviously hear it in my voice. 'I'm a big girl, you know. I'm sure I can keep away from any straying hands.'

My mind went back to six months ago when I'd wavered in Pete's kitchen, and let Pete kiss me, or more accurately, participated in a full-scale smooch. It wasn't that he had wandering hands. It was just that he made you feel so special and gave you his full attention. Then throw in intelligence, amazing good looks and immaculate clothes, and it was easy to be the one with wandering hands yourself, particularly if you'd had a glass or two of wine.

I was suddenly decisive. 'John may be with Sally in the evening. Can you follow him all day tomorrow, please? Get yourself to Sally's house early. You did say he doesn't have a car?'

'Yes, I did, so I should be able to manage on buses and walking. If I'm stuck, I'll take a taxi and you can charge it to the Major.'

'Okay. See how you go. Contact me if he goes out alone in the evening, and I'll come over to wherever you end up. First of all, though, can you draw up all the details you have on John and fax them over to Pete tonight, please? Then ring him and ask how long it'll take him. Tell him it's more urgent than tracing the heirs, and ask if he can let you know when he's got some answers. Then we'll nip round together to see him, pick up what he has, and brief him on the other stuff.'

'No problem.'

'Thanks, Carly. Good luck with your investigation tomorrow, and by the way, good work!'

'Thanks. Talk tomorrow. Bye.'

Good job Steve can't read my mind. I was just thinking that I should be safe with Pete if Carly was with me, as would she, if I was with her, when he came home.

'Hi, love. Had a good day?' he asked.

'Just steady, thanks. Not really made any headway, but it's been alright. What about you?'

'One of the constables found a witness, but it's not likely to help us much at the moment. Down one of the back lanes near Faxfleet there's a place where you can pull off the road - just a dried mud verge really, but the ground was quite churned up and scuffed with footprints. While he was looking, an old bloke came out of a nearby farm building. It turned out he owned the farm, and he said there'd been a right rumpus there a week or so back. He'd not seen much, just heard some shouts and what sounded like a scuffle, but when he'd got to the corner of the barn, all he saw was a car driving off, kicking up dust as it went.'

'Didn't he get the plate number?'

'No. He only knew it was a red car. He didn't get a glimpse of anyone involved. He thought about reporting it, particularly as another car, a silver one, was still parked there, but he thought it was lads larking about, and when he looked out again before it got dark, the silver car was gone. He didn't take the plate down, but when the bobby showed him a photo of Cuthbert's car, he seemed to think it might have been the same silver one he'd seen. Forensics cordoned off the area and erected a tent, and they'll do a thorough sweep of the area, take casts of any tyre tracks and footprints tomorrow, but I don't know if they'll find anything after all this time. And it's likely only to be of use if we get a suspect. Still, it's something, to have found the place where Cuthbert was abducted. He wouldn't have been killed there. It was too exposed for them to have worked on him to try to get him to talk.'

'Where did Cuthbert's car end up? I presume they came back to move it after they killed him and dumped his body?'

'Outside his shop. And before you ask, there's no CCTV there to catch the killer parking it. His wife didn't seem surprised he'd left it there when he went to catch the ferry. She doesn't drive and probably thought he'd caught a taxi to the terminal from the shop and left it there for safety reasons. We sent men to ask around the other shopkeepers in case anyone saw the car arrive outside the shop, but that's drawn a blank so far. It seems likely it was left there after they left for the day. There's a slim hope that someone in one of the flats above saw something, so they'll make enquiries tonight when people get in from work. We're also looking at any CCTV cameras on nearby roads that evening, to see if we can find someone driving Cuthbert's car. There aren't any CCTV cameras out near the Humber, or else we'd have picked up the incident at the farm before now, so I don't think the red car's going to lead us to anything, but as a long shot, I've allocated a probationer to look at the cameras on the A63 near the area of the turning to the farm, for the suitable time frame. You never know, we might get lucky and spot a stolen car being used.'

'Well, it's progress of a sort, Steve. Are you ready to eat? Tea'll be ready soon.' At that moment the phone rang. 'Whoever it is, I hope they're quick. I'm starving.' Luckily I needn't have worried. It was Tony Fitzwilliam calling to tell me that Rob had just gone out as usual, but not before telling his parents all about the dance class. Tony didn't need to have rung me, but I was glad he had, and I'm sure Carly would be pleased to know Rob had taken her advice and broached the subject.

16

On Tuesday morning, I logged onto my laptop to find I had an email from Clare Brenner acknowledging receipt of my report and confirming the transfer of a further twelve hundred pounds into my bank account. Can you believe it? I'd forgotten I'd be getting more money. I transferred it to my online savings account to earn a few precious pennies' interest for when I needed it in leaner times, then buoyed up by the good news, I made several appointments in the Pocklington area. They included one at the home of a private collector who had not been robbed.

It took me about an hour to get up to Pocklington, lying between Beverley and York, not only due to commuter traffic in Hull but also to a frustrating mixture of a bus that called at every stop but allowed no room to pass, and lorries blocking the road as they waited to turn right or crawled uphill with heavy loads. Alexander Larson lived in a substantial period property in Millington but had gone down to London in person to buy his French Impressionist painting at auction. He came up with a long list of people who may have known he would be away from home on the night his Manet was stolen. He was particularly suspicious of the new Eastern European owner of the newsagents in Pocklington who delivered his Times. I had the feeling the suspicion stemmed from Mr Larson's racist tendencies rather than anything more concrete, but who was I to say we weren't dealing with an international gang of painting smugglers?

Somewhat mischievously, I asked him, 'Do you by any chance come from European ancestry, with a name like Larson?'

'Funny you should ask. My people originated in Sweden. My great-great grandfather was related to the ancestors of the current royal family. They dropped one of the s's from Larsson when they settled in England. Do come and have a look at the artefacts I have from that time.'

When I eventually escaped an hour later, exhausted by his lecture on the uses of reindeer hide and hooves, I swore to myself that I'd concentrate on the matter in hand for the rest of the day, rather than let myself be distracted. I'd felt the need to prove to someone with European ancestry, that he was no more a Yorkshireman than the Lithuanian newsagent was, and anyway, what did it matter? We're all descendants of people who came from somewhere else originally.

Steve says I can be racist in my feelings towards Americans, but I don't think so. It's only the thick ones who think all Englishmen walk around in dense fog in bowler hats or England is joined to the European mainland, whom I find irritating. I'm not ignorant enough to tar them all with the same brush.

As for the French, well, President Sarkozy was about as irritating as you can get, and my Auntie Lesley was offered brains to eat, as well as horse, in a French café when she was a student, but I don't seriously suggest that all French people should be tarred with the same brush.

Although I was running late, I just had to stop at a shop in Pocklington, probably the one belonging to the charming newsagent, from whom Mr Larson bought his newspaper. Not, you understand, to show my solidarity and lack of racism, although that was a bonus, but because I was a woman in need. I bought a large bar of chocolate and ate it all at one sitting, washed down with a couple of mouthfuls of bottled water.

My next call was in nearby Fangfoss, but revealed nothing of interest. It was nearly lunchtime by the time I left, so I detoured to Stamford Bridge to eat by the river, remembering when Mum had brought Sis and me here once. Guess who'd leant over too far and fallen in? I had many mishaps even as a child, but Mum was prepared as usual and had a change of clothes for me in the car.

Anthony Wharton's home, on the outskirts of the quaint village of Bishop Wilton, was massive. It was tucked down a lane behind St Edith's church, but I found it eventually. People keep telling me I should get a sat-nav, but I'm not a great fan of modern gadgets, and anyway, I'm with Dad on the issue. He loves maps and passed his love on to me. I could get car-sick unless I sat in the front seat, so I was appointed chief navigator on family outings. Both he and I prefer choosing a scenic route or going completely off-piste if we want.

I'd spoken to Mr Wharton on the phone and asked if I could visit him at his home, enquiring when he'd be available. As I suspected of the owner of a massive import and export business, he was only free in the evenings. I then said that I really only needed to drop off some documents concerning recent art thefts, and if possible, briefly review the security for the paintings he had insured with Thompson and Brenner. I asked if he had any staff at the house during the day. As luck would have it, there was a housekeeper, and I hoped to quiz her about any new pieces of art which Anthony Wharton might have recently acquired, and check them against those he had declared to his insurers.

Mrs Lloyd was as far removed from the Mrs Danvers-type housekeeper in Daphne du Maurier's "Rebecca" as I could imagine. She was probably in her early thirties and wore jeans and a checked shirt. She greeted me with a friendly smile, introduced herself as Charlotte and invited me into the hallway. Far from being frosty, and highly defensive, she was easy-going and chatty, telling me she'd grown up in the village and married her childhood sweetheart, Darren, whose dad was the gardener for the Whartons. She'd done a level one NVQ in Hospitality and then a further NVQ in Domestic Services and Housekeeping and when this job had come up right on her doorstep, she was over the moon.

'Anthony and his wife Josephine are lovely people. They treat me like their daughter. Sometimes I have to cater for parties but mainly my job involves preparing their meals, ordering food and getting Darren's dad to provide some of the veg, organising the cleaner, and other bits and pieces. The old coach house has been converted into cottages and Darren and I rent one of them. He trained as a carpenter, but can turn his hand to fixing most things, and he's Anthony's driver, so he takes him to Hull and business meetings in the Bentley.'

'Did Anthony tell you why I was calling?'

'Yes. It's to do with his paintings. Checking they're all secure for the insurance, isn't it? There are some in most of the rooms, even the bedrooms, but he also has a separate wing of the house which just contains paintings, like a private art gallery. Shall I show you around?'

'If it's not too much trouble. Do you know if he's bought a lot of new paintings recently, Charlotte?'

'Yes, quite a lot, actually. Josephine had a little moan the other week. She said he had enough, but he said he couldn't help it; there were some paintings he just had to have.'

'Are they all on display?'

'The new ones? I wouldn't know, I'm afraid. I know he swaps the paintings round sometimes in the gallery, though not in the house. And he keeps the ones he has no room for in a walk-in safe. He may not have put all of the new ones on the walls yet.'

'Did you see any of them when he first bought them?'

'He showed me one he knew I'd like. It was really pretty, children on a beach with sparkling sea. Can't remember the name though. I'm hopeless on names. He said it was painted in Cornwall.'

I didn't want to raise her suspicion by showing her pictures of the seventeen stolen paintings. I knew already that there was only one by a Newlyn artist and it wasn't as she had described. Nothing else came close. But that didn't necessarily mean anything. Wharton might buy paintings as well as having some stolen to order, if he felt he wouldn't get them any other way. The gallery was full of very expensive artwork, encompassing all periods and styles. I counted the paintings, and whilst openly admiring them, I jotted down the titles and the names of the artists where they were shown. I then checked the room was alarmed, for Charlotte's benefit. I hadn't a clue what I was looking at, but that was why I was supposedly there. If the gang targeted Mr Wharton, they would disarm the system in the same way as at the other houses, by hacking into the computer controls, but the insurers were keeping that information to themselves.

We continued round the rest of the house in the same way. I'd email my list to Clare Brenner and get her to check there weren't any paintings included that they didn't insure. I told myself not to feel excited, as Wharton might have legitimately bought his recent acquisitions. Charlotte had openly mentioned the safe, but he may not have wanted to raise suspicion, by telling her not to. If it was full of stolen paintings, then how could it be proved, other than by asking Wharton to open the safe, or finding grounds for the police to get a search warrant? He could of course move any stolen paintings in advance, if he was forewarned. This was one reason why I was keeping it all low-key and not drawing attention to anything suspicious, whilst at the same time hoping that my list of the paintings on the wall might prove invaluable.

When we'd toured the house, Charlotte gave me a cup of tea, I left her some literature about taking extra precautions against theft, and then I drove back to Hull before rush hour.

Steve was a bit late and I'd already decimated the contents of the biscuit barrel when he arrived. He looked a bit troubled. 'What's up, love?'

'They've let Banks out on bail. His solicitor convinced the judge that there's only circumstantial evidence linking him to the attack on you and your imprisonment afterwards.'

'What?!'

'I knew you'd be upset. They said there's no proof that he was the person responsible, even though you followed his car to the road in which the attack occurred, and you were found tied up in one of his premises.'

'That's ridiculous!'

'I know, but they say that someone else could have attacked you, because you lost sight of Banks on the industrial estate, and although you followed his car, you didn't actually see who was driving it, or who attacked you. Neither could you describe how you came to be in the lock-up.'

'That's because I was unconscious when he put me in the car and drove me there! I just don't believe he's going to get away with it. Isn't there anything to prove I was in his car, like a hair or something?'

'Unfortunately not. We got the lab report back this morning, and the car was clean. He'd have had it deep-cleaned at one of his workshops. We thought there'd be traces of blood or saliva. You can't vacuum or clean away dried specks of spilt fluids, but he must have wrapped you in something, which we haven't been able to trace or which has since been burned. We'll just have to try to find a witness, or hope when it gets to court, that circumstantial evidence is enough to convict. It's not enough to prevent bail, though. The offence wasn't considered serious enough to keep him in jail while we made further enquiries, particularly as you've recovered without any serious injuries.'

'Bloody brilliant.' I stopped cutting potatoes in case I chopped my finger, I was that angry.

'Rach, I'm just as livid as you are, but I'm afraid I've run into this brick wall so many times, I shouldn't be surprised any more. I'm so angry he could do what he did to you and walk away scot-free. I'll just have to try harder to see if I can link him in to those diamonds somehow. It would seem too much of a coincidence for him not to be involved. Anyway, enough of work, let's try and put it out of our minds and eat, then have a quiet night in front of the TV together.'

But for once it was me who couldn't leave Steve's work where it belonged, back in the office. 'Will he come after me now he's free?' I was scared. Memories of that night haunted me as I considered the possibility.

'Definitely not. One, he doesn't want to make himself look any guiltier. And two, you never saw his face after he left his house. He would be quite happy for his activity that evening to be limited to that of a suspected adulterer - one who met his girlfriend somewhere on an industrial estate. He might contend that you followed a different car from the industrial estate, thinking it was his, or even that his car was taken from the industrial estate by someone unknown to him, but returned in time for him to drive home after his assignation.'

'So he's going to find some woman to say she was with him the whole time in her car on the industrial estate, and also find a reason for his car having been thoroughly cleaned before you called at his house to arrest him?'

'Something like that. His car wasn't there when we arrived, and by the time we'd located it, it had been cleaned. And to think I was certain we had him this time. But you never know, Rach. Like I said before, maybe a witness will turn up before it gets to court, and the whole thing might sound as fishy to a jury as it does to us. Now, come on, you tell me about your day.'

After I'd filled him in on my various calls, Steve agreed that Wharton warranted further investigation and said he would get someone to look into his background and his company. He raised the possibility that Wharton might also import stolen paintings from abroad through his own import-export company.

Mum rang me on Wednesday morning. She wanted to know what we'd been up to over the weekend and remind me that Gran's birthday was coming up. I told a white lie and said of course I'd not forgotten. The truth was, having Steve's family around had put it out of my mind. 'I'm getting her a big box of her favourite chocs. Unless you have any other ideas, Mum?'

'No. I've given Laura the only idea I had left over after getting Gran something myself. You don't need to get her something else though. She'll be really pleased with the chocs, and anyway, you know she keeps saying she has enough things in the house and there's no point buying her anything else. And as for clothes, she says what she has will see her out. Anyone would think she's a hundred, to hear her talk!'

'Mm… If you think that's alright, then?' Trust my sister to pick Mum's brain for ideas first. She's so much more organised than I am.

'Get her a nice big card with flowers on and a good old-fashioned verse, if you can find one. You will be coming for tea, won't you? I'm making her favourite chocolate cake.'

'It's my favourite too. Yes, I'll be there, though I'm sure I'll see you before then. It's not for a while, is it?'

'I know, but I wanted to be sure you'd remembered and have you put it on your calendar. Well, I'd better go. I've got a lot to do today, and your dad's promised we'll take our neighbour's dog to the kennels. It's far too big for us to look after while she's on holiday. I don't know why she has to have such a big one. I wouldn't be surprised if it doesn't take a lump out of one of the cats there. Did I tell you it's a cattery as well as kennels? Seems crackers to me.'

'I'm sure they must keep the dogs and cats separate, Mum. They can't have them fighting. I can't imagine people would be too pleased if they went to pick up their cat, and got told that their little tabby Stripy had lost its ear because it upset a large dog. They'd never go there again.'

'I suppose you're right. Well, if I don't see you before, see you a week on Tuesday for Gran's birthday tea.'

I scribbled a post-it note to remind myself about the card and chocs for Gran and stuck it on my bag, then typed up the list of paintings I'd seen at Wharton's house and faxed it off to Clare Brenner. I also sent a brief note asking her to kindly check if they matched with the paintings he insured with them. Then I rang Carly and asked how she'd got on the previous day.

'I almost rang you last night. John Munro visited three of those money-lending places today. I hung around outside and saw him getting cash from each of them. He showed them some documents. He doesn't have a payslip, so I was wondering if he showed them some copies of Sally's bills. They'd be in her name, though.'

'I'm not sure whether they'd loan money to a different person.'

'We don't know how closely they check things out. They're just trying to make loads of interest off people.'

'I think they must be regulated in some way, though, Carly. And I thought the whole idea of those places was loans until payday. I think you have to be working to get a loan from them. Maybe he does have a little job - one we don't know anything about? Where else did he go?'

'He went to one class and then he hung around the union on the machines for a while, before going in a nearby pub and doing the same. He slammed the machine a few times and then went to Sally's.'

'Right. Have you heard back from Pete about John Munro's background?'

'Not yet, no. Shall I chase him up?'

'No, it's OK. I need to speak to him anyway. I'll ring him and if he's got any information, then we'll go and see him together. I'll get back to you in ten minutes or so. Why don't you make yourself another coffee?' The white lie didn't bother me. I didn't have anything else I needed to talk to him about. I just wanted to make sure that Carly didn't see Pete on her own.

'Hi, Pete. It's Rach.'

'Hi, Rach. How's it going? I spoke to your charming assistant the other day. Is work taking off so much that your little empire is expanding?'

'No, it's just temporary. I've got the usual stuff and then I landed a much bigger case. As luck would have it, Carly was looking for a few weeks' work and so it suits both of us. She's Steve's baby sister, so I hope you were nice to her.'

'Are you warning me off before we even get to meet and she sees what a gentleman I am? I've got the information she asked for. I was going to call her today in fact, and arrange for her to come over.'

'Great news that you've got it so soon, Pete. However, although you're a great guy, do you really think I'll let you loose on a young defenceless student, and more importantly, one whose mother may be my mother-in-law one day?'

'Don't tell me he's popped the question?'

'No, he hasn't. I said 'may' be my mother-in-law, not 'will'. Anyway, joking apart, Carly and I saw Major Ferris together and I'll have to do most of the talking when we report back to him about his grand-daughter's fiancé. So I thought we'd come over to see you today sometime, if you can fit us in?'

'No problem. It must be my lucky day. Two delectable women instead of one. Can you come round about eleven? It'll give me time to get everything together for you?'

'That's fine. See you then. Bye.'

I rang Carly and arranged to pick her up at around ten thirty. I reckoned that would give me enough time to get Gran's birthday sorted out before I forgot, and I was right. I had to call at the local post office for a card. That's the only place apart from the market where they still sell cards with long flowery verses - the kind Gran loves so much. The chocs were easier. They sell them at Asda and I needed something for tea anyway.

When we got to Pete's house, I could tell Carly was impressed. He has a small mansion in Sutton on the outskirts of Hull. You couldn't see his pool and gym from the outside, but I think she got the picture anyway, even before we walked into an entrance hall big enough to accommodate the bedroom in my flat. That was nothing to the effect Pete had on her. Now, I've said it before, but it's true. Pete is extremely sexy. Dressed in dark well-cut jeans and a navy and white checked shirt, he looked casual, yet at the same time, dressed for a date. His eyes crinkled into a smile when he opened the door, and I remembered his lips on mine. I knew the effect he was having on Carly, because I was in danger of falling under the same spell.

'Rach. Great to see you. You're looking as beautiful as ever. And you must be Carly? You look as lovely as I imagined from your voice on the phone.'

She sort of squeaked 'Hello.' I guessed how she must be feeling. I'd felt like that once, although in my defence, I had been drinking and I was feeling lonely and unappreciated at the time. Carly was single and I doubted she'd come across many blokes like Pete before, so I was fairly sure she'd be weak at the knees, particularly as Pete was still holding her hand.

'Pete,' I reminded him, 'have you had time to get everything together for us?'

'Sure, come in. I'm forgetting my manners. Would you like coffee?'

While he was making it, Carly whispered, 'he's gorgeous. Is he single?'

'He is, but you'd have to join the queue. Love them and leave them, that's Pete.' Just as well I'd not let Carly come round alone, or she'd never have been seen again. However, I was now sober and well-adjusted and could remember the things Steve had, which were lacking in Pete's character. Pete might be a great-looking guy, rich, and know how to treat a woman on a date, but Steve was loyal, had a good sense of humour and we had fun together without it costing a fortune. But, more important, he cared about me as a person, not as a conquest, and he wasn't concerned with appearances all the time.

I'd not wanted to tell Carly about the times I'd gone out with Pete when Steve was working twenty-four-seven. They belonged in the past, when we weren't living together, and in any case, nothing had happened other than one drunken kiss. I could have told her plenty about his string of girlfriends, starting back in our schooldays, but without giving her any details, she could only go on face value. Best thing was to get the info and get us out of there as soon as I could. When he came back with coffee, I cut short any attempt Pete made to charm Carly further. 'We haven't got long, I'm afraid, Pete. Could you summarise what you found out while we drink, please?'

He gave me a look - one which said, 'she's young, pretty and I'd like to get to know her better.' I gave him one back - one which I hope said, 'don't you dare, or I'll kill you.' I thought he was going to ignore me, so I muttered half under my breath, 'please…' He leant back in his chair and I knew he'd given up the offensive this time. He behaved like a gentleman, cutting out all personal remarks and compliments, but still managing to remain very charming.

'Munro's family come from Kent. I called in a favour from a mate down there and he did a bit of digging around for me. The lad's parents split up when he was ten and he was brought up by his mother, but as far as I can tell, the family is free from debt, and she seems to have done her best for him. He was an only child. He played football at school, performed well academically and wasn't known as a problem pupil. He saw his father very occasionally, but when Munro was seventeen, his dad died in a car accident and that's when a few problems started. His mum got some sort of compensation payout from the accident, as they'd never actually divorced, and she must have given John a bit of a lump sum from the money. I don't know whether she intended it to pay his way through university, but the word in his home town is that he ran through it all by the end of his first term at Hull University. I don't know whether his dad's premature death had anything to do with it. I'm no psychologist. What have you found out about him in Hull?'

I summarised what Carly had been able to find out, and continued, 'Maybe he's a nice bloke going through a rough patch. Maybe he'll come through this phase and pay off his debts. We've got one more day before we report back to the Major. As to how he handles it, though, that's difficult, but we can only give him the information. Telling your grown-up child, or grandchild, in this case, what they should do in a relationship is a recipe for disaster. She's more likely to run into Munro's arms if she thinks the Major is set against the idea, and speaking to Munro might make things even worse.'

'I think you're right there, Rach.' Pete passed me the paperwork he'd assembled.

'Thanks anyway, Pete.' I stood up to leave. 'You'll send me a bill for your work, won't you?'

Before he could answer, Carly broke in with 'We can't leave yet.' I gulped and stared at Carly in amazement, until she continued 'Pete was also looking into the whereabouts of the will beneficiaries for me. Unless you've not had time yet, Pete?'

'I managed to find the time, especially for you, Carly. I've tracked them all down and the paperwork's with the stuff on Munro.'

'Oh, right, thanks. I hope you didn't think I was implying you'd only done half a job?'

'Not at all, Carly. It's been lovely to meet you. I hope you've enjoyed your stay in Hull. I gather you'll be off back to Leeds before long, but maybe we'll meet again another time.' Pete grinned at me behind her back, and mouthed, 'you owe me one.'

I put that thought to the back of my mind as we said our goodbyes and drove off.

To my surprise, Carly didn't mention Pete in the car. 'Do you think we have enough to go back to the Major, yet, Rach?'

'The Major gave us a week, so we'll have to get back to him on Friday. The only thing I think we're missing is Munro's career prospects. If he's a brilliant student, and in the near future he'll be earning huge sums, that might make a difference, although I don't see how. There's just a slim chance that he got into gambling because his debts and student loans worried him. Initially he may have won a bit, so he saw that as a way out, but then got on the slippery slope of losing and then trying harder to win the losses back. But gambling's addictive, and now he's in the hands of those loan companies. Even if he were suddenly earning well, I can't see him stopping, and that's really bad news for Sally as he would gamble her money away as well.'

'It's really sad if she loves him.'

'I know, Carly, but maybe she's not seeing the real person. I'm sure he can be charming and loving, and that's what she fell in love with, but until you've spent a lot of time with someone in all situations - probably until you've actually lived with someone - you can't know whether he's the right one to spend the rest of your life with. Hormones have a lot to answer for when you first fall in love, but you know the old saying, that you have to agree on money, sex and children, because they're the things most likely to break up a relationship.'

'What about you and Steve then, Rach?'

'I think we'll be alright. About the only thing that gets me down, is that when he gets a big case, I don't see him hardly at all, but I've come to accept that it's par for the course for a policeman, and he makes it up to me when things are quieter.'

'So you think you'll get married?'

'If he asks me - but don't you dare tell him that. I want him to be sure it's what he wants too, and the only way I'll be sure, is if he asks me without any prompting, from me or from anyone else.'

'Well, it'd be great to have you as a sister-in-law, and I know Mum would like it too.'

'Oh, that's good. I didn't know if she liked me or thought I was a bit too scatty for Steve.'

'No, she really likes you. What about your parents? Do they like Steve?'

'What's not to like? They're a bit old-fashioned really. They can't wait for a wedding, though they're not as bad as Gran. She doesn't really know I already live with Steve. She thinks I'm saving myself for the big day!'

Luckily, before my brain could fully switch to images of last night, with Steve and me lying naked on the settee, we'd got back to my flat and the subject changed to lunch. Carly made us cheese on toast whilst we discussed whether she could feasibly approach one of Munro's lecturers. I quickly decided it was a step too far for Carly, and that she would be better employed trying to get information from people on his course as to career chances for geography students in general. We decided she could then ask if anyone on the course was likely to outshine the others, and come at it that way.

I wasn't sure whether I would be any more successful with the lecturers, but I was going to give it a try. I'd taken half a day out from the insurance case already, so I might as well make it a full day and make up for it by working one day at the weekend. I rang Major Ferris and told him we'd been making steady progress and arranged to call round on the coming Friday morning. When he pressed for details, I said I thought it was best if we had a full picture first, and thankfully he accepted that.

'Right then, Carly. If you wouldn't mind spending this afternoon and tomorrow morning talking again to Munro's fellow students and friends, we'll see how much more we can find out. Besides the career prospects for geography graduates, see if you can also determine whether he has a job. It goes without saying that we mustn't tip Munro off, so if it looks like anyone is starting to get suspicious, then gradually change the subject and charm them into forgetting that you were asking about Munro. Do you think you're up to it?'

'I'll do my best, Rach.'

'Great. Remember, don't push it. We already have a lot of information. We just need to give the Major his money's worth, and you may come up with an interesting snippet that we might otherwise have missed. I'll come over tomorrow afternoon and we can draw up a full report to take on Friday.'

18

I rang the Geography department and struck lucky. One of the lecturers was in the office, and better still, it turned out that he was John Munro's tutor, and amazingly, was prepared to speak to me. I'd decided there was nothing to gain by hiding the reason for my call. I didn't tell him anything we'd discovered about John's gambling and debts, but explained about Sally's grandfather being worried about their engagement, and could he just supply a character reference and give me some idea of John's likely prospects.

'I can't see a problem in that. John's a quiet lad. I've known him two years now. He always hands in his work on time and it's of a very high standard. I've no doubts he'll do well in life. Obviously with the recession, there are no guaranteed jobs out there for graduates, but he's got a better chance than most. He has a personable manner and would probably shine at interview, and he can spell and write grammatically, which has become increasingly rare these days, so that's another positive.'

'So, as far as you're concerned, would he be a suitable prospect for Sally, from her grandfather's point of view?'

'I couldn't go so far as to say that I think he'd make a good husband. Personally, I agree with his fiancée's grandfather. I think he's rather young to be considering marriage.'

'That's fine. Sorry to have pushed you. I understand it's far from your place to say. I'm grateful for the information you've been able to give me, and I trust you will treat this conversation in confidence, Dr Stapleton.'

'Naturally. I shan't say anything to the lad about our chat. I'm sorry, but I must be going now. Good afternoon.'

Well, that was interesting. Maybe John would be able to pull his life around, after all, but first he needed to come clean to Sally about his gambling and how he'd got sucked into it to start with. Then he'd have to promise to stop, using whatever help available, and see how she reacted. It certainly didn't seem like marriage should be on the cards anytime soon. I made a few notes. I'd start the report before Carly gave me her feedback later, but since I'd been able to speak to Dr Stapleton without driving out to the University, I now had time to visit another of the burgled houses. There was one not far from the outskirts of Hull, in Hedon.

Hedon pre-dates Hull as the first town on the Humber, although changes in the estuary now mean that it lies inland. As I drove towards its impressive eight hundred year-old parish church, St Augustine's, nicknamed 'King of the Holderness', I kept my eyes peeled for the turn that would lead to

Atley Hall. It was hard for me to concentrate, as memories kept flooding my brain of the last time I'd driven down this road, out beyond Hedon and then south on to the almost other-worldly landscape of Sunk Island.

It hadn't been an island for over four hundred years, but the name stuck, although it was now part of a large area of reclaimed farmland. Despite being so close to Hull, it was desolate and windswept, and therefore suitable for a murderer to carry out his vicious crimes unobserved. Unwittingly, I had almost been killed too, when I attempted to free one of the murderer's victims. Although it was only a few months ago, I had succeeded in blocking it out until now, and I shook my head to banish it again. I'd convinced myself I was tough, though my recent encounter with Banks told me otherwise. I prayed that violence would give me a wide berth in the future.

Atley Hall was owned by Mr and Mrs Shuttleworth and was a large, pleasant 1930s house, built in the art deco style. They were both retired and were agreeable to my calling at short notice. Mrs Shuttleworth had been on her way to her afternoon ladies' bridge session, but was happy to cancel if it meant they could help the insurers with their enquiries. Their painting was by John Atkinson Grimshaw, an artist born in Leeds who also lived in Scarborough. He's well-known for night-time scenes, and his trademark is his brilliant use of light in his paintings. I'm not that interested in art, but even I would recognise a Grimshaw, as I'd seen quite a few in art galleries, and I'd read a while ago in the local press that one of his paintings of Whitby had fetched half a million at auction. It transpired that the Shuttleworths had owned another of the finest examples of his many paintings of Whitby, so it was obvious why it had been a target for the mysterious art-loving thief.

'We didn't pay a massive amount for the painting. We bought it just after we married, almost forty years ago. We just loved it, and it reminded us of our honeymoon in Whitby. Prices have shot up since then. I'm not sure what we'll do if it's not recovered. I know we'd get a considerable amount of money, but however much it is, it can't make up for the loss of the painting.' Mr Shuttleworth sounded downcast, but I was no longer giving his words my full attention, as I puzzled over how the thieves knew where to find it, when the Shuttleworths hadn't bought it at a recent auction. Did records of purchasers go back that far, I wondered?

'Stuart says he'd rather get a good print of our painting, if that's possible, rather than spend the money on an original painting by someone else. Paintings by Grimshaw hardly ever come up at auction these days and we want to enjoy it now, rather than wait.'

'I can understand that,' I said as I looked at the small photograph in my folder. 'The insurers haven't given up hope of recovering the paintings yet, but I do need to run through your previous statements and see if you've thought of anything since. For instance, were there any unexplained visitors or members of staff who might have left with a grudge?'

'No, I only have a lady in once a week to help with the heavy cleaning, and she's been with me for fifteen years now. I trust her as much as if she were one of my closest friends.'

'I'm afraid I have to cover all the possibilities. Sometimes the nicest people have a son in difficulties and maternal love robs them of their usual scruples. Can I have her name and address, please?' I followed the now-familiar script of the last week or so, taking notes but not learning anything that piqued my interest. They couldn't shed any light on my dilemma of it having been purchased such a long time ago. They hadn't shown it or mentioned it to anyone outside the family recently. When I was explaining my theory about the thieves having inside information, perhaps having an accomplice working in an auction house, Mr Shuttleworth interrupted, 'but we didn't buy the painting at auction. It came from an antique shop in York.'

'Really? That's very interesting. I've visited ten owners so far, and all their stolen paintings were bought at auction. You wouldn't happen to remember the name of the antique shop, would you?'

'I can do better than that. I must have the receipt somewhere. Patricia, why don't you make us all some tea while I look for it?'

The tea in the pot must have been going cold, because Patricia Shuttleworth and I had drunk a couple of cups each by the time he reappeared, clutching a worn receipt from Clifford Antiques and

Fine Art. There was no mention of a proprietor, and the phone number was unobtainable when Mr Shuttleworth tried it, but I hoped to track down Mr Clifford if he was still alive, and see if I could find out how news of the painting's current owner might have reached the thieves.

'Thanks very much for your time. You've been most helpful.'

When I got home I trawled the internet for Mr Clifford and the address of the Antique shop. The only thing I found was that the shop had been on a street close to Clifford's Tower, which made me doubt the usefulness of looking for a Mr Clifford, as the shop title probably referred to its vicinity to the tower. I determined to dig a bit deeper when I got chance, but at any rate, I'd learned something useful for my next report.

Steve was working late that night. He sent a text telling me not to wait up. They'd been searching through hours of CCTV coverage both around Cuthbert's shop and on the A63, and now faced the equally lengthy job of tracking down and interviewing the owners of dozens of possible cars that might have been involved in the torture and killing of the jeweller. After speaking to Carly, I used the time profitably to type up the draft of my report on John Munro. She was rather down as she'd learned nothing new, but I thought it was no bad thing, as she'd been getting too keen on following in my footsteps. It didn't hurt for her to find out that there were days when you made no progress at all, and seemed to be wasting your time. I arranged to meet her at midday at my flat the next day to finalise the report, before our meeting with the Major on the Friday.

That done, I curled up in front of my all-time favourite film, "While You Were Sleeping", and imagined myself in Sandra Bullock's shoes, whilst I indulged in a bar of chocolate and a glass or two of wine. Bliss! I was so sleepy after the wine that I didn't hear Steve come in. When I woke, he was already up and about to leave. I had a dry mouth from the wine and a bit of a headache and cursed myself for not drinking enough water before I went to bed. He put his head round the door on his way out.

'Morning, sexy!'

'I don't feel sexy. I had a couple of glasses of wine. Feels like a couple too many this morning.'

'You can't take it, can you, love? One of these days, you'll remember that. No, strike that. By the time you get that sensible, you'll be at the age where you forget everything.'

I threw a pillow at him.

'Hey, I did say you looked sexy. That tousled hair look suits you.'

I wondered why I spent time trying to tame it, if he liked it best when it looked a mess. 'Did you get anywhere with the CCTV last night? I didn't hear you come in.'

'No, it's a long haul. We've eliminated a lot of cars but it'll take a few days to get round all the drivers. I might be late again tonight, so don't wait tea for me. How's your heiress case coming along? Is Carly okay?'

I filled him in quickly on John Munro and told him I thought Carly would be finished by the weekend. 'I hope you don't mind I only found two weeks' work for her?'

'Course not. She had nothing else lined up, and you've paid her well. It's been nice to see a bit more of her than usual as well. Better go now, though, Rach. See you later. I'll try to get in before you go to bed but I can't promise.'

'Okay. Bye, love. Have a good day.'

I showered and washed my hair, drank a load of water with a couple of paracetemol and made myself eat a sensible breakfast. I'd arranged to meet Carly at twelve to finish the report, so, once I felt a bit more human, I made a couple of appointments for the afternoon, and one for mid-morning. I was getting through them now. I just needed to draw some insightful conclusions and break the case, or else get a lucky break. Speaking of which, I placed a quick call to Pete, giving him the details of Clifford Antiques and Fine Art, and asking him to try and track down the current whereabouts of the owner or any employees.

'I'll do anything I can, Rach. It'd be great if I can make your life easier by helping you earn the reward money.'

'That'd be super, thanks.'

'I'm still hoping you'll let me take you out for a meal again soon. When you come round, we'll have to arrange something.'

'I'm a bit pushed with having Carly here at the moment, Pete, so I'd prefer it if you just email me or ring with any information.' I thought that sounded a bit short, and I needed the information, so I added, 'but next time I need something, we'll definitely have that meal.'

'I'll hold you to it, Rach.'

I put the phone down with the sinking feeling that I'd agreed to something stupid, but pushed it aside, grabbed my keys and set off for my appointment in North Ferriby. I needed to be back for twelve, so had picked somewhere near to Hull.

19

North Ferriby is a commuter village, near the banks of the Humber, just west of Hull, and by the time I got there that sunny Thursday morning, it was as quiet as the grave. I found Rydal Grange without much difficulty and by half past ten I was sitting in Jason Lambert's lounge, looking at the gap where his Paul Nash painting had hung until recently.

Mr Lambert was much younger than my previous interviewees. In his late twenties, he'd either done very well for himself, or possibly inherited the money to buy his modern designer house with its manicured gardens. It reminded me a little of George Best's house, not that I'd ever seen it, except on the telly. It was all glass and angular shapes. Not my cup of tea, but most definitely expensive.

I didn't want to like him. I didn't like the house, and at the same time I suppose I was rather envious of the fact that he had the money, at my age, to afford it. But that changed when he told me what he did for a living.

'I bought the painting to challenge myself to produce something comparable in my own line of work.' I must have looked as puzzled as I felt, because he continued, 'I'm a war photographer. It pays well, because of the risks attached, and I'm not ashamed to say that I'm very good at it. I hope you don't think I'm bragging, but I just have a knack for taking the shots that newspapers want. But at the end of the day, that's all they are - glorified snapshots. When I saw the Paul Nash painting I knew that, although I could never be a great war artist, I could try my best to make my photographs as near to art as possible. Buying it and hanging it on my wall was vital to remind me of my goal. And that's why I agreed to fit you in at short notice, Miss Hodges. I miss that painting badly.'

I felt humbled. I could never bring myself to visit a war-torn country by choice, let alone immerse myself in the heart of the fighting to get photos the way that Jason Lambert did. I no longer begrudged him his expensive home and furniture.

I filled him in on the reason for my visit and asked the same questions about his recent visitors and his staff. He'd been away for three weeks when the theft took place. Anyone knowing he was the owner of the house, might have guessed he was away in Afghanistan, but he couldn't remember telling anyone specifically, except his mother, who came in to water his plants and check on the place. It turned out that he paid her a small sum to do his cleaning and laundry, and there were no other staff employed.

'Looks like I've kept you from other things for very little, I'm afraid, but before I leave, would you mind telling me how you came to purchase the painting? There's just a chance that the paintings were stolen to order and the buyers targeted through sale records.'

'I bought it from a gallery in London a couple of years ago. I'm not sure of the name. I was just walking by on my way to meet a client at a restaurant, and the gallery was holding a major retrospective of his work.'

'That's interesting. Most paintings were bought at auction, and I was starting to believe that the thieves had gained access to auction house records. Could you find out the name of the gallery for me, so I can investigate the staff, please?'

'I'd be glad to. I can't remember offhand but I probably have a record of the gallery's name on an old bank statement. Failing that, I'll try to locate the restaurant and Google galleries in the area until I come up with the information for you. Do you want to wait while I dig around?'

'Oh, I'm really sorry, but I have another appointment. Would it be too much trouble for you to email me the details, please? It could be crucial in finding a link between the thefts, and hopefully lead us to the thieves themselves.'

'No problem, and thanks for your visit. You've made me feel much more positive, knowing there's something I can do.'

I took my leave and drove back to my flat to meet Carly. She'd managed to speak to some of the girls on John Munro's course. They didn't know him well, as he carried out his social life mainly off campus with Sally, but they thought he was 'an okay sort of a bloke'. He was also known for getting his work in on time and achieving high grades. One of them had heard him mention he'd been working in his holidays for his local council, in the town planning department, and she got the impression he might have the promise of a job to go to, when he graduated. Granted it was just opinion, but it did put his future in a more positive light and explained why he had a payslip.

'I drafted the report last night. I've got a couple of appointments on the art insurance case this afternoon, so I was wondering if you could finalise the report for me and print it off? You need to add in what you heard this morning, saying it's hearsay but you've included it to give a full picture, then check the whole thing for errors, spelling mistakes and slips in grammar before you print it off. You don't need to draw any conclusions. It's not part of our brief to do so, and Major Ferris will want to decide for himself how best to proceed.'

'What do you think he'll do?'

'I really don't know him well enough to second-guess him, but I think he'll handle it sensitively. Do you mind finishing the report?'

'No, not at all, though I'd be happier if you saw it before we go to see the Major. I can also type up the report on the will beneficiaries for the solicitors this afternoon. They said they'd pay me on receipt, so I'll call round before they close. How much is Pete charging for the information on the beneficiaries I couldn't trace myself?'

'Nothing. He won't take a penny.'

'Really? Why?'

'It's nothing to him. Just half an hour's diversion from his usual corporate IT work. And anyway, it amuses him to have me in his debt.'

'So I can keep all the solicitors' fees?'

'Yes, and you can have the fee from Major Ferris too.'

'Oh no, I couldn't take all that. Including tomorrow and seeing Pete, you'll have come with me on three occasions, and you spoke to the lecturer. You must have done a quarter of the work.'

'Call it a gift to a future sister-in-law to keep her student debts to a minimum.'

Carly protested a bit more, but eventually gave in when I said I had to get off or I'd miss my next appointment. 'Why don't you bring the finished report over on a memory stick so I can give it my seal of approval before we print it out? You can eat here too, although I'll be the only one in. Steve said he'd likely not get back till late. We can have a girls' night in, if you'd like?'

'That'd be great, though I thought I'd head off tomorrow afternoon, so I ought to do some packing, and I have lots of bits left in the fridge. Why don't I come over after I've eaten and packed? It'll only be eightish, no later?'

'Good idea. I could do with typing up my notes so far this week, ready for emailing to Clare on Monday night, anyway.'

'Fine. You've been so good to me, Rachel. The money'll be a great help. It'll be a shame to go home, and if I go tomorrow afternoon it means I'll miss seeing Steve, but we'll catch up again before long.'

'He'll be fine with it, don't worry. But now I really must go.'

I rushed out and then remembered I was almost out of petrol. I didn't have far to go, but I had to go over the Humber Bridge and didn't want to risk running out and blocking one of the lanes, so I called at the garage. For once I did the sensible thing and called ahead to say I was running about twenty minutes late. Good job, as there was a torrential rain shower and even with my wipers on super-fast, I had to slow right down to a crawl till it eased.

Cavendish House was in Winteringham, Lincolnshire. I paid the toll to cross the Humber and drove through South Ferriby, which is separated from North Ferriby by less than three miles as the bird flies, and now a mere seven or so miles by road across the river. However, before the bridge was built, as recently as 1981, it would have taken a round trip through Goole of well over fifty miles. Winteringham is still a quiet village, but has had an influx of Hull commuters since the bridge opened.

I found David Gaskell waiting at Cavendish House, eager to tell me all about his painting by Pissarro, one of the greatest Spanish Impressionist painters ever to have lived, or at least that's how he described him. I'm not a big fan of those soft fuzzy impressionist painters, but maybe that's my loss. He graciously accepted my apology for being late. 'Ten minutes here or there doesn't matter at this time of day. The restaurant's closed till the evening. We don't serve afternoon tea.'

'Oh, do you own the restaurant in the village?'

'Yes. It's how I made my money. I've got a marvellous chef and we draw in people from Lincoln as well as north Lincolnshire, Hull and the East Riding.'

I confessed that I'd never eaten there myself, but that I'd heard great reports of the food, which was true, as Pete had mentioned it when he was trying to entice me to dine with him. He could afford the best restaurants. I wasn't sure that Steve and I were quite in that league except for a special occasion, but I did assure Mr Gaskell that we'd try and visit sometime soon. I ran through the usual questions, but learned nothing of interest. Anyone who wanted to, could have found out that he was at his restaurant every evening, leaving the house empty the night it was burgled.

Next stop was Elsham, a village further south towards Scunthorpe, and I was back on schedule. I was beginning to think I wouldn't learn anything else new, but Quentin Black soon dispelled that thought. 'I was until recently the proud owner of one of the few Van Goghs in private hands. I kept my identity secret, but was persuaded to loan the painting to an exhibition in London. Basically,' he explained, 'although on paper I'm worth a fortune, at the moment cash flow is very tight and the gallery offered me a tidy sum of money, so I agreed, somewhat reluctantly, to let the painting out of my sight. I have regretted it every minute since.'

'So it was stolen from the exhibition?'

'No, it wasn't. However, I believe it was stolen because it appeared in the exhibition. I think someone unscrupulous connected to the exhibition's organisers sold the information that I own the painting.'

'Have you any proof of that? Any idea who it might have been?'

'No, I'm afraid not. It's the only logical solution. As you can see, my home is not a country estate. It's a lovely country vicarage, and as such, would hardly attract an art thief. No-one knew the painting was here.'

'Sorry to interrupt, but you must have visitors, tradesmen, repair men, or a cleaner?' As I mentioned each category, he shook his head.

'The Van Gogh was in the study. I work from home, and it's my office. No-one, and I do mean no-one, Miss Hodges, has ever set foot in my office apart from me. I lock the door when I leave and the window is alarmed along with the rest of the house. It's been safe for over forty years since I inherited it from my dear aunt Edith, and no-one would ever suspect that there was a Van Gogh here. When the security system was fitted, I moved the painting temporarily to my wardrobe. The only other people who know of its whereabouts are the insurers, and I am assured by them that the information is known only to a select few. In any case, the timing of the robbery, a mere six months after the exhibition, would seem to indicate the source of the leaked information.'

'Excuse me for saying so, but I would imagine you've raised these concerns with the insurers already?'

'They told me that none of the other stolen paintings had been exhibited, nor did they have any connection with the gallery concerned, but without wishing to sound boastful, mine was a particularly rare and valuable painting, and the thieves might have felt it worth going the extra mile to locate it. Just because the other paintings were located in a different way, doesn't mean anything.'

'I can understand what you're saying, Mr Black, and believe me, I'll be sure to have all exhibition and gallery employees cross-referenced with people who came into contact in any way with the other paintings before they were stolen.'

'That's all I can ask of you, and I'm glad you called round.'

We exchanged a few more words, Mr Black gave me full details of the exhibitors and gallery concerned, and then I left, feeling quite excited, and wondering if Pete could do any digging for me into the people on the list and their relatives and near acquaintances.

It was only when I was driving back over the Humber Bridge that I remembered something Quentin Black had said, and realised that there was another lead that had totally been ignored by the insurers. Someone in their own offices could have leaked the whereabouts of the Van Gogh and all the other paintings. Two immediate questions sprang to mind.

Firstly, had any other insurers dealt with any paintings that had been stolen lately in the area? I had taken Clare Brennan at her word when she said that they were the major art insurers in the country, and obviously she was keen to recover the paintings her company insured. She may not have exchanged information regarding thefts of paintings insured by other companies, or she might be correct in her assumption that all major art in the area was insured by Thompson & Brenner. If theirs was the only insurer, or if there were no paintings covered by other insurance companies stolen, it could have been an inside job.

Secondly, I presumed that the insurers kept a list of all artworks insured with them. A list with addresses, a list held on computer, which could be accessed by other employees - or hacked into by someone in the IT department?

There was just a chance that Thompson and Brenner had never considered these possibilities. By the time I had finished mulling it all over, I was back at Steve's flat. I dashed up the stairs and made copious notes on my laptop before taking my shoes off. I didn't even put the kettle on first. That's how important I considered my latest theories. I hadn't totally disregarded the other possibilities - a connection to auction houses, or Anthony Wharton's growing collection of paintings without being robbed himself, but they didn't seem as high a priority any more.

When I'd written down what seemed like the entire contents of my head, I made a drink and raided the biscuit tin. At that moment Carly knocked at the door, and it was only then that I realised it was way past teatime, and I'd not given a thought to food, which shows you how engrossed I was. I put a pizza in the oven while I read through her finished report. There were no corrections necessary, which pleased her greatly, so I printed it off, got the pizza out and discovered Carly had bought wine and chocolates 'as a little thank you present.'

'You didn't have to.'

'I know. But I wanted to. I really appreciate everything you've done the last couple of weeks. Not just the money, but putting me up and showing me how you do things.' It was my turn to look pleased, before we laid waste to the chocs and wine.

20

I'd drunk too much to drive Carly home so she stayed on the settee, and the following morning Steve did get to see her before she left, after all. After they'd finished chatting, Steve got up to go.

'I nearly forgot, Rach. I had a phone call from Anna Rijkhart yesterday. The Dutch police have a lead on the diamond smuggling, though it seems to connect to Germany rather than England. They were hoping to make at least one arrest today. She said if there's any likelihood it connects with Cuthbert's murder, then she'll let me know. Maybe I will get to Holland after all, if the Super thinks it's worth paying for a trip.'

As he left, I was wondering whether I could sneak in on the trip, whilst at the same time hunting for something fairly formal that was clean. 'Washing tomorrow,' I muttered.

'Sorry, what did you say?' Carly came out of the bathroom, looking far better than I felt. She's still at the age when an evening of chocs and wine has no effect on the figure or head at all.

'Nothing. I just realised I need to do laundry.'

'I see. Well, I'm ready when you are.'

'Better get off then. We've to be at Saxilby Hall by ten thirty.' It was a lovely morning for a drive up onto the Wolds. I handed Major Ferris the report and gave him a verbal summary.

'I had a gut feeling that something wasn't right. Don't worry, Miss Hodges. I've been thinking it over, and I'll tread carefully with my granddaughter. I don't want Sally digging her heels in, just to be contrary, and rushing into marriage. Maybe this John of hers will come good in the end. I've just got to somehow hope she waits until they've graduated. Maybe he'll turn his back on gambling and then he can clear his debts. If he doesn't, then I'm sure she's sensible enough to realise he wouldn't be the man for her.'

'That would be my opinion too, for what it's worth.'

The Major handed me a cheque and we got back in the car.

As we set off back to Hull, Carly was obviously still thinking things over. After a few minutes, she turned to me and said, 'he seemed to take that better than I thought. Do you think John will be able to stop gambling, Rachel? If he doesn't, I'm not sure how the Major could tell Sally about it, without her being angry that her grandfather's been checking up on her boyfriend.'

'Who knows, Carly? I'm afraid we can only do our job and then it's up to other people. It's frustrating, but there aren't always easy solutions in real life. It's not like being a private detective in a

TV programme or a book. I don't always find out how things end.'

We ate sandwiches for lunch at my flat, and I wrote a cheque for Carly for the amount Major Ferris had paid me, whilst she packed her last few things. After lunch I dropped her at the railway station and paid the Major's cheque into my bank account.

I looked at the brief from the insurers again. I had now visited fourteen of the seventeen houses that had been robbed, and there weren't many to go. Clare had promised me four weeks' salary as a minimum, and I'd only been working for two weeks. I had some open leads to follow up on auction houses and gallery owners and besides the remaining three houses, there were two or three more owners whom she'd listed as major art collectors who hadn't been robbed. I know she'd guaranteed the four weeks, but I couldn't help but worry that I'd run out of leads before the time was up, and she might change her mind.

I was also fretting over how I could raise the possibility with Clare that it might have been an inside job. Then it occurred to me that I could play on the possibility that their computer system might have been hacked into, adding as an afterthought, that might or might not be meant to be taken seriously, that of course, no hacking would be necessary if the information was handed over by a member of her staff. She could then tell me that was impossible or investigate herself.

I had just filled the washer when my mobile rang. It was my old friend, DI Jordan. 'Are you still working on the art robberies for the insurers, Rachel?'

'Yes, I am, and I must thank you for recommending me to Thompson and Brenner.'

'You're welcome. The reason I'm ringing you, is because there was another robbery last night, and I thought you might like to come along with me when I visit the owner. I'm going over at five today, when he gets in from work. I'm sure you'll have the background fresh in your mind, so if you could come, it would help me, as well as giving you a chance to see if you can come up with anything.'

'That would be great. Thanks. Shall I come to the police station or meet you there?'

'It would look better if we arrive together, I think, and it's quite a way, actually. Sewerby, just past Bridlington. Can I pick you up?'

'Yes, no problem, or else I can walk round. I'm actually at Steve's flat at the moment, just around the corner from the station in Dagger Lane. What time do you want me?'

'I'd say we need to set off by three forty-five in case of traffic.'

'Right. I'll meet you at the front desk. It'll only take ten minutes to walk over from here, so I'll set off at three thirty and bring everything I have.'

'Great. You can fill me in on what you've learned so far, and I'll bring you up to speed on this robbery in the car on the way there.'

'It wouldn't be Simon Keaton's house, would it?'

'How on earth did you guess that?'

'I'm not psychic. Clare Brennan gave me a list of four collectors who haven't been targeted by the thieves yet, and I was just looking at it ten minutes ago. Seems there's now only three. See you soon.'

I had about half an hour to get everything together, but that still gave me time to email Pete and ask him if he would look into the gallery who arranged the Van Gogh exhibition. It dawned on me that I'd not asked him if he knew any hackers on the wrong side of the law, so I threw that in too. Whilst I was walking over to the station, I wondered if that had been wise. In the past, Steve had expressed doubts about the legality of some of Pete's business methods. I'd always thought that was prompted by jealousy, but what if he was right? If Pete did have acquaintances or even friends who might have been involved in the IT side of the robbery, he was hardly going to tell me. Of course, it could have been Pete himself. I'd be willing to bet he was capable of it from the technical viewpoint, but surely he'd not knowingly be an accessory to robbery? Of course not. That was ridiculous. I dismissed the thought as quickly as it had appeared in my head, ran up the steps of the station and pushed open the door. DI Jordan was waiting for me.

'Am I late?'

'No, right on time. Let's go the back way down to the car park. How are you, Rachel? Found any dead bodies lately?'

I laughed and said I hadn't, and then he concentrated on driving through the busy afternoon traffic in Hull. After we'd skirted Beverley via the bypass and then taken the A164 to Driffield, I asked him if all the owners of stolen paintings had been insured by Thompson and Brenner, and he confirmed that was the case.

'Did you not find that a coincidence?'

'Yes, of course, but when we looked into it, it seems that there are only two other specialist insurers of artwork, and one of those is a small affair in Scotland. The other is in London but operates exclusively in the capital. Thompson and Brennan have subsidiary offices in Leeds, Manchester, Liverpool, Birmingham and Exeter, and they have links to several major general house insurers, thus simplifying things for the customer, as they can arrange insurance for the rest of the house contents at the same time. I've been assured that it wasn't surprising that all the owners concerned used the same firm. I did take the precaution of checking a list of their employees against the criminal records system, and satisfying myself that they have no convicted criminals working for them.'

Once we were free of the Driffield bypass and on the A614 to Bridlington, he told me what little he knew about the robbery at Simon Keaton's house.

'He arrived home late last night from the theatre in York to find one of his paintings had been stolen. His wife had left the house at around four to catch a train to York to meet him for dinner before the play. She's adamant she'd set the alarm before leaving. It was exactly the same as in the other thefts. The system controls at the alarm company had evidently been bypassed to turn the alarm off, and then re-set after the break-in. The times were logged at the security company, but of course, as no alarm was triggered, their system didn't flag it up as a break-in. It merely assumed the owner had returned briefly and then gone out again. In the initial robberies it was assumed that the owner must have told someone else the password to disable the alarm, whether by intention or by having the instructions written somewhere that an unscrupulous or disgruntled employee could find, but that theory didn't hold water, as the robberies piled up. The only solution had to be that someone had hacked into the system.'

'Did you have any suspects?'

'A few, but they all had alibis. One was locked up, two now live abroad and the last one was at a Rotarians' dinner at the time of one of the thefts. I think you know him - Peter Shannon.'

I blushed, as much at the knowledge that he had somehow connected me with Pete, as at the memory that only an hour previously, I'd been entertaining vague doubts myself as to whether Pete might have been somehow involved with the robberies. I quickly recovered from my surprise and said, 'Why was he a suspect, if you don't mind me asking?'

'He's extremely wealthy, has a first in Computing from Oxford, and there have been unsubstantiated rumours about the legality of some of his business methods.'

'I see. I wouldn't know much about his business, I'm afraid. He's helped me track down people on the internet occasionally, but that's all.' Maybe I was being naïve but I wasn't going to tell DI Jordan that I used Pete's business services frequently, particularly as I wasn't sure all the information he found out for me was always obtained legally, so I decided to lead him down a more personal route. 'I went to school with him, and ran into him again about six months ago. I saw him a couple of times and he helped me out with when my car was in an accident. Then of course I was attacked by his crazy ex-girlfriend.'

'Ah, yes. The mud-wrestling and her black eye.'

Word had obviously gone right round Hull Central Police Station. I groaned. 'I really don't want to be reminded of that. Was it my fault she wouldn't stop trying to kill me?'

'You mean to tell me you can't you see the funny side yet?'

'Maybe, but if you don't mind, can we go back to discussing Simon Keaton instead of me, please?'

'We're nearly there now, but take a look at his preliminary statement to the constable who responded to his 999 call, and then you'll know as much as I do.'

We bypassed most of the Bridlington traffic, and were soon entering Sewerby, which has become almost a suburb since new estates were built along the main road from Brid. Surprisingly, the Keatons lived in a new house on one of those estates. But this was no average newly-built estate, where people lived cheek by jowl with their neighbours. No. The houses were massive, with well-proportioned rooms, high ceilings matching the style of times gone by, and enormous gardens with trees shielding the houses from unwelcome intrusion. It looked like the builders had bought an extremely large field and built a mere six houses. The Keatons must have paid a hefty sum.

I didn't take to Keaton and his wife. It didn't help that they looked at me as if I was something they'd trodden in, and weren't much more polite to DI Jordan. They'd lived in France prior to moving to Sewerby. Madame Keaton was herself French and was exquisitely dressed in a pale green silk dress. She had her hair in a chignon, which is nothing more than a posh bun and was wearing a diamond necklace, which I thought ludicrous for the afternoon. She looked at my unruly long hair as if it belonged to an animal.

I learned little at the interview that was useful to my investigation. My interest was awakened when Keaton handed DI Jordan a photograph of the missing painting. The Chagall painting was certainly unusual. It was entitled "Picture of Vava", and in a way it matched Mrs Keaton's dress, except it was the woman's face that was green. Maybe she was jealous. I don't know. The painting wasn't bad apart from the green. I asked if I could have a copy of the photograph. That caused a bit of a fuss as they'd assumed I was with the police, and DI Jordan had let them do so. Mrs Keaton was most insistent that they would have rung the insurers as soon as they had spoken to DI Jordan.

I asked why they hadn't reported it stolen to the insurers as soon as the constable had given them an incident number. Keaton then surprised us all by shame-facedly admitting he'd hoped that there'd be a ransom demand so he could get the painting back before the insurers got involved. I gave him a sharp look. That made no sense to me. Why tell the police but not the insurers? Something niggled at me, but I couldn't put my finger on it.

'Why would you expect a ransom demand, Mr Keaton?'

'I don't know. I've never had a painting stolen before, and it is very valuable.'

He didn't look like he was lying, and I like to think I have a sixth sense for detecting liars. I decided to give him the benefit of the doubt. Maybe his thinking had just been muddled.

The scene of crime people were dusting for prints and whatever else they do when they are looking for clues, so I didn't get in the study to see where the painting had hung. DI Jordan told me I wasn't missing anything, but I'd have liked to have made my own mind up. We asked all the usual questions between us - I chipped in to ask where they'd bought the painting. The answer was an auction in Paris. Now that was a completely new answer, but I couldn't say what it told me. I took the details and we left. On the way back to Hull I realised I'd not got my copy photograph, but I imagined Clare Brenner would forward me one in due course.

DI Jordan, or Mike, as he said to call me, asked how my investigation was going. I felt a bit awkward, not only calling him Mike, but also because he seemed to be implying I'd been keeping things from the police, but then he said he was getting copies of my weekly reports to Clare, so that was okay. In fact he'd just had the first report the previous day, but he wanted to know if there'd been any new leads since that report.

'If there have, I could do with knowing what they are, now there's been a new robbery.'

'No problem, Mike. Anything I can do to help. I wouldn't have the case if it wasn't for you. I update the draft of my report daily, while things are fresh in my head, and I printed out the latest version this morning. You can take it. I can print a new copy when I get home.'

'That's great, Rachel. Thanks a lot. Now, where do you want dropping? The station? Or your flat?'

I was about to say 'Steve's flat would be better', when I realised Steve might not like his colleagues to share that piece of personal information, so I said, 'my flat would be great as we're coming back down Holderness Road.' I decided I could call in on Mum and Dad for a cuppa and then get a bus into town afterwards.

21

'Hello, Rachel. I'm glad you've dropped by. You can tell me what you think of the cardigan I've got your Gran for her birthday.'

'That's a nice shade of mauve, Mum. Where's it from?'

'Marks and Spencer's. She'll say I've paid too much and I should take it back. Then I'll tell her you get better quality there, so it'll last for years. Then she'll say she's only got a few years left, so it'll be a waste. Then I'll tell her not to be silly, and that she's got decades ahead of her. I can predict the whole conversation. It's the same every time I get her something to wear, but some of her woollies are wearing thin.'

'Just tell her she'll not find a lovely mauve like that in any cheap shop, and that'll sort her out.'

'That's a good idea. It is a pretty colour, isn't it?'

I just hoped Gran didn't decide to pay a visit to one of her neighbours for a home perm and colour, any time soon. In the past she'd emerged with her hair that mauve colour, and I'd hate her hair to clash with her cardi. Prudently, I kept that thought to myself. No use upsetting Mum.

We had a cuppa and I brought her up-to-date on the houses I'd visited since I last saw her. She wasn't interested in the robberies, though she was pleased for me that I was getting paid so much. No, she wanted to know all the details of the furnishings in the houses of the rich and famous. I was so parched when I finished talking that I had to have another cup of tea.

'Where's Dad?'

'Didn't I tell you? I'm sure I did. We've heard nothing else since City got through. He's gone to Wembley to the Championship play-off finals.'

'That's great. How are they doing?' I looked at my watch. The game should have been over now, surely? I hoped they hadn't lost. Dad would have been so excited at the thought of them going back into the Premiership. How could I have missed such a vital piece of news?

'It's only Friday, Rachel. They don't play till tomorrow. Your dad's gone down to London to stay overnight with Uncle Jack.'

I made a mental note to keep an eye on the result at a quarter to five the next day so I could congratulate or commiserate with Dad, and then I left, clutching an apple crumble for Steve's tea, and Mum's words echoing in my head, 'I'm sure you don't feed that lad properly and he's a policeman. He needs a good meal inside him.'

When he got in, Steve had a surprise for me. 'I'm going to have to work on Sunday, I'm afraid. So how's about we have a day out tomorrow?'

'That sounds great.' My mind half occupied with where we could go, I suddenly remembered my trip to Sewerby with Mike Jordan and I told Steve all about it.

'Oh, so it's Mike now, is it? I'll have to keep my eye on him.'

'Stop teasing. You know he's coming up to retirement and can't wait to spend his time gardening with his wife.' Then I told him Dad had gone to Wembley and he suggested I go over for one of Mum's Sunday salad teas, so Dad could tell me all about it. It seemed like a good idea with Steve out at work, so I rang Mum after we'd eaten, and arranged it.

Of course, on Saturday morning Steve remembered something he just had to nip into work to see to. It was nearly eleven by the time he got back from the station. His idea of an hour at work is always a couple at least. In fact I'd had in my mind he wouldn't get back till lunchtime. I was all set for every eventuality with umbrella and sunglasses in my bag, and picnic packed, so off we went. I'd had in mind to go to Castle Howard so we headed up towards Malton. Then the sun came out and it warmed up, so we cut across to Helmsley, and had our picnic on the terrace overlooking Rievaulx Abbey. It's rare you get a vantage point above a ruined abbey, but this is where the owners of Duncombe Park would come and promenade and picnic. They'd built small temples at either end of the long terrace. After lunch we went down to the abbey ruins and then drove back into Helmsley for a potter round the shops. Being Saturday, it was difficult to park, but we squeezed into a spot near the castle.

After lunch I spotted someone I recognised. I couldn't place him at first. I only noticed him because he was behaving rather furtively and so caught my attention. He was looking in every direction as he unlocked his car boot and pulled out a large square parcel wrapped in brown paper. Then I realised it was Brian Mills from Cottingham, the owner who'd been so eager to get rid of me. I pointed him out to Steve, just as he disappeared into a shop doorway some distance down the street. You won't be surprised to hear that policemen are naturally suspicious, and it didn't take much prompting from me, for us to take a closer look. The shop was an antique shop, selling paintings.

'Maybe he wants to buy a painting to replace the one he lost, but, on the other hand, with that parcel in his hand, I'm thinking he's up to no good.'

'I'm sure you're right. Sorry I didn't chase up the enquiry I made about him, Rach.'

Mills emerged shortly afterwards into the sunlight and we followed him to a nearby café.

'You stay here and ring me if he leaves. I'm going to make a few enquiries in the shop in my official capacity.' I was dying to go with him, but someone needed to watch Mills. Steve'd only been gone a moment when Mills came out of the café, looking in all directions once more. He took the parcel back to his car. I wrote down the number plate and rang Steve. Fortunately, Mills didn't seem to be in a hurry to leave, and Steve got back as he was pulling out. We jumped in the car and pulled out a couple of cars behind Mills.

'Well, that was interesting. Mills was trying to sell a painting.'

'It wouldn't happen to be an expressionist painting of horses, would it?'

'Funny you should say that. The shop owner thought it might be by Franz Marc. Does that ring a bell?'

'Yippee. His own stolen painting! Do you think he's behind all the robberies?'

'No, sweetheart. I think he's an amateur. He reported it stolen for the insurance money, but held onto the painting and now he's trying to dispose of it. Smacks to me that he must be desperate for money, otherwise he'd have laid low until it'd all been forgotten.'

'You're right. He's got some nerve. The insurance hasn't paid out yet.'

'The owner of that shop didn't know Mills personally. When he asked him where he'd got the painting, Mills said it was from an antiques fair in Newark. The shop owner was a bit suspicious as the painting, if authentic, was too valuable to have been sold at an antiques fair. He thought it was either a good copy, or had been stolen. He asked Mills to leave it with him for a proper evaluation, at which point Mills left rather hurriedly. The owner was just thinking about ringing the police, when I popped in. I gave him Mike Jordan's name and number.' As

Steve spoke, he was now speeding up fast, overtaking cars to keep Mills in his sight.

'But Steve, surely he must have realised they'd need to know the provenance of a valuable painting?'

'Maybe he thought a small shop in a small town might not ask too many questions, or maybe he hoped they might give him something for it, not realising its true worth. I'm guessing by his behaviour, he has no idea how to go about selling a stolen painting. As I said, he's an amateur, Rach. He must have jumped on the bandwagon when he heard about the other thefts. We could really do with catching him with the painting, though.'

Steve's mobile rang. Before he could switch to hands-free, I answered it for him. 'Hello, Mike. Yes, it's Rachel. Steve can't talk at the moment. He's driving.' I filled him in on what we knew, and reported we were following Mills on the A170 heading towards the top of Sutton Bank. 'We're just passing the bend where there's the turn-off to Oswaldkirk and Ampleforth. You know, where caravans have to turn because they can't go down Sutton Bank.'

A moment later he'd rung off. I filled Steve in on the rest of the conversation. 'He's going to get onto the police in Thirsk and see if they can catch him at the bottom of the Bank. He asked if we'd follow him a bit longer in case he turns off onto one of the minor roads. It's exciting, this, isn't it?'

'Yes, love.' Steve grinned. 'And I tell you what. If he really does have the so-called stolen painting in that brown parcel in his boot, then you'll be in line for a reward from the insurers.'

'Yippee! I'm glad we went to Helmsley instead of Castle Howard.'

'I doubt if he'd have managed to sell it anyway. He'd probably end up dumping it somewhere, to be found and returned to him.'

'Yes, but then he'd have got away with it. I can't understand why he didn't just sell it, if he was short of money.'

'Greed, possibly. Maybe he wanted to make money on it twice over, by claiming on the insurance and selling it as well. Maybe he paid too much for it and he would have lost money if he'd sold it. Maybe the market had dropped. Or maybe he just thought he was clever enough to get away with it, and wanted to see if he could. I don't know. I've learnt in this job, people do the craziest things.'

The phone rang again. I relayed the information to Steve. 'We're in luck. It's the Thirsk police. They're ringing from a patrol car that was on the A19. They're almost at Sutton-under-Whitestoncliffe. Once they get through the village and past the little road to Osgodby Hall, there should be nowhere for Mills to escape, providing he goes down Sutton Bank.'

'Tell them we're approaching the top now, and it doesn't look like Mills is turning off onto one of the side roads.'

'He's asking us to pull back and stay on the line,' I told Steve, before confirming to the police that Mills had started to go down the Bank. 'He wants you to turn round in the entrance to the country park, ready to pull out across the road, should Mills manage to turn round at the bottom when he sees them, and come back up the Bank.'

'OK, Rach. Give me my phone back, please, and pop out of the car for a few minutes. I'll take over.' I was a bit scared, with visions of Mills ramming Steve's car, but I needn't have worried. A couple of minutes later, Steve got out of the car and came over. 'It's OK. Mills is in custody. He didn't suspect a thing apparently, even when he saw the police car in the road. He probably thought there'd been an accident. When the police approached his car, and said they wanted to search his boot, they said he just went pale, and confessed. He didn't even make a run for it.' Steve sounded a bit disappointed. I know him. He'd have liked to have arrested Mills himself.

'So, what now?'

'That's it. Mike's sending a car to pick up Mills and the painting from Thirsk.'

'So we can go?'

'Yes, love. They have a witness statement from the shop owner in Helmsley, the painting and the confession. We don't need to give statements, so let's enjoy the rest of the day. How's about we watch the gliders taking off, take a look at the White Horse, and then find ourselves a nice pub for a meal?'

'That's a good idea. We can celebrate. First thing tomorrow I can fax Clare Brenner and claim that reward!'

After admiring the gliders and discussing who kept the white horse on the hillside white, and how, we stopped to eat in Hovingham. I celebrated with two glasses of wine, glad Steve was driving. The days had lengthened considerably so it was still sunny and I suggested we drive through the Castle Howard parkland. Good job Steve's not one of those men who only drives from A to B by satnav. Like Dad, we have a stack of ordnance survey maps in the boot. Even after drinking, I still managed to find the road that goes south from Slingsby.

It's always been one of my favourite drives. The road's dead straight with fantastic views across the lake to the hall. You drive through battlements and pass an obelisk, and you can imagine yourself in a horse and carriage in a costume from Jane Austen's day. Of course, the wine kicked in before long and I got us lost among the many little lanes, but Steve didn't mind getting lost as he was able to indulge in one of his favourite pastimes - outdoor amorous activity. Needless to say, it was dark and very late when we got in and we went straight to sleep. When I looked at my phone, it told me I'd had a missed call from Pete. He must have rung while Steve and I had been otherwise engaged, but it would have to wait.

22

We got up a bit late on Sunday morning, so Steve was in a rush to get to work. As soon as he'd gone, I drafted my weekly report for Clare Brenner and attached it to an email, in which I claimed the reward for the recovery of the painting that Mills had reported stolen. I tried to return Pete's call to see if he had information on Clifford's Antiques, but his mobile was turned off. Maybe he was having a lie-in, with it being Sunday. I didn't try his landline. I wanted the information, but not that urgently. I was acutely aware I'd promised to go for a meal with him, which had been incredibly stupid.

For once I had a bit of spare time so I put some washing on, then read the last couple of chapters of the book I'd been trying to finish for over a week. Since I took over the detective agency from my friend Julie when she emigrated to New Zealand, I seemed to have less, not more, time to read. Sometimes I wondered if I'd dreamt up the fact that I'd got a degree in English Literature from Hull University, but I only need to take one look at the rest of my life, namely Steve, to remind me of that time. I met him when we took the same Psychology module. He was studying law.

Some hours later, I was toying with the choice between cleaning and another good book, when the phone rang. It was Sarah.

'It's ages since we last met up. What's been going on in your life? Are you and Steve alright, now the Dutch policewoman's out of the picture?'

I couldn't believe I'd been so stupid as to be jealous of her, and told Sarah so. 'After our day out yesterday, Steve and I have never been closer. I've loads of news, Sarah. I had so much work, Steve's sister Carly came over to help. That's why I've not been in touch. I'm sorry.'

'Hey, it doesn't matter. Just don't forget me completely. Are you still busy or can you find time to help me pick a dress for our wedding anniversary? John's taking me to that posh place you went to with Pete. And you can bring me up to date with everything.'

'Great. Can you make tomorrow afternoon?'

'Yes. I can leave Josh with my mum. Have you time for lunch?'

We arranged to meet in a café in town and I put the phone down, happy that she wasn't upset I'd been neglecting her. I felt so upbeat, I got the vacuum out and set to with a vengeance, and even threw in a bit of dusting and tidying. The flat hadn't been as spotless in ages. I got so carried away it was almost two before I ate a sandwich for lunch. I restrained myself from eating afters, knowing Mum would have a good spread set out for tea.

Mum and Dad's house looked a bit different as I pulled up outside. A flag and a Hull City shirt were hanging from the windows. How could I have forgotten to turn on the news and check the result? City must have won, but Dad would expect me to know the score - and the goal scorers. Luckily Mum was in the kitchen and after a whispered conversation when I came in the back door, I had all the information I needed to rush in the living room and congratulate Dad on their return to the Premiership.

'Just wait, Dad. This time you'll take points off Man United.'

'We might at that, but don't get over-excited. As ever with the Tigers, we have no money to strengthen our squad.' He had a nerve talking about me getting over-excited when Mum had just told me Dad was driving her crazy. But what was new? It didn't take a win at Wembley for her to say that.

When Gran arrived we had tea. Being a Sunday in Hull, tea means salad, which in turn means tinned ham, lettuce, tomatoes, Branston Pickle and lashings of bread and butter. If you're really trendy, you serve coleslaw as well. I loved it. Afterwards Mum unveiled a cake decorated in yellow and black.

'I didn't know you could get black icing, Mum,' I said warily.

'It's liquorice, Rachel.'

'Oh, that's a good idea.' I had my doubts about mixing chocolate cake, yellow icing with God knows what E numbers in the colouring and liquorice, but my addiction to chocolate cake overcame all doubts, and it tasted surprisingly … interesting. I wasn't sure Gran should have had three slices, though.

'So, what's all this about you capturing a criminal and claiming a reward yesterday?' Dad asked after we'd eventually exhausted the topic of the Wembley game.

I'd only told Mum the bare bones when I'd arrived, so I filled them all in, stressing how I was never in any danger, and that I would be getting a reward for my efforts.

Gran butted in with the inevitable. 'That's good, our Rachel. A few more cases like that and you'll have enough money to put down on a house. Then we can have a nice wedding.'

'I'm sure it won't be long now, Gran.' I hadn't the heart to tell her or Mum that Steve still hadn't actually proposed. I'd let them believe a wedding was in the offing when I moved into Steve's flat, because otherwise they'd have been horrified. As I feared, Mum had obviously continued to buy wedding magazines, because she brought out that month's edition, and insisted I look at the latest fashion in dressing the chairs for the reception.

I saw Dad's face drop and inwardly I sagged too. How was I ever going to tell her that I was sure Steve would rather elope than go through with a grand affair that included dressed chairs? Mind you, by the time Steve got round to putting a ring on my finger, if he ever did, they'd surely be so pleased, they wouldn't mind what the ceremony was like. 'They look pretty, Mum, but don't you think Auntie Lesley could rustle up something simpler and more sophisticated with plain white cotton and coloured ribbons?'

'What a good idea, Rachel.' Dad visibly brightened at the thought of saving money. There was no way we'd expect him to pay for a wedding, but he'd be offended if he didn't. Another reason for Steve and me to elope.

'Any news, Gran?' I asked, knowing she couldn't resist, and the subject would move safely away from weddings.

'Well, you know Betty next door?' Not pausing for an answer, she continued, 'that new woman next door to her had her car towed away this week. She can't have paid for it. I didn't like the look of her when she moved in.' I wondered if the car had simply broken down, but knew better than to say so. 'And Mavis from the church, she's started walking out with Ted who lives over the road from me. I don't know what she sees in him. He's bald and has a limp. I like a good head of hair on a man, myself. And he can't even keep his garden tidy.'

After half an hour of similar titbits, I decided enough was enough, and took my leave. I got home and watched Downton Abbey and then Steve came home.

'It was hard getting some of them to concentrate on work today. All they really wanted to do was discuss yesterday's match,' he moaned.

'So you think you've been hard done by because of the Wembley victory, do you, love? Well, there's more to come. Mum's sent a piece of the cake she made for Dad,' I told him as I unwrapped the kitchen roll to reveal the icing in all its glory.

'They broke the mould when they made your family. It's no wonder you're crackers, Rach, but I do love you.'

We curled up on the settee and watched a bit of TV but we both were having trouble staying awake after the previous late night and were soon in bed.

The next morning, we were awake early. I put the kettle on while Steve took a shower. When he came out, he asked me what I had planned.

'I'm having lunch with Sarah and then we're going shopping for a dress for their anniversary. Before that I have to try and chase up some loose ends and then send my weekly report to Clare Brenner. What about you?'

'I'm hoping to hear from Holland about whether it's worth a trip to interview this Pieter Meerdink they've arrested, although I'm not sure it's connected to Cuthbert's murder.'

'So they did make an arrest, after all?'

'Yes, an email came in about it yesterday. Apparently, he was caught with a bag of diamonds and the Dutch think they must've come from the same source as those found on Jan Petersen, the man who fell in the Marina.'

At that precise moment, Steve's mobile rang. 'Yes. I'm on my way now. Oh, that's great news. See you in a few minutes, then.'

'Good news?'

'Yes. Or at least it could be. One of the red cars on the A63, in the right area and in the right time frame, was stolen at the time. The owner's only just reported it, because he's just got back from a long holiday in Australia.'

'Good luck, then. See you later.'

I knew better than to ask what time he'd be in. CID time was a flexible entity as it was, and if they had a lead on the murder case, well, who knew? I tried Pete again, this time his landline as well as his mobile, but there was no reply from the landline and his mobile was still turned off. I emailed the report as it was, wondering how much the reward might be, and if I'd get the cash included in my weekly payment.

I'd hoped to go through all my notes on the stolen paintings and make a list of loose ends that wanted chasing up, but somehow there was only time left for a drink, a quick change and then I had to leave to meet Sarah. I still had the last three owners to visit, as well as two who'd not been robbed.

I realised that, once again, I'd let the dreaded internet suck me into that black hole where time disappears.

Sarah's my best friend and even though she and John have a baby, Josh, we still have plenty to talk about that doesn't involve children. We went to school together in Hull, which is a bond that couldn't be broken even by years apart. You grow up cut off from the rest of the country, so you're always several years behind the current fashions, combined with being part of a unique Hull variation of the Yorkshire family identity. It's hard to describe to outsiders.

On top of that, Sarah and I studied English together so we swap books and talk about articles we've read and new books we've heard of. She's like a sister to me. We keep saying we'll start a book group, but neither of us has much free time, and we're our own miniature book club anyway.

She was really pleased for me when she heard about the well-paid insurance job, and when I got to the part about chasing Mills across North Yorkshire, I swear she was as excited as I was.

'As soon as Josh gets to nursery, I'll be enrolling as your assistant, if you'll have me.'

'You know you don't mean it. John would be horrified, and it wouldn't be exciting, because I'd have to give you run-of-the-mill errands to keep you safe,' I laughed. 'You need to find something a bit more literary where you leave work behind when you come home. A book shop would be ideal. You can get advance copies and lend them to me.'

'I must admit that sounds good, and I can always get my fix of excitement vicariously through you.'

'If you've finished eating, we'd better get shopping. There can't be many perfect dresses in Hull and they'll take some rooting out. Although I did a little search online this morning, and found a couple of new shops that specialise in vintage dresses. Would you fancy anything that's been worn before?'

'If it'll turn me into someone desirable without costing the earth, then it sounds great.'

We arrived at the first shop. Unfortunately, there were some ugly dresses that had probably only survived in good condition because it's doubtful they were worn very often when they were first bought. Then they'd been pushed away somewhere to emerge now there was a trend for vintage. There was the odd decent item but not in Sarah's size. 'I'm beginning to think this is a mistake. I'm sorry.'

'No. It was worth a try. Let's try the other shop before we give up. It's only further along this road,' Sarah replied.

And we struck gold. There was a much better selection of quality dresses, all of them perfect for a special night out. Sarah tried on three before settling on a pretty midnight blue lace dress, with the tiniest of blue ribbon straps. 'I look very sophisticated.'

'Very sexy, more like. It's perfect.'

'I agree and the price is brilliant.'

There was time for a drink and cake. We went to my favourite café overlooking the old market place and had enormous scones that filled the plates. I made Sarah promise to let me know how her evening went, and walked back to Steve's. I felt a bit guilty taking most of the day off work, but our day out on Saturday had turned into work which, although fun, had achieved a lot. I tried Pete's numbers again, but got nowhere. Maybe he'd had to go away on business. I sat down and tried to list the loose ends I needed to follow up, but my brain refused to function. I decided to give up and read, concluding I'd be better starting afresh in the morning. Around half past five, Steve texted to say he'd be late and to eat without him. I cooked healthy salmon in foil in the oven, peas and not-so-healthy spicy potato wedges.

I buried myself in a book, with Adele singing in the background. He was so late, I couldn't keep my eyes open and went to bed at around eleven. I didn't even hear him come in.

23

When I woke, Steve was still asleep. I got up as quietly as I could, but he must have heard me, because he appeared in the kitchen by the time the kettle had boiled. 'So, what's new?' I asked.

'Well, quite a lot, for once. The IT people managed to enhance the photos from the CCTV cameras and we identified the driver of the stolen red car. He's a thug called Bob Giggs, and he's been inside several times for stealing cars and GBH. And wait till you hear this! We've had him down for stealing for Howard Banks in the past, even though we couldn't make the connection stick, and Banks walked free while Giggs did the time. I just knew Banks was involved with those diamonds. I'll get him back for what he did to you, Rach.'

'But will he give up Banks this time, if he didn't before? Have you had him in for questioning yet?'

'Yes, but he won't even admit to stealing the car. Says a bloke in a pub sold it to him for cash. I ask you! He said he didn't know it was stolen, but when this bloke couldn't find the registration documents, he gave him it back. Said he only had it a day or so, and that must've been when he was caught on camera driving it. We've kept him in for more questioning, but even if he admits to stealing, we can't place him definitely at the scene of the scuffle, let alone taking part in a beating that presumably went too far and ended in Cuthbert's murder.'

'So, without wanting to sound critical, you haven't really got that far, then?'

'Well, we have got a link to Banks, which makes me feel we're on the right track and gives us enough grounds for having his workshop kept under surveillance. And I'm trying to get a phone tap organised. I'm going to call round and ask Banks about his links to Giggs, see if that rattles his cage at all, but we'll have to let Giggs go soon. We're just trying to let him know he's in deeper than he's ever been before, try and frighten him, if you will. Then we'll have him followed and see if he leads us anywhere. The most we can charge him with is 'receiving stolen goods' at the moment. We're looking into his known associates to see who might have driven Cuthbert's silver car and left it outside his flat. We've not managed to catch it on the CCTV in the surrounding area, and as I think I told you, there's none in the close vicinity. I mustn't forget to chase up the financial team looking into Cuthbert's finances as well.'

'Well, sounds like you'll be busy. I'll keep my fingers crossed for you.'

After Steve left, I rang to make appointments to visit the last three owners who'd been robbed, before I turned on the computer, ready to look at the files on each of the paintings and see if I'd overlooked anything. I made myself another cup of tea whilst it whirred into action, but before I could sit down and get to work, my mobile rang. I answered, and a familiar voice, though not one I could immediately place, asked, 'Rachel?'

'Yes, sorry, but who's calling?'

'It's DI Jordan. Mike. I wonder if you can spare me ten minutes?'

'When?'

'Now, preferably, if you can manage it.'

A little surprised to hear from him, I agreed to him calling at Steve's flat, rather than mine. Knowing it would only take DI Jordan ten minutes to come over from the station, I rushed round like a whirling dervish, tidying things away and moving the pile of washing-up into the sink, all the time wondering what he wanted. Maybe he'd got a lead on the latest robbery? But he could have told me that over the phone. Maybe they'd made an arrest and found all the paintings, and he was going to commiserate with me because I wouldn't get the reward money? But it sounded urgent. I would know soon enough. I'd only just brushed my unruly hair when there was a knock at the door, and I invited him in.

'Hello, Rachel. Thanks for meeting me so quickly. You remember we spoke about Peter Shannon? Well, I was wondering if you'd heard from him lately?'

I wondered why he wanted to know that, but decided it was better not to ask if Pete was in trouble. Instead I answered, 'I saw him one morning about a week ago. He'd been looking into the background of a young man for one of my clients. Then I spoke to him the same evening to ask him to try to locate the owner and employees of Clifford Antiques in York for me. I'm not that efficient when it comes to the internet and it saves me time to have him trawl through the electoral rolls and such like, instead of doing it myself.'

'Do you know what day that was?'

Tiny alarm bells were ringing as I racked my brain. 'Let me see. It was the day I saw the people who bought their Grimshaw painting from Clifford Antiques.' Continuing to think aloud, I said, 'the next day I went over the bridge to North Lincs, and the following day you took me to Sewerby.'

'That was Friday.'

'So it must have been last Wednesday when I spoke to Pete.'

'Mmm... Have you tried contacting him since then?'

'Yes. Just let me check my notes. That's right. I emailed him last Friday to look into another gallery owner, in connection with the stolen Van Gogh. Funnily enough he's not come back to me at all, though I did have a missed call on my mobile from him. I presume he wanted to talk rather than email, but I've not been able to get an answer on his landline, and his mobile's turned off.'

'Might I ask what day the missed call was?'

'Has something happened? I seem to remember you said you'd ruled him out of any involvement in hacking into the alarm systems because he had an alibi, didn't you?'

'He's gone missing and we're anxious to contact him. If you could tell me when you had the missed call, it might prove helpful.'

'Of course.' I fumbled with my phone, feeling a bit shaky. What did he mean by 'gone missing?' Who would report that - a neighbour? A girlfriend? And where could he be? Eventually I found the details of the missed call. 'It was Saturday night. Eight forty-seven.'

'Saturday? You're sure it was Saturday?'

'Yes, why?' I remembered exactly why I hadn't answered. Steve and I were too busy in the back seat of the car to answer a phone. It was the day we'd helped capture Mills, celebrated with a meal, then stopped the car somewhere near Castle Howard to celebrate some more.

'His neighbours told us he'd called round on Friday morning to say he'd be going away for a while.'

'I see. But why are you concerned?'

'I'm afraid we have reason to believe Mr Shannon may be involved with the robberies after all. It's now come to light that his alibi isn't watertight. He was absent from the meal for a while, and another guest recalls him using his laptop earlier in the evening. He thought it odd that Shannon had felt it necessary to take it along to such an event.'

'Oh, no! But surely there could be an innocent explanation for that?'

'Perhaps, but the fact that he has now gone missing makes that less likely. I'm sorry to be the bearer of such news, but I need to be sure that you understand the seriousness of the situation and tell me everything you know.'

'Of course. But I'm not sure what I can tell you. The case I met him about last Wednesday can't be involved, I'm certain. It concerned a young student who'd got engaged to my client's orphaned granddaughter. My client, Major Ferris, was concerned the lad was after her money, but the case all ended amicably. I can let you have the details, in confidence, of course.'

'Thank you.'

'Then I spoke to Pete that evening about the stolen Grimshaw. In the copy of my notes I gave you last Friday, you'll find details of the lead on Clifford Antiques. And that's it really, apart from the email I sent him on Friday evening about the Van Gogh exhibition. I can't be sure he even read that, as I've not had a reply. I can give you a copy, although if you're checking his computer, you should be able to see if he's read it.'

'Thank you, Rachel. We can't check his computer until we get a warrant, so that would be good.'

I ran a copy off for him. 'Is there anything else I can do to help? Are you sure he hasn't just gone away on business or away with one of his girlfriends?'

'I doubt it very much, but if you can tell me about any women in his life, that would be very helpful.'

'I don't think I can. I presume Stella Cooper's still in jail?'

'Yes, I've checked.'

'Well, I did meet him once about a case in a wine bar... There were quite a few girls hanging around who seemed to know him, and he was talking to one in particular, but I can't remember her name, I'm afraid. I'll let you know if it comes back to me. But someone at the wine bar might know something.' I wracked my brains for the name and gave him it.

'One last thing, though. I know you might not find it easy to answer as your boyfriend is a policeman, but I should advise you strongly to give me an honest answer. Do you yourself know of anything illegal that Mr Shannon might have been involved with, either now or in the past?'

'No. Definitely not. I don't think he would have been involved in anything nasty, but even if he had, he'd never have told me, because he would know I'd have no option but to tell Steve.'

'That's exactly what I hoped I'd hear from you, Rachel, even if it doesn't help me. Now I'll look into the places you'd asked Shannon to check out. What were they, now? Clifford Antiques - in the notes you gave me, and the gallery that organised the Van Gogh exhibition - in this email. I'll let you know if we find out anything concerning the robberies.'

'I appreciate that. I know it's none of my business, but if you could at least let me know when you locate Pete, I'd be grateful. I'm sure his going away must be entirely innocent, but if you could let me know for my own peace of mind...'

'Of course. We may know something later this morning. Like I said, we're applying for a search warrant for his house and computers. Thanks again, Rachel. I'll be in touch.'

And with that he left. I sat down, my head in a whirl. I didn't know what to believe. I'd only just asked Pete if he knew of any hackers on the wrong side of the law. Maybe he was guilty and he'd taken that as a hint to do a runner. Surely not? And why had he rung me after he'd told his neighbours he was going away?

I didn't know what to think. I wished I'd answered that call, then I might have some answers, but I couldn't regret the perfect evening I'd spent with Steve. I made a cup of tea, and tried to put it out of my mind. I didn't feel like work, but I had no option. I had an appointment to go to.

Fortunately it was only ten minutes away in Sutton, which didn't really help, as it was the same upmarket satellite village where Pete had his mansion. I resolutely glanced the other way when my route took me past the pretty little country lane where his house lay. I desperately wanted to go and see if he'd returned.

Maybe the neighbours were confused and he hadn't gone away, but just wasn't answering the door to the police. Not, of course, because he was hiding from them, but because he was busy or just liked to have as little to do with them as possible. But in my heart I knew there'd be a police car watching the house, so it would be a complete waste of time to go there.

24

Miranda Parkinson was much younger than I'd expected, but far from having made her fortune at a young age and putting me to shame for my penury, she had in fact inherited her painting, along with the splendid Georgian house, which I admired as I parked my Fiesta on the immaculate gravel drive. Miranda's parents had been killed in the tsunami in the Far East a few years previously, whilst on holiday.

When she told me this, I felt suitably awful for my initial feeling of envy. I still had my parents and couldn't imagine life without them. With visible emotion, she said, 'I never got to say goodbye. They were only in their early fifties. It was such a waste.'

I uttered my condolences, and then ran through the usual questions, reeling them off by heart after so many repetitions. She couldn't come up with anything to help me, and I was about to leave when I thought of something. 'Just one last question. The police report says that you were in the house at the time of the burglary?'

'Yes. It seems incredible, but I didn't hear a thing. The alarm was disabled and I'm a heavy sleeper, so I didn't hear the large circle of glass being cut from the window and removed by a suction device, before the burglars entered and removed the painting. It was the only painting of any value, so, as you say, they must have known it was here. I presume they're no nearer to finding it?'

'No, I'm sorry. I'm the last line of investigation. Fresh face, new look at things, that sort of thing. They were also hoping that people might remember more after the trauma of the event had faded.'

'Well, I can't help you any more, I'm afraid. Will the insurers be releasing their payments soon, do you know?'

'Probably it won't take them much longer now.'

'That's good. I'd like to take a holiday in the sun and forget all about it.'

I took my leave and wrote notes in the car before leaving. Yet another painting that someone knew where to find. If not someone who targeted auction records, it pointed to the insurers, not to Pete, but I suspected the police had other ideas.

With those unhappy thoughts, I drove home for lunch.

I was making a sandwich when Steve rang.

'Rach, I thought I'd better let you know. Pete Shannon's gone missing in suspicious circumstances.'

'I know. Mike Jordan was round first thing to ask if I knew anything.'

'But they've only just searched the house and found the blood.'

'What blood?' I had difficulty thinking. 'Steve, are you saying they found blood at his house?'

'Calm down, love. Tell me what you know first and then I'll bring you up-to-date.'

I struggled but managed to give him an account of DI Jordan's visit.

'Okay, Rach. Well, firstly, while they were waiting for a search warrant, someone linked up his address with a minor report that had come in over the weekend. It seems his burglar alarm was triggered on Friday night. It's linked up to a company who call back to see if it's a false alarm. If they don't get an answer, someone goes to check. When they got there, one of the French windows at the rear was slightly open. They had a quick glance and saw that his many paintings and other valuables hadn't been removed, so concluded the window hadn't been fastened correctly and had blown open. It was very windy that night. They got a locksmith out to secure the building, sent in a routine report to the police, and left it to the burglar alarm company to chase Pete up.'

'Maybe he'd already gone away, and someone took advantage to burgle his house? The burglar alarm could have spooked the thieves and they ran for it,' I said hopefully, determined to ignore the mention of blood.

Steve ignored my comments and continued. 'Unfortunately the minor report wasn't linked to Jordan's investigation straightaway. Today, they finally searched the house and found a quantity of blood in the hall, with marks suggesting something

216

had been dragged through it. I'm sorry, but it looks like Pete may have been assaulted and then taken forcibly from the house.'

'Oh, my God!' The icy cold shock hit me immediately and I felt short of breath. 'Do you think he's dead? How much blood was there?'

'It's not sufficient to convince them he's dead, Rach. I haven't a clue what's going on, but Jordan and his men will find him, I'm sure.'

'Oh, Steve, I can't see him being involved in these robberies, I really can't. It must be my fault he's in trouble. I asked him to look into Clifford Antiques and the Van Gogh exhibition organisers.'

'I really can't see those investigations triggering such a response, Rach. No-one's come after you. This has to be something different.'

'What does Mike Jordan think now, then?'

'He's still going with the same theory - that Pete was the hacker who bypassed the alarms, and that the gang probably found out he was going to run and wanted to silence him.'

'What do you think?'

'If they'd wanted to silence him, they could have killed him there and then, and made it look like a burglary that had gone wrong. I don't understand it. I'm guessing he's still alive and they wanted him to go with them for some reason, but he put up a fight. As to why, I haven't a clue, though.'

'But you think he's still alive?' I was clutching at straws.

'I think there's every chance, Rach. I'm fairly sure he was alive when he was taken, or there'd have been more blood at the scene. And now you've just told me you had a missed call from him on Saturday.'

'Someone else could have used his phone.'

'But why pick you to ring out of his entire address list? Look, Rach, I know he's a friend of yours, but try not to worry. All of Mike's team are working on this. Although his computer leads were ripped out and the computer's missing, they found a laptop pushed under the sofa and they're going through that now. They may come up with a lead. They're also checking the blood for DNA to match against hairs from his bathroom. The blood may not even be Pete's.'

'That's a bit of a long shot, but thanks, Steve.'

'I almost wish I hadn't called you, but I didn't want you to hear about it on the local news.'

'I know Steve. It's alright. Just let me know if you hear anything, please. I think I'll have a walk around the pier front this afternoon to clear my head before reviewing my casework on the robberies, but if I'm out, you can catch me on my mobile.'

True to my word, I took a brisk walk along the river front by Victoria Pier and let the wind blow away the befuddled thoughts in my head. I couldn't dwell on how, why or when, Pete had been dragged into the art thefts. All I could do was move forward, whilst saying a prayer that it would all end well. I made a cup of strong tea when I got back and broke out a packet of quadruple choc chip cookies, then spent the rest of the afternoon doing the best I could to help Pete, which was reviewing the robbery casework.

If I could find something I'd overlooked or follow through on leads, it might help in some small way to catch the robbers and find Pete. I took a large sheet of paper and drew up a list of all the stolen paintings in date order. There were eighteen in total, including the latest one. When I'd finished, I made a list of the outstanding enquiries. They read as follows:

1) Can non-employees access auction house records?

2) Pete, now DI Jordan, to track down owner of Clifford Antiques.

3) Jason Lambert to send me details of gallery where he bought war painting.

4) Pete, now DI Jordan, to look into Van Gogh organisers

5) Still to visit -Edward Satterthwaite, Anlaby (appointment Weds am) and Keith Sankey, Hornsea (appointment Thurs pm)

6) Owners not robbed - Steve to look into background of Anthony Wharton. Also Christopher Styles and Fiona Carlisle, still to visit (appointments Weds pm and Thurs am respectively).

I sat back and reviewed the sheet of paper. There didn't seem to be much to go on, apart from any possible links between auction house, gallery and exhibition staff. However, I put in a call to Jason Lambert to see if he had tracked down the name of the gallery where he'd bought his painting. I was in luck. He answered almost immediately.

'Hello, Miss Hodges. I'm really sorry I didn't get back to you earlier. I've been away on assignment and only flew home yesterday. The name of the gallery is "The Hanging Corner".'

Jason gave me the address and other contact details before asking how things were going with the investigation. 'Nothing new to report, I'm afraid, apart from one robbery turned out to be no such thing, just an owner who made a fraudulent claim. We found him out when he tried to sell his painting.'

'Well that's some progress and it will serve as an example to anyone who thinks of doing the same. You mustn't be too hard on yourself. If nothing else, you'll have moved things on and maybe convinced the insurers it's about time they paid up. To be honest there'll be a lot of people waiting to have the thing settled now, get a payout and buy something else.'

'I know. It just seems like I've failed, that's all. I'm usually in the business of solving cases. I'm not used to admitting defeat.' He probably didn't understand why I sounded so down, but of course I couldn't tell him about Pete. I took my leave and made a note in the case notes and on my summary sheet.

Then I rang the nearest auction house connected to the robberies, the one at Ilkley, and asked for the person in charge of payments from buyers. I hoped that whoever entered them on computer would know the answer to my questions. I was put through to someone called Duncan. I introduced myself as a private investigator working for the fine art insurers Thompson & Brenner and asked if auction house sales records were accessible to non-employees.

'I'm not sure what you mean.'

'I'm following a line of enquiry that suggests the thieves may have targeted paintings to steal via auction records. Is that possible?'

'The only way an outsider could get that information would be if they went to auctions and ask bidders for their names, but a lot of bidding is by phone and online these days, and it's unlikely even that people bidding on the day in person would give their names to a complete stranger, don't you agree?'

'I understand, but what about lists of paintings in Wikipedia and the like. They tell you which paintings are in which art gallery.'

'That's because the information is in the public domain. The art galleries publish lists of their paintings because they want the public to go and see them.'

'Of course. That was a stupid notion of mine. So you're saying no-one could get a list of private buyers?'

'Not from an auction house. Not unless an employee broke the rules. And I believe you said only two paintings were bought at our auction house and there've been more than two robberies, so you'd need staff at other auction houses. Added to which, I doubt whether all the paintings were bought recently. The only other way would be if someone broke into our computer records, but I have to say that auction houses were for a long time somewhat old-fashioned establishments, so computerised records don't go back very far. It took most of us a long while to join the digital age.'

'Thanks ever so much, Duncan. You might have found my questions a bit ill-informed, but I just wanted to make sure I understood the process completely, so thanks for your patience.'

'No problem.'

'You've been very helpful. Goodbye.'

At least I'd learnt something - that it would probably take a computer expert to target specific paintings to steal, and more than likely the only place where all the records could be targeted, would be at the insurers. That didn't look good for Pete. However, there was just a chance that the thieves had a contact who worked at various places. I was being paid to do a complete review of the thefts, so I couldn't leave any leads unfollowed, however unlikely. There was an awful lot of money riding on it for the insurers.

With Pete unable to help, I'd have to try to do the job myself. I had a clue where to start looking for the Clifford Antiques records - at Companies House. So I got on the phone to them first to get the names of the owner and company secretary, and attempted to track them down in the electoral rolls of York and when that failed, surrounding areas. Eventually I had to admit defeat and concede I wasn't as good at this job as Pete. I spent the rest of the afternoon ringing round auction houses and the few galleries involved, asking to be emailed lists of employees to compare.

Steve was late in again that night. I said I thought it was best if we didn't talk about Pete until he or Mike Jordan could tell me any more, and wisely he said he thought that was a good idea. Just before we watched a bit of TV and went to sleep, I remembered my notes, and reminded Steve that he was going to look into Anthony Wharton for me, if he had time.

'I'm sorry. It must have slipped my mind. I was probably too pre-occupied with Banks at the time. Speaking of him, I'm afraid he's off my personal agenda for a while. I spoke to him today about Giggs, and I was hardly back in the office before his lawyers called to say that they'd be putting in an official complaint about police harassment, if I visited him again with tenuous enquiries. It pains me to comply, but if I don't play ball and keep away, then a complaint'll go up higher and I might have to pull the watch on his premises.'

25

Wednesday morning dawned bright and sunny, but I hadn't slept well, worrying about Pete. I couldn't get it out of my head, that he might have been hurt because of one of my cases. He'd been so keen to help. Maybe he went a bit further than his usual digging into paperwork. I lay there thinking back to our recent conversations, and how he'd been hinting he still wanted a relationship with me. How did that make me feel about him? To be honest, I didn't know.

I loved Steve, but I did care about Pete, and it wasn't that long ago that I'd been happy to go out with him, because when Steve was so busy working, he seemed to forget I existed. I was sure it had only been neglect that had made me act as I had done, but there's a lot of that for a policeman's wife, and I had to be sure we could make it work.

Enough of brooding, though. Steve was already up, showered, dressed and grabbing a bite to eat. I had to get moving. I had an appointment to keep as well, although it wasn't far from Hull at all, in the neighbouring village of Anlaby, in fact.

Edward Satterthwaite and his wife couldn't conceal their disappointment that I hadn't brought them news of their missing painting, "Fatima", by Edward Burne-Jones.

'We counted ourselves so lucky to have been able to buy the painting for a reasonable price before the Pre-Raphaelites became so popular. I believe Andrew Lloyd Webber did the same and built up quite a collection. I can't understand why the paintings fell so much out of favour, but apparently they were deemed too romantic, too outlandish for modern tastes. Of course, they're now worth an absolute fortune, along with everything else art nouveau.'

'But our luck changed, didn't it, dear,' broke in his wife. 'It was taken from us.'

'Yes, you're right. Are you really sure there's nothing you can tell us to give us a shred of hope, Miss Hodges?'

They seemed a bit melodramatic about the loss of their painting, but I did have a partiality for Burne Jones and the other pre-Raphaelites myself, particularly since meeting Richard Staithes, so I answered sympathetically. 'I'm sorry to dishearten you, but I've just come with a few questions, to see if anything's occurred to you since the burglary. Sometimes there are things which don't seem important at the time, but do in retrospect.'

'We'll try and help you all we can. Ask away.'

I ran through the usual questions, but it was another fruitless visit. I took my leave before long and went back to the flat, arriving just as the phone was ringing.

It was DI Jordan. With scarcely a nod to the expected polite pleasantries, he rushed straight in. 'Good morning, Rachel. I don't suppose you've heard from Peter Shannon, or even had a missed call, have you?

'If I'd had, I would have rung you. Honestly.'

'Mm… Thought not, but I had to ask. I know you think I'm being harsh on your friend, but I'm afraid I have to follow every line of enquiry, and I'm beginning to wonder if your friendship and trust in Shannon might have been misplaced.' Before I could protest, he continued. 'You see, we've found some pretty damning evidence on his laptop. It certainly looks like he was researching computerised alarm systems and he's made notes in a document which would seem to be a method he'd devised for hacking into those systems.'

'But surely, that's not proof he was involved in the robberies? I can't believe it of him. I'm sorry, but I can't.'

'Well, we'll see. I just thought I'd better tell you, and ask that you think back on conversations you had with him and try and see them in a different light. Also, I did say I'd let you know if we found out anything about Clifford Antiques and Fine Art. There were a few notes on Shannon's computer referring to the owners, but he seems to have hit a dead end, and his notes finish with, "Tell Rach, no viable leads." Hopefully that's of use to you.'

When I'd put the phone down, I wondered if I could have been so wrong about Pete. I was beginning to lose faith in my own judgement. Had he been playing me for a fool all along? I admit I'd had the feeling that he might sometimes sail a little close to the wind as far as the law was concerned, and I didn't enquire too closely as to where he got information from for me. In fact, I wouldn't admit it to Steve, but Pete probably did use some of those illegal sources that Steve told me about. But he only seemed to do that whilst working for the better good. I knew I was splitting hairs, but I just couldn't see him spending his time as an out-and-out hacker for criminal purposes.

The only tiny consolation I could take from the phone call was that Pete had hit a brick wall tracing the owners of Clifford Antiques as well. It made me feel marginally less useless.

That reminded me to check my emails. The auction houses had been remarkably co-operative. Probably it was the magic name of Thompson and Brenner, renowned insurers of fine art, which had produced that effect. I arranged the lists of employees in alphabetical order and printed them out. A couple of names jumped out as being in more than one list. I guessed it was inevitable that some people would move companies, either to gain more experience or for promotion. The world of auction houses was a small one, and none of them employed many people. I would ask for further information on those concerned, but there was only one person, a Stuart Cottle, who had worked at three places. The others only featured in two lists.

Just then the phone rang. 'Someone in Forensics just tipped me off that the blood found in Pete's house belonged to two people: his and that of another, as yet unidentified, person. Thought you should know. Sounds like Pete put up a fight. If the other person was wounded, and you think Pete was investigating a hacker, then that strengthens your case, I'd think. Hope that makes you feel a bit better.'

'Oh, thanks Steve. I think that's good news, even if we still don't know if he's alright. You are a love, taking time to call.'

I told him briefly of Jordan's call, and he said, 'If you think he's innocent, then so do I, Rach. I have great faith in your gut instinct and I can't see you making a friend of a crook. Sorry I can't chat longer. See you later.'

Bless him. He still had faith in me and my judgement, even though his police colleagues might think differently, and what's more, he'd taken time out of his busy day to let me know he did. I did love Steve.

Encouraged by Steve's call, I managed to eat lunch - quite a lot actually. I realised I'd only been pecking at my food since I'd heard Pete was missing.

Afterwards, I set off to visit Christopher Styles, owner of a large collection of art and an imposing house in the tiny village of Wilfhome on the banks of the river Hull, deep in the countryside north-east of Beverley. It was a lovely day for a drive, and I relaxed a little for the first time in over twenty-four hours.

The moment I arrived, I had an inkling as to why he'd not been targeted by the art thieves. His house was protected by high thick walls, and an electronic steel gate. But that wasn't all. There were signs everywhere declaring 'Private. Keep Out. Protected by 24 Hour Surveillance and Dobermans.' The people I'd visited so far had relied on anonymity and, where that failed, advanced burglar alarm systems, to protect their works of art.

Once I'd negotiated the intercom at the gate and had been escorted to the house by a man who was best described as the sort you wouldn't want to meet down an alley on a dark night, Christopher Styles told me that he didn't care what the outside of the house looked like to anyone, nor what it cost to protect his assets. When he got home from his office, where he was head of a large chain of estate agencies, he just wanted to be able to shut the world outside, confident in the knowledge that his paintings would be there to enjoy.

He showed me round his extensive collection and didn't appear to have anything to hide. I thanked him for his time. He was a very pleasant man, and didn't seem to be at all smug that his methods of protection had worked, where those of other unfortunate art lovers had failed.

When I got home, I ate some more of those yummy quadruple chocolate chip cookies. White and brown chocolate chips in chocolate cookie, coated on the bottom with a layer of chocolate. They're massive and expensive as well, so I usually manage to ration myself to two, but I had three. Steve had said he didn't expect to be late, but I didn't think I'd be too full to eat my tea, if by some miracle he was right.

I realised I'd only been jotting the odd note on my summary sheet, when I should have been typing up daily notes for the following week's report to Clare Brenner, so I rectified that. When I'd finished, I sent emails to the current employers of Stuart Cottle, who'd worked at three auction houses, as well as to the employers of the people who'd worked at two different ones. Then I pondered whether there was anything else I needed to do to finish the assignment, apart from the next day's appointments.

The way things were going, Mike Jordan would have Pete locked up for the robberies, if he ever found him. But even if Pete were involved, he'd hardly have been acting alone. I looked through the list of stolen paintings, hoping there might be a link which would indicate what sort of person would steal these particular paintings, but they ranged from old to new, from portraits to landscapes to abstracts, from cubism to impressionism to Pre-Raphaelites. The only link was that they were among the best of their kind, and therefore rare and extremely valuable.

Steve arrived home as I was adding this conclusion to my draft report, and I told him about the visits I'd made, before we made tea together.

'How's your day been?'

'Since I was warned off Banks, I've taken a step back on the murder enquiry, but it's bogged down in routine investigation at the moment, anyway. We've not got anything new we can talk to Giggs about and he'll get released on bail unless anything turns up soon. All we can charge him with is receiving stolen goods, since he claims he bought the car from a bloke in a pub. It came with no documents, and at least he now admits he bought it, knowing it might be stolen. Because he was linked with stealing cars for Banks in the past, we're sure he stole this one, with or without the knowledge of Banks, but can't prove it.'

'Is there no way you can link him in to Cuthbert's car?'

'There is, but it's a long job. My team are taking turns to watch CCTV footage because after a while their eyes glaze over. They're looking to see if they can spot Giggs driving Cuthbert's own car to his office, which would link him in to the murder, and mean we could keep him longer for questioning. At the same time, they're looking at footage around the area the stolen car was dumped and set on fire, after Cuthbert's body was thrown in the Humber, to see if they can get a face for the other bloke.'

'You're sure there were two of them?'

'Yeah. We think it would probably take two of them to throw the body in the Humber, even if one was only keeping an eye out, and in any case the logistics of dumping the stolen car and then going back to get Cuthbert's car only works if there were two people involved. It could be that the other bloke drove Cuthbert's car to his office, and Giggs dumped the car. Either way, we'd get somewhere.'

'Well, maybe there'll be a breakthrough tomorrow.'

'Maybe. Shall we have a glass of wine?'

One glass turned into several and when I went into the kitchen with the empty plates, Steve followed me in and pinned me against the worktop, caressing my breasts from behind. I leant back against him, getting more turned on as I felt him pushing against me. He undid my jeans and gently stroked me.

In the morning, I woke in a relaxed haze. 'You took advantage of the wine,' I joked.

'As if. You were begging for it in the end. Anyway, you've been saying all week you needed to get to bed early.'

'Mmm...' I pointed at my raggedy stuffed monkey, Maisie, sitting on the shelf above the worktop. 'If only I could train her to do the washing up when we go to bed early, so the kitchen doesn't look like a bomb's hit it the next morning.'

'She could do with a good scrub herself. Come on, I'll give you a hand with the pans, show you how big and strong I am.'

'I thought you did that last night,' I joked.

'I could always manage an action replay.'

'I'm sure you could, but I'm going out soon, you're going to be late for work if you don't shift, and these pans won't clean themselves, as Gran would say.'

26

Half an hour later, Steve was long gone and I was looking as respectable as I ever can, and on the way to Fiona Carlisle's house. She lived at Goodmanham, near Market Weighton, and I was beginning to wish I'd set off earlier. I was stuck in a line of cars behind a tractor and I was going to be late. Ms Carlisle had specifically asked that I meet her at half past nine as she had a string of appointments later. The house was fairly small but with an attractive garden filled with exotic plants.

'I'm so sorry I'm late.'

'Well, I'm not sure I've much I can tell you anyway, but if we've not finished by ten, then I'm sure my secretary Alex will be able to answer any questions you still have. I gather you're wondering why I haven't been burgled?'

'That's about it, yes. You have a number of expensive paintings insured with Thompson and Brenner and, as you're aware, there have been a lot of art thefts in the area.'

'Well, I'll show you the paintings and then you can judge.'

I followed her upstairs and she showed me into a bedroom. There were seven paintings in ornate gold frames arranged in a group on one wall. They were different sizes but none of them was large. 'Is this your bedroom?'

'Yes, it is. I do most of my thinking up here and they inspire me. Do you like the way they're grouped? People are so stuffy about paintings, hanging them at intervals or singly along a wall. You get more impact in a group. That's what I tell my clients.'

'Are you an interior designer?'

'I'm an interior artist. I dress rooms which are already decorated. I source paintings and decorative objects and arrange them along with those a client already owns, to create the ultimate display for the room.'

'That's interesting.' I was trying to imagine what type of person would employ Fiona. Who would want things they hadn't chosen themselves, displayed as she wished? Whoever these people were, I suspected they had a lot of money to throw at her to create the effect she chose.

'As you can see, being an interior artist pays well if you're good at your job, and recommendations are everything in this line of work. I really don't know why I've not been targeted by these thieves, but all the same, I'm very grateful. I've ploughed all my profits into those paintings. They're an investment, but also proof of how far I've come from the council estate in Hull where I grew up. Is there anything else you could suggest that might improve their safety?'

'You might want to fit a second burglar alarm system.'

'Well, I could, I suppose, but is that really necessary? My father installed this one for me. He normally only does smaller houses, but he fitted the most expensive up-to-date model he had, and it's linked to the cottage next door where Alex lives, as well as to the police station that covers the village. No-one has seen the paintings except those I trust, and as Dad said, the paintings are on an inside wall in the bedroom where I sleep.'

'So the burglar alarm system is computerised?'

'I don't think so. When I said it was up-to-date, I meant the most modern one that Dad fits, and he's not computer-minded. Neither am I.'

'Well, that may be why you haven't been targeted. I'm not saying that another thief or gang might not target you, but I can tell you in confidence that these thieves have been gaining access by disabling the burglar alarms, and that appears to have been done remotely by someone hacking into the computer system controlling them.'

'Good to know there's still a place for the traditional way of doing things, then. Thanks for that information. I'll think about some sort of back-up system, but after what you've just said, that might not be necessary. Now, I'm sorry, but I'm afraid I have to leave now. Is there anything else you need to know?'

'No, I think that's it. Thanks very much for being so forthcoming and helpful.'

As I drove away, I realised I should perhaps have spoken to Alex as well. I could have asked if Fiona Carlisle had another stash of paintings, but my instinct was to believe every word she'd told me. I wondered if I'd be any good at dressing rooms.

I had a quicker drive home and was soon demolishing what was left of the packet of biscuits. They are delicious, but they should put more in a packet. Eight is simply not enough.

I wrote up details of the visit in my draft report, exonerating Fiona Carlisle from any suspicion of involvement in the thefts, and looked in the fridge to see if I had anything fresh to put in a sandwich. There was nothing. I opened a tin of tuna instead and decided to eat early and then nip to the shops before my afternoon appointment. There was nothing in the fridge or freezer for that evening's meal, or any other meal, and the cupboards were looking a bit empty too. A major shop was called for, but that could wait till I had more time. I'd just get something for the evening meal.

I was waiting for the kettle to boil, when the phone rang. It was Mike Jordan again. I braced myself for more bad news.

'Hello Mike. Have you any news?'

'I was about to ask you the same. Have you heard from Shannon?'

'I did promise to call you if I did, and I will. Don't you trust me?'

'I just thought you'd maybe not had time. I rang earlier and you were out.'

'Just doing my job for the insurers. Not out meeting Pete.'

'Right. Anyway, that wasn't the only reason for my call. We found a list in Shannon's house of names and email addresses, and there's a folder on his laptop with copies of emails he'd sent to these people. He'd obviously deleted them from his email's sent register. That's not unusual. People don't tend to let their email boxes fill up but they generally archive things rather than delete them totally, or they save them elsewhere.'

I don't do either. My inbox and sent boxes are a mess, overflowing with rubbish so I can never find what I'm looking for, but I said, 'Pete's a computer expert. He probably doesn't want his archive area to reach its limit.' I had no idea if an archive could overflow, but I sounded knowledgeable.

'Hm... That's not the point. These emails are all asking detailed questions about hacking. I was wondering if any of the names mean anything to you?'

'I doubt it. I told you I don't know any of Pete's friends, but read them out to me and I'll tell you.'

He read a list, but as I expected, I'd not heard of any of them, and told him so. 'You're sure you've never heard of Ian Pottinger?'

'No. Should I have done?' Surely he didn't go to school with me and Pete? I might not remember much about a lot of people from school, but I think a name would ring a bell.

'Shannon's emails to him refer to Oxford.'

'Well, Pete went to Oxford University, but I went to Hull, and Pete's never mentioned him. Why is he important?'

'His name's ringed on the list and he was taking Computer Science with Shannon until he dropped out.'

'Gosh. It looks like Pete stumbled on something. I told you it was my fault he was in trouble.'

'Actually, we think they may have been working together. Shannon finds out how to hack into burglar alarms. He draws up a list of people who seem to be hackers, and then identifies who might be willing to assist him in his criminal activities.'

'Well, I think it's more likely that he found out what skills were necessary to access the burglar alarm systems and that led him onto people he had heard were hackers. Surely rumours must circulate about hacking in the legitimate computer business world. I still don't believe Pete was involved. And why would there be blood belonging to both Pete and this Pottinger if they were in cahoots with each other?'

'So Steve told you we'd found blood belonging to someone else besides Shannon, then? We've not identified it as Pottinger's blood yet, but I think Shannon thought you were on to him and so planned to do a runner. Pottinger found out and either came after him, or sent someone else, to stop him talking.'

'I'm sorry, but you're completely wrong about Pete. I have to go now. My lunch is ready.'

I slammed the phone down. I couldn't believe that I'd previously thought DI Jordan was a decent, intelligent sort. He was pig-headed and couldn't see further than his original theory that Pete was a crook. Maybe Steve could convince him otherwise. I resolved to talk it through with him when he got home, but for the moment bolted down my sandwich and rushed off to the shops.

It's not far to Hornsea. It sits on the coast, halfway between Bridlington and Spurn Point, and even though I'd had to nip out and do that shopping after lunch, I made it on time for my two o'clock appointment. Keith Sankey shook me warmly by the hand and invited me into his tiny cottage. I was wondering where he'd find room for the large Dutch seascape by Jan van de Cappelle that he'd had stolen. He offered me a cup of tea, and invited me to join him in the kitchen. As we walked towards the rear, I realised that the cottage was like Doctor Who's Tardis - much bigger on the inside. The deceptively small frontage hid a series of rooms extending backward from the road, culminating in a massive sunny modern extension, with a large empty space on one wall.

'Yes, that's where it hung,' he said, as he followed my gaze.

Keith had retired from the Merchant Navy a few years previously and he'd sunk his savings into the painting. 'I saw it at an antique fair at Kedleston Hall, out Derby way. I've never been married. Being away for weeks at a time doesn't lend itself easily to married life. I had my share of romance, if you know what I mean,' he grinned, 'but never settled down with one lass. When I retired I joined the National Trust. Thought it'd get me out to go to all these places and I might meet people. There are always volunteers to talk to, and you get to see a bit of the country. I go on holiday to different parts of the UK and visit the properties there. Anyway, the day I visited Kedleston, there was this antique fair, and as soon as I clapped my eyes on the painting, I had to buy it to remind me of my days at sea. Different sort of ships, but the sea was painted so well, it takes me back every time I look - sorry, looked - at it.'

'Well, I'm sorry to say there's no news on its whereabouts for you, but if you could cast your mind back and see if there's anything you missed out of the account you gave to the police?'

'Sorry, Miss, there's nothing else. I've been thinking since you rang. I wouldn't know how they knew I had it. You don't get paperwork when you buy at an antique fair usually. I couldn't even tell you the name of the dealer. He didn't have a machine for processing cards and I didn't have a cheque book with me. We hardly use them these days, do we? Anyway, he held the painting for me while I went to the nearest town to a branch of my bank to draw cash. I didn't even get a receipt from the dealer. I never thought about it. I'm really sorry, if you've had a wasted trip.'

I drank my tea and assured him it was nothing of the sort, and that was true. It was very interesting that he'd bought from someone who had no idea of his address. So, to all intents and purposes, out of all the people who could have known he had a valuable painting, the only links to any other paintings were the insurers. Ironically, at the last home I was given to investigate, I had my instincts confirmed. There had to be a leak at the insurers. I was positive now.

As I was driving back, my mobile rang. I ignored it. I refuse to take calls when I'm driving. Hands-free or not, I think it's dangerous, and as Dad says, there's nothing so important that it can't wait till you have chance to pull over and return the call. I hate being at the beck and call of people. If I'm waiting to hear from someone, then I'll stop somewhere safe and check if it's them. Otherwise, I usually wait till I've got where I'm going, which was what I did on this occasion.

Just as well, as I'd have been in too bad a mood to continue driving, because when I got home I discovered it had been DI Jordan yet again. I couldn't face speaking to him, so instead of calling him back, I wrote up my report from my afternoon appointment and made myself a cup of tea. I was just going to start cooking when my mobile rang again. Fortified by the tea, I took Mike Jordan's call. 'I've just got off the phone from talking to Clare Brenner, Rachel. Ian Pottinger works for Thompson and Brenner.'

'Really? That's strange. I'm positive his name wasn't in the list she sent me. It's unusual and I would've remembered it. Surely she can't have left it off on purpose?'

'I said I was surprised you didn't react to the name, but she said she only sent us a list of people

241

working in the Fine Art and the IT departments, as they were the only ones with access to the names of paintings and their owners. Pottinger works in the accounts department, and as such shouldn't have been able to gain access. He's only been working there since shortly before the robberies began. It's a wonder no-one picked up on that.'

'Well I might have, if she'd given me the complete list of all employees. I did check on the employment history of the ones she'd given me, and they'd all been there at least two years. She also said she'd checked into their backgrounds and was convinced none of them could be the source of the leak. I couldn't do a good job, if I was only given part of the information. It's not my fault. I thought you said he did the same computer course at Oxford as Pete. Didn't she consider he might have been able to access records he shouldn't have?'

'I asked her that. He never mentioned any IT qualifications. He worked at an import company before joining the insurers. I've since checked with Oxford and he never finished his degree course so didn't get his qualification. He got thrown out. Some scandal regarding hacking into exam results. He must have joined the insurers after Shannon hatched the robbery plan, so he could hack into the art records.'

'Why won't you consider that Pete somehow suspected Pottinger, and he sent emails to draw him out, but got more than he bargained for?'

'Your concern for your friend is admirable, but I see nothing to back that theory up.'

That night, after we'd eaten, I told Steve everything Mike Jordan had said, and how I felt he had made up his mind that Pete was guilty and was blind to any other possibility.

'This Pottinger bloke could have been passing the information on to someone else, not Pete.'

'I'm sure he was,' Steve agreed. 'Even if Pete were hacking into the alarm systems, someone else has to have been arranging the robberies and selling the stolen paintings. It couldn't just be the two IT experts running the whole show.'

'I know, but DI Jordan's never got anywhere trying to find out what happens to the paintings, or who the thieves are. Once the paintings leave the owners' homes, they disappear into thin air.'

'I may be missing something here, as I've not been involved with investigating these thefts, but why pay two people when you have one expert hacker? It doesn't make sense. The major theft squad seem fixated on the alarm hacker being local to the Hull area, when a hacker is a name for someone who gets into computer systems from afar. Just because the information at the insurers was in the same building in London as the hacker, doesn't mean that the same hacker couldn't be targeting the alarms in East Yorkshire.'

'That's brilliant, Steve. Why the hell didn't I think of that? If Pottinger's the hacker, he could find the location of the paintings and also hack into the alarm system on the night of the robbery. I'll ring Jordan back right now.'

'Don't bother, Rach. He'll have gone home by now. You can ring him in the morning, or I'll talk to him if you want.'

'I think it might be better coming from you. He wouldn't like me pointing out something like that to him, but he'd take it from you. Not to mention it was your remarkable insight anyway. I'm so lucky to have you. You're really clever. You ought to be a police inspector.'

'Very funny! You're clever too, Rach. You were just a bit too near to it, like Jordan was. You follow a line of enquiry and it leads to something else and something else, and sometimes it's not easy to see the wood for the trees. It can help to have someone take a fresh look. Now, shall we go to bed early or watch some mindless TV?'

'Mindless TV, please. Sorry, but I feel drained tonight.'

'What have you got on tomorrow? Why don't you take the day off?'

'I might just do that.'

27

I got up late the next morning. My body must have wanted me to catch up on sleep. Steve rang at about half past nine.

'Hi, Rach. You'll be glad to know that Mike Jordan's come round to our way of thinking after all. He was even beginning to think you might be right about Pete before I spoke to him. One of his officers found a sheet of paper in Pete's house with a list of all Thompson and Brenner's employees, and it had Pottinger's name ringed. It had got pushed to the back of the settee on the floor, probably when Pete kicked his laptop to safety under there. Presumably he was writing on it when he heard Pottinger breaking in. Like you thought, my guess is he identified potential hackers then emailed them. He'd probably identified a few possibles, then somehow got hold of the list of employees and cross-referenced them.

'Jordan accepts that if Pete had known about Pottinger first, or even encouraged him to get the job in the first place, he wouldn't have a list of all employees with his name circled. He also thanked me for my suggestion that the head of the gang would only want one hacker, and Pottinger fits the bill.'

'So Pete's in the clear, and he probably went on the run because Pottinger came after him to shut him up? I'm presuming Pottinger's not sitting at his desk in London?' I asked.

'He's not. He didn't turn up on Monday, the first working day after Pete's house was broken into. And he hasn't been seen since.'

'All we have to worry about now, is whether Pete's alright.'

There was a pause before Steve answered. I guessed he was wondering how much I was worrying, and why. 'We're doing all we can. Hospitals have already been told to look out for young men with knife wounds and Jordan's men are going to question all Pete's known girlfriends again. Someone could be hiding him. After all, Pottinger's still missing, so Pete might feel he's not safe. There's nothing you can do, Rach.'

'I know. Thanks for letting me know, love. See you later.'

After I put the phone down, I let my thoughts wander and asked myself the question: How much did I care? And if I cared a lot, then why? I'd rejected DI Jordan's theories that Pete was involved, so I believed that Pete was basically a good guy. I felt worried when the blood had been found, because I didn't want anything awful to have happened to him. I'd felt relieved when Steve supported my view that Pete wasn't a crook - but that probably said more about how I felt about Steve than Pete. I

246

wanted Steve not to have his convictions clouded by jealousy. I wanted him to feel sure that there was nothing between Pete and me. Because there wasn't. Reassured, I came to that conclusion. I didn't feel jealous that Pete might be hiding out with another woman. I felt guilty that it was my fault he was in trouble, and that made me particularly worried about Pete. But he didn't mean as much to me as Steve.

The day meandered away from me. I checked my emails. There was one from the auction house where Stuart Cottle was now working. They gave him a fantastic character reference, saying he'd worked his way up from glorified dogsbody, to porter, to assistant auctioneer, by gaining experience at several firms. The employer of one of the others came back to say the bloke had changed companies but, as 'they paid more', there didn't seem to be anything suspicious behind the move. The other two hadn't replied, but I didn't really expect anything to come of the answers either. I paid some bills, cleaned up a bit and then went over to my flat. I'd not been there since Carly went home. She'd left it tidy so I didn't need to start cleaning there as well. I sat in my little office and caught up on bills, and generally tidied my paperwork up. I'd not got any new cases, which was something of a relief as I'd been so busy over the previous few weeks, and for once I didn't need the money.

I needed to do a proper shop, and called at the supermarket near Gran's. With bags safely stowed in the car, before I knew it, I was sitting in front of a plate of custard creams, and Gran was saying, 'if you'd said you were coming, our Rachel, I'd have bought a Swiss roll.'

'Don't worry. These are lovely, Gran. Now tell me what you've been up to since I last saw you.'

'Let me try and remember. My friend Elsie's got shingles. She can't stop scratching. It's driving me mad.' I stopped myself in time from saying that it was probably driving Elsie mad too, but I wouldn't have got a word in edgeways anyway. Gran was on a roll. 'Those people from the X Factor want me over for filming a fortnight tomorrow. I was wondering about looking for a new outfit, but don't worry, I'll ask your mam to go with me next time.' I choked on my tea. 'Are you alright, Rachel? You shouldn't gulp it. It's hot. Let it cool down a bit. What was I saying? Yes, your mam. She might have more idea than you. Although I suppose that slip of a lass, what's her name? Steve's sister?'

'Carly'.

'Yes, her. She'd be more the right age.'

'She's gone back to Leeds, Gran.' A lucky escape for Carly, though it'd have been an education for her, shopping with Gran for tight sparkly low-cut dresses in lurid colours. 'Are you looking forward to being on the telly, Gran?'

'Course I am. I wouldn't have entered otherwise. Jack at the centre's going to organise a bit of a party and we can all watch together. He's going to video it and sell copies, but I'll get you one for free, to give to your kids, when you have them, though I'm beginning to wonder if I'll be dead before I get a great-grandchild.'

Poor Mum. She was already cringing at the thought of what the neighbours would say when Gran was on TV. Now it looked like Gran was going to turn it into a circus. How would she cope? But as that thought was going through my mind, Gran was off again, on another of her favourite subjects. 'I hear your cousin Suzy got wed. Lovely do, your mam was saying, must have cost a bit. Is that what's putting you and Steve off, the money?'

The chasm yawned open in front of me. I'd told a white lie to her to keep her happy, a while back, but the truth was, Steve hadn't actually proposed, and I wasn't asking him. I wanted to be sure it's what he wanted, and he might just agree because it's the easiest thing to do. How did I get round Gran's question?

I needn't have worried. Although she was usually like a dog worrying at a bone on the subject, she moved seamlessly on. 'I nearly forgot. We had a coach trip to Withernsea, organised by the centre last Tuesday.'

I thought back. 'It was a lovely day, Tuesday.'

'It was sunny alright, but the old ones spoiled it. We had to come home early.'

'Why, Gran. What happened?'

'We went on the beach and they plonked themselves in a row, with windbreaks to keep the draught off them. Elsie and I sat for a bit, but she couldn't sit still with the itching. The sun was making it worse. I was a bit bored anyway. It's nice to look at the sea but there weren't many other people. They'd dropped us off at the far end and it

249

was too quiet. So Elsie and me, we went for a walk down to the slot machines. Do you know they still have one of those old machines where an elephant brings a box round on its back and drops it down a hole? Only plastic beads but we had a go for old times' sake. Made twelve pence in the tuppeny machines, got talking to the coach driver, Ron his name was, had a cup of tea and a good laugh. Elsie even forgot the itching. Then Ron realised the time and we had to rush back. We were nearly too late, even so. They'd all dropped off and the tide had come in sudden-like. When it woke them up, they were ankle-deep in water, trying to move their handbags and fold up the chairs, and moaning their sandals and nylons were wet. We had to go home. They wouldn't hear of going to the café for our tea in wet shoes. Spoiled the day for me. I'd been looking forward to a thick slice of Yorkshire ham and some chips. And I was in with a chance with Ron.'

I laughed. 'Oh, Gran, I can just picture it.'

'It was funny, I suppose. Do you want another cup of tea? Mine seems to have gone cold. It's with you keeping me talking.'

We had another cup and Gran ate the last biscuit, while I told her that the police thought they'd identified the man who disabled the burglar alarms so the paintings could be stolen. I didn't mention Pete. She had a soft spot for him and his mansion. I looked at my watch and said, 'Just look at the time. Sorry, Gran, but I'll have to go and get Steve's tea on,' and escaped.

When he got home from work, Steve had news. He was going to Amsterdam after all, to interview the bloke the Dutch police had arrested in connection with diamond smuggling. They'd found information linking him to Cuthbert. 'I'm due there first thing Monday, so I'm flying Sunday lunchtime.'

'I bet you're excited. I don't suppose I could come?'

'It's just work, Rach. I'll only be going to the police station. I won't get to sightsee or anything. Tell you what, why don't we have a run out tomorrow afternoon? I'll have to go into work in the morning but I could spare half a day.'

'That'd be good. I'll have to attack the mountain of ironing in the morning, anyway, or you'll be going naked.'

'You're just trying to get me to stay home, flaunting the idea of naked bodies. I know you.'

'I didn't say I'd be naked.'

'But you could be, couldn't you?' Steve reached for me and undid my skirt. It fell to the ground.

'After a night like that, I won't need to visit all those sex shops and brothels.'

'So you had thought about them?' I smacked his bottom playfully.

'Don't get me started again or I'll be late and I won't be back by lunchtime.'

'Alright then, spoilsport. I'll pack a picnic so we can get straight off, and I'll try to think of somewhere to go.'

I chained myself to the ironing board and got it all cleared, then gave Mum a ring for suggestions. 'Why don't you have a run to Market Weighton? There's a nice farmer's market there.'

Before I could answer, Dad must have snatched the phone from her. 'You can go and see the statue of the giant. Lovely one carved in wood. It's not been done long, so I never took you and Laura when you were kids. There's his house, specially made to let him get through the doors, and as I recall, a footprint on the wall. I can't remember his name, but it'll maybe come to me.'

A moment later, Mum was back. 'Don't mind him; he thinks he's talking to Mikey and Johnnie, giving them one of his history lessons. If you don't fancy the farmer's market, then what about Pocklington? There's Burnby Hall Gardens with the water lilies. We've not been there for years, but I think they've done it all up. Or else there's Millington Woods.'

'The gardens sound nice, Mum. Thanks. I'd better go. We can catch up on news tomorrow.'

Steve was home by one, and agreed on Burnby Hall. We got most of the way before hunger forced us to stop down a side road and eat our picnic. I brought him up to date on Gran's exploits, and he told me what had gone on at work, which was not a lot, otherwise he'd not have been out with me, with an unsolved murder case still on the go.

'The accountants haven't come up with anything from Cuthbert's records. They say that if he was

252

receiving diamonds and making them into jewellery to sell, then he's managed to hide the cost of the diamonds. He hasn't any records of selling rings he's made. The only rings he's bought have been job lots at auction or antique fairs. His widow knows nothing and if he was alive, he'd probably say he bought low and sold high. Even if he had, he should have paid tax on the profit. Basically, he's guilty of false accounting and tax evasion at the very least, but as he's dead, he can't be charged, and a lack of proper records means there's no paper chain for us to follow to anyone.'

'And the CCTV?'

'Barry and Kate have got square eyes but nothing to show for it.'

'Never mind. Maybe this Dutch trip will throw up some new information.'

'That's what I'm hoping, but let's forget work for now. I think we're here.'

I'd never been to the gardens and didn't realise they were almost in the centre of Pocklington. The hall isn't open to the public, apart from a museum, but it was a fine afternoon and we walked through the different gardens, did the woodland walk, saw the aviary and then sauntered around the two lakes, admiring the water-lilies. There were so many different types and colours, but it wasn't until we reached the visitor centre that I realised it was actually the National Collection of hardy water lilies, and there were over one hundred varieties.

'We're lucky we came now, while they're in bloom, Steve.'

'It wouldn't have mattered when we came. It says here that water-lilies bloom all year. I must admit I never knew that.'

We drove back through Market Weighton and stopped for a civilised pot of tea and cake. I told Steve about the giant, and he said, 'We may as well call as it's on our way, keep your dad happy.'

To be honest, we were actually impressed by the life-size carved and varnished wooden statue, and the fact that William Bradley was still the tallest man on record to be born in England.

We drove on till we found his house and a life-size footprint on the wall. Fifteen inches long and five and three-quarter inches wide. Steve had picked up a leaflet along the way, and read from it. 'He was seven foot nine, which was in fact 5 mm taller than the Chinese Guinness Book of Records holder of "world's tallest man".'

'Maybe it's too long ago to accurately verify, so they won't count him.'

'I suppose so. He weighed fourteen pounds or six point three five kilos at his birth in 1787. Like two big twins.'

'Yes, but you don't have to push out two twins at once. Must have been murder for his mother.'

'Well, it says he was the fourth of thirteen children, so it can't have put her off. He was only thirty-three when he died of TB. He'd done the rounds as a freak show exhibit, along with a huge Yorkshire pig and a dwarf, but fell out with the organisers over non-payment, so he hired a room in towns up and down the country, charging a shilling for people to see him. He was presented to King George the third at Windsor, who gave him a gold chain which he wore for the rest of his life. When he died they had to put his grave in the church to be safe from grave-robbers making money from exhibiting the bones.'

'Just like current day newspapers, flogging stories and pictures of celebrities.'

'At least he wasn't exposed to international paparazzi.'

We left Market Weighton and its famous son, stopping for a delicious Italian meal in Beverley on the way home. As usual I couldn't resist dessert.

I sat on the bed while he did his packing.

'What are you going to do tomorrow, Rach?'

'I thought I might go shopping in the morning. Spend a small amount of my recent earnings. Then I'm seeing Mum and Dad for tea.'

'And Monday?'

'I've got to file my report to Clare. I might risk asking how much I'll get as a reward for finding the Mills painting. Then I've got nothing to do. Maybe some new cases will come in.'

'You know what I'm worried about, Rach, don't you? That you'll be sitting around twiddling your thumbs and think there's no harm in looking for Pete, or delving into what got him abducted. I don't want you landing yourself in hot water again. Pottinger's still out there and he's dangerous.'

'I won't get into trouble, Steve. I promise.'

'Do you mean it? You won't get involved in anything to do with Pete's disappearance? You'll leave it to Mike Jordan, whatever you think of him? Because I'd not feel so bad about leaving you if I could be sure.'

'Promise.'

'Let's get an early night then, sweetheart. I don't know how many days I'll be away. Hopefully only a couple, but I'm going to miss my sexy Rach.'

'You mean you've got energy left after last night?'

'I have if you have.'

28

Sunday was heavily overcast. We woke much later than planned and it was a bit of a scramble, but Steve eventually got away by half past ten. The flight wasn't till two thirty in the afternoon, but he had to be at Leeds/Bradford airport a couple of hours before, and what with the traffic and parking, he wanted to have time to spare.

I had another cup of tea when he'd gone, ate toast and got jam on the paper. My first thought was that at least Steve wouldn't be complaining about it. My second was, I missed him already and I felt a bit low. I wondered what I could do with myself until it was time to go to Mum's. I'd promised Steve I'd not start looking for Pete, but I felt frustrated I couldn't do anything. I put some washing on, before settling down to read. I got so immersed in the book, when I eventually looked at the time, it was already eleven o'clock, and I realised the shops would be open. I decided to treat myself to a new dress out of my insurance earnings.

When I got back, I tried on the turquoise blue sundress. For once it looked as good on me as on the hanger. The straps tied in bows on my shoulders, something which I was sure Steve would find irresistible. I just hoped we'd get enough sun to wear it.

I was just finishing lunch, when my mobile rang. It was Ida, Gran's friend. She told me People were banging in the caravan factory again, and I should go over now, if I wanted to catch the cat-murderers. I still had plenty of time before going to Mum's for tea, so I tootled over there.

I parked round the corner from the factory and got out. As I grabbed my bag, I didn't notice that my mobile had slipped out onto the seat. As a result I missed Steve's phone call a short while later, and his voicemail message saying, 'Rach, it's Steve. They've cancelled all the flights because of some volcanic eruption in Iceland. Apparently there's loads of ash in the air and it's not safe. It must have been on the news. I'm going to have to catch the overnight ferry to Rotterdam to make the interview in Amsterdam in the morning. By the time I get back to Hull you'll probably be at your mum's, and I'll have to go straight to the docks, so I'll speak to you tomorrow. Behave yourself in the meantime. Love you. Bye.'

When I knocked at Ida's, the door opened straightaway. Like a whirlwind, she was out of the door and past me, before I could even hope for a cup of tea. She shouted, 'I'm off to a social afternoon at the church. Let me know how you get on,' and fairly dashed off down the road. I thought she'd got a bit of a nerve, but Gran did say she was a bit weird. On the other hand, I could hear some banging, so thought I'd take a look anyway, if only for Gran's sake.

As I crossed the road, a Mercedes drove out. I recognised the driver, but couldn't place where I'd seen him before. Seeing no-one in the yard, I went through the open gates of the factory and crossed the yard undetected towards the source of the banging. It was coming from inside one of the motorhomes - the only one with lights on. I pressed myself up against a wall, deep in the shadows. I reasoned I was unlikely to be seen there on such a gloomy day. A small weasly-faced man wearing a hideous lime green t-shirt, with a picture of a scary octopus and 'screw you, suckers' emblazoned across the front, climbed down from the motorhome, and went across the yard into what looked like an office.

He'd left the door open, and I slid inside quickly. If he came back, I could always claim I thought it was open for prospective customers to look around. Behind the driver's and passenger's seats, the small lounge part looked immaculate apart from a hammer, a small tool bag and an open newspaper covered in what looked like sawdust, on one of the upholstered benches. More interesting, a panel had been removed from the side of the motorhome, and was propped up against the bench.

Before I could look any further, I heard the sound of voices and footsteps crossing the yard. All thoughts of my flimsy excuse fled from my brain as I hauled myself up into the small sleeping compartment over the driver's seat. Anyway, I wanted to know what was going on, or my foray into the factory yard would have been wasted. I knew it wasn't kidnapping or murdering cats, even if Ida didn't. I just didn't know what else it could be. There was still a slim chance it could be an innocent bit of overtime on a Sunday, but Gran's words about Simon Robinson, the factory owner, being a bad sort, reverberated round my head.

The motorhome shook a little as the men entered below me. 'Okay, Terry. You can fix it now. He's happy. It's the right one and it's not damaged. You didn't have any trouble picking it up?' a smooth voice asked. I needed to know who was talking and from my prone position almost above their heads, I squinted over the edge of the sleeping compartment, but the two men were bending over the bench, looking at something, their backs obscuring my view.

'Nah. It went the same as always. The police may have picked up Bob but they've got nowt to go on and he'll keep stumm, you can bank on it. I got it from the lock-up, used the spare key. I double-checked but the place was deserted.'

'Well, it'll be the last one for a while. We've all got to lie low, but his client was getting impatient about this one and we don't want to let him down. There'll be more orders in the future. Here's half your cut, Terry. You'll get the rest when the delivery's made, as usual.'

'Okay, Mr Robinson.'

As the men turned to leave, I edged back into the shadows. I lay still, waiting to see if they were leaving. Two minutes later, someone returned and banging, scraping, and other noises carried on for about fifteen minutes, and then I heard the door slam and footsteps receding, accompanied by a rattling noise. I presumed that the weasly-faced man had returned to the motorhome to finish off the job he'd started, and had now gathered up his tools into the rattling toolbox, and left.

I waited for a good fifteen minutes before climbing down. Cautiously looking out of the window, I saw no-one. Inside the motorhome, at first I saw nothing out of place, but then I noticed some of the screws in the panelling didn't match. I could have left and told Steve what I'd seen, but he was away, and anyway, what did I actually have to report? I'd seen nothing so far. I needed to undo the screws which held the side panel of the motorhome in place, and see what was hidden in there.

Luckily my nephews had bought me a small but well-accessorised Swiss army knife for Christmas, and I congratulated myself on thinking to keep it in my handbag for just such an occasion. The screws came away easily as they were newly inserted. I removed the panel and lifted out a large package wrapped in old curtaining. From its size, I had my suspicions, and these were soon confirmed. It was a painting, and although I couldn't recall it in its entirety from the brief glance I'd had of a photograph the previous Friday, the portrait's green face told me without a doubt, that it was the very same painting by Chagall that had been stolen from the Keatons in Sewerby.

This was no isolated amateur theft like the one Mills had committed. Ida had said there'd been banging for months at odd times of the night or at weekends. I reached for my phone, and that was when I discovered it wasn't in my bag. The weasly-faced man might well have returned at any moment but I had to empty my bag out onto the small table to double-check. Steve told me I had to ring him first if I ever got into any kind of situation, and I was trying to do as I was told for once. Only when I was sure the phone was missing, did I think to put the panel back, just in case. It took a while longer than I'd hoped, but I was happy with my efforts and better still, the task was completed without interruption.

All I had to do now was creep out and return to my car. If by any chance the factory gate was locked, I'd have to climb the fence somehow. But the motorhome door wouldn't open. I hadn't heard a key turning, so I assumed it had some kind of automatic lock. I didn't panic. I was sure my Swiss army knife would be equal to the task. Failing that, one of the hairgrips holding my unruly mane in place. After half an hour's jiggling, however, it didn't look like I was going anywhere fast, and I was just wondering if I could squeeze through one of the extremely tiny windows, when I heard a noise.

I scrambled back into my hiding-place above the cab. I heard someone climb into the driver's seat and the engine started. The motorhome drove a few yards, I was jostled about and pitched at an angle, then the engine died, the driver slammed the door and I heard a clanking of chains. I crept down and tried the door again. I was desperate enough to risk detection, but it was locked once more. I risked a surreptitious peek out of the windows to confirm my suspicions. The motorhome had been loaded, and now secured, onto a low-loader with cab.

Moments later, we were moving. I couldn't get out, and I had no idea where I was headed. Added to which, only Ida knew that I'd been to the factory that afternoon, and as she'd gone out, she wasn't expecting me to report back anytime soon. It was, as the saying goes, another fine mess I'd got myself into.

Contrary to my expectations, the drive didn't last long. Only about ten minutes. I pulled myself together. I was bound to get a chance to get out when the motorhome door opened. If it didn't, then I'd be able to try to get out of the window, whilst we were stopped. I risked a look outside but couldn't quite make out where we were. It looked like a massive car park with some buildings in the distance. What was about ten minutes drive from Simon Robinson's factory on Hedon Road? I couldn't think, but there was a chance I could attract someone's attention.

Unfortunately there seemed to be no-one around, so I turned my attention to the windows, only to discover they were all fitted with tiny locks. I was running out of ideas and conscious that it was almost tea-time. I'd had nothing to eat since lunch and I was starving. Which reminded me - Mum and Dad would soon be wondering where I was, when I didn't turn up for tea as agreed. I had to get out.

First things first. I ate the half Twix I'd spotted in my handbag earlier, saving the almost full tube of Werthers Originals toffees in case of dire need. I must have forgotten I had them, or else there wouldn't be many, if any, left in the packet. I checked the cupboards but they were all empty. I then had the presence of mind to check out if there was water on board, and gratefully filled up the half empty bottle of water in my bag, as well as going to the loo, for good measure.

I scoured the motorhome from top to bottom for an escape route. I'd just concluded there wasn't one, when we set off again. I was jerked violently to the floor and hit my head as I fell.

I must have been knocked out, because when I came to, it was dark and I felt sick. I felt really bad, so much so that the motorhome seemed to be swaying. I closed my eyes and waited for the sensation to pass, but it didn't. Eventually I pulled myself up into a sitting position and reached for my bag. I took a gulp or two of water, and felt my head for lumps and bruises, but there was only a small lump on my temple. This was no good. How could I think about escape when I felt as if I was seasick? Bracing myself, I stood up and looked out of the window. Out of the far corner of my eye I could see daylight. I couldn't have been unconscious for long, after all. It was still daytime. The darkness was because I was underground. In an unlit car park, perhaps, I thought as I registered the lorries towering alongside.

Call me slow, or put it down to the bump on my head, however minor, but it took me far too long to work out that I was in the hold of a car ferry. This meant I was on my way to Zeebrugge or Rotterdam. I knew the ferries left in the evening from King George Dock on Hedon Road and travelled overnight. My parents would be really worried if they didn't hear from me until the following morning. I felt so desperate I tried to break the windows of the motorhome, but they must have been well reinforced to protect the occupants from being assaulted in their beds or robbed when on an isolated campsite, because I couldn't produce so much as the tiniest of cracks.

It was dark. I was hungry. I ate half of the toffees, drank more water and refilled the bottle. I had no ticket for the ferry, but couldn't get out anyway. If I didn't get back by Tuesday, I wouldn't be able to submit my next report to the insurers, and get my next payment. I had so much to report as well. More than that, I'd not got round to faxing over the information that I'd recovered Brian Mills' painting, and claiming my reward.

I hoped I'd be home soon, but it was beginning to look like I would have to wait at least until the low loader reached its destination and delivered the motorhome and its painting. At that thought I brightened a little. I'd be able to see where the painting ended up, and after contacting the police, get a further chunk of the reward fund, which would be more than my fee anyway. Of course, I had no passport and no foreign money, but I had to stay positive, and assume I could find help quickly. One point in my favour was that Steve said the Dutch all seemed to speak English.

A bulb went on in my head. Steve had flown to Amsterdam. All I had to do was ring the Amsterdam police station and he would take care of everything, including the locking-up of the thieves. Simplistic and totally implausible, considering my lack of phone and euros, but those thoughts were enough to console me as I lay down to sleep. I had to get back before Tuesday for a more important reason. Gran would kill me if I didn't go round for tea on her birthday with her card and present. I knew I'd need all my energy for the day ahead, but I tossed and turned on the hard bunk.

I was still trying to place the other man I'd seen leaving Simon Robinson's factory as I'd arrived. It sounded as if he'd been there to check the painting before it was shipped abroad. He had to be the one behind the art thefts, so it was vital I worked it out. I was sure I remembered seeing his face very recently, so I went through all the owners I'd met, but he wasn't one of them. I spread the net wider and went through anyone else new I'd visited or come into contact with over the previous few weeks, but it was no good. It was really annoying.

My mind switched to imagining the various items of food I could have been eating in the ship's restaurant, far above my head. I was starving. That was a worse form of agony.

Determined, I forced my mind back to the picture I had in my head. And that's when the penny dropped. I hadn't seen the man in person before; I'd only seen him in a picture. I'd been shown a photo of him and his wife by Charlotte Lloyd, his housekeeper. The man behind the thefts was Anthony Wharton. I was sure of it.

I'd thought there was something fishy about his locked vault of paintings, but it looked like he was shipping them elsewhere, rather than stealing them for himself. From the conversation I'd overheard between my 'driver', Terry, and Robinson, this wasn't the first painting they'd shipped. Wharton owned an import / export business, I recalled. Simple for him to do a deal with Simon Robinson, a nasty piece of work and a crook, according to Gran, to smuggle paintings out in the motorhomes, which Robinson legitimately made and sold. Clare Brenner had assumed the paintings were somewhere in the UK because none had been discovered at the ports, but now I had the answer.

No doubt Wharton produced legitimate paperwork to export the motorhomes. Maybe that's how he met Robinson. His housekeeper said he was always buying paintings, so he probably went to loads of auctions and met people who had specific tastes. It might be that he stole paintings to order and used the payments to fund what she called his 'obsession' to buy art. It would be too risky to own paintings he'd stolen in this country, and with his clients paying over the odds for the painting of their dreams, Wharton would have more than enough money to buy whatever he fancied at auction.

29

At exactly the same time as I was lying in the motorhome thinking things through, a couple of decks above me, Steve's phone rang as he was tucking into a steak.

- -

When Steve took out his phone, he didn't recognise the number, and was surprised when he heard Rach's dad ask, 'Is that Steve?'

'Yes. Is anything wrong, Mr Hodges?'

'Is Rachel with you, by any chance?'

'No, sorry, she's not. Is there a problem?'

'She didn't turn up for tea. We thought she might be late, but after half an hour or so I rang her mobile, her flat and yours, but there was no reply on any number. Eventually, after we'd eaten, I went round to both flats but no-one answered, and so I thought maybe she'd flown to Amsterdam with you after all and forgotten to tell us. But if she's not with you, then can you give me Carly's number, please. She might be out with her.'

'I'm sorry but Carly went back to Leeds on Friday. Is Rach's, I mean Rachel's, car outside my flat?'

'No sign of it. I played it down to Rachel's mother, but I'm starting to worry now. Please tell me you've been in touch with her since you flew to Amsterdam.'

'All flights were cancelled. I'm on the overnight ferry to Rotterdam instead. I tried to ring Rach but assumed she was driving round to your house when she didn't answer, so I left a voicemail message instead to update her, and say I'd be in touch tomorrow. She hasn't replied, but I didn't think anything of it at the time, because I imagined her to be chatting to you. I was going to ring her when I got off the ship. So the short answer is "No"; I haven't heard from her.'

'Oh dear. If she hasn't been in touch with you, even, then it sounds like something's happened to her.'

'Look, try not to worry, Mr Hodges. I'm sure she's fine. She's probably had a call about a case and got involved in following someone, completely forgetting she was going to your house for tea. You know how focussed she gets when she's working, and maybe she left her phone in the flat. But to set your mind at rest, I'll ring the station. I can ask one of my team to put out a discreet call for patrol cars to look out for her car.'

'Thanks, Steve. I'd be grateful if you'd do that. Would you ring me back if you hear anything, please?'

'Of course, I will. Leave it with me. I'll track her down.'

Steve disconnected and swore under his breath. Rach was thoughtless sometimes, but she wouldn't forget she was going to her mum and dad's. It sounded like she was in trouble, and he couldn't do much about it. He couldn't turn round in the middle of the North Sea and go back to Hull. He hoped Banks hadn't got to her. He put that thought from his mind and concentrated on doing what he could.

Once he'd spoken to Matt, his sergeant, he felt better. He could rely on Matt to act as if it was one of his own loved ones who'd gone missing. He'd asked him to send someone round to check up on Banks and his various premises, as well as putting out a search for Rach's car. He knew he shouldn't abuse his police connections to track down his girlfriend, but Steve had the sinking feeling that Rach's disappearance was linked to a crime, and he wasn't prepared to wait. If they couldn't find her car, he'd see if Matt could get a fix on her mobile, but that would take longer. Then he rang Carly. He kept the conversation short and light. He didn't want to worry her. He told a white lie and said that Rach didn't have her phone switched on, but he thought there'd been someone suspicious she'd wanted him to check out and he had a spare minute to do it.

'She thought there was something fishy about that Mills bloke who got rid of her quickly.'

'No, it can't be him. He's been arrested for fraud. He faked the theft and tried to sell his own painting. I'm sure Rach will tell you about it when you next speak, but you'll be glad to know she's getting a reward.'

'Oh, that's great. The only other owner she had doubts about was the man who hadn't been robbed. Now what was his name? Yeah, Wharton. She said he'd got a load of new paintings recently.'

'Right, thanks. You couldn't remind me of his address, could you?'

'Sorry, no. I didn't go to his house, and I don't know if she ever told me. Clare Brennan would know, but it's Sunday so they'll be shut. I guess you'll have to wait till you speak to Rach.'

'I will. How's thing with you?' Steve was dying to get off the phone but forced himself to exchange pleasantries for a few minutes, so as not to worry Carly. When he put down the phone he rang Matt again, knowing he wouldn't be able to track down a man who hadn't been robbed, on the basis of his surname and the fact he lived somewhere in the East or West Riding of Yorkshire, but hoping he might try, nonetheless.

'Hello, Steve. I'm glad you rang. I wasn't sure how easy it would be to ring the ship from my mobile. I hope you don't mind, but I took your spare flat key from your desk and nipped over myself to see if Rach has left any clue as to her whereabouts. There doesn't seem to be anything obvious, I'm afraid.'

'Could you have a look at her case notes, please, see what she was working on, and dig out the contact details for a bloke called Wharton, someone she visited in connection with the art thefts. In case you can't get through, I'll ring you in an hour. I'm glad you're on duty tonight, Matt. It means a lot to me, that you're looking for her.'

'No worries. We'll find her soon, I'm sure.'

Steve returned to the restaurant and finished his steak, even though it was cold. If there's one thing a policeman understands, it's never to waste the opportunity of a meal. You may not get chance of another for a long time when you're on an active case. He followed it up with hot chocolate fudge cake, though it reminded him of Rach and her love of chocolate. Drat the girl. He loved her to bits, but she just couldn't get it through her head not to go off without telling anyone.

He paid his bill, and went through to the bar, ordering an alcohol-free lager. He heard a voice asking for a Black Velvet, calling up another reminder of Rach, in the dress he'd bought for her birthday, and of him undressing her later that evening.

He turned to see what sort of man drank a sickly mixture of champagne and stout. The bloke with the scrunched-up face looked familiar, he was sure. Another thing about coppers, they try not to forget a face. He couldn't remember his name but recalled he'd locked him up a few years previously for thieving lead off church roofs. To pass the time until he could ring Matt again, he kept an eye on the man in the lime green t-shirt, and when he left the bar, Steve followed him down to the car deck.

He saw the man get a holdall from the cab of a low-loader. Knowing the bloke couldn't afford the brand new motorhome on the trailer, he hung around out of habit after the man left, to note down both number-plates, in case either vehicle was stolen.

All the time he was oblivious to the fact that Rach was mere yards away, fast asleep.

Back in the bar there was no sign of his thief. He pondered the brand new motorhome. How could a lowlife thief get a job delivering a vehicle like that? Maybe he'd turned over a new leaf? But there was something else skittering around in his mind. He felt sure there was a link between the bloke and Banks, but he didn't know what. He thought again of Banks and the stolen BMWs that had been spirited away before the police raid. It was a long shot but maybe, just maybe, there was a link. His intuition rarely let him down. He'd pass on the information to Matt when he called him. For now though, Rach was the priority.

About twenty minutes later, Steve rang Matt again. He answered on the second ring. 'Good news and not-so-good, Steve. We found Rach's car, but her mobile was on the floor in front of the passenger seat, and there's no sign of where she might have gone. The car was parked down a side street just off Hedon Road. Other good news, I think, is that Banks is at home. A patrol eyeballed him through his lounge window. No movement, lights or anything at any of his business properties.'

'I've got a couple of men knocking on doors near where the car was found, and I'm about to plough through this folder I picked up from your flat, with details of her latest cases, to see if there's any link to Hedon Road. I'll look out for that address you wanted as well.'

'That's great, Matt. Can you run a plate for me as well, please? I've just seen a thief I collared a couple of years back, and he's driving a low loader with a brand new motorhome. It's nothing to do with Rach, but I'm curious who it belongs to.'

'You're never off the job, are you? That reminds me, though. I've another piece of good news. You were talking to DI Jordan before you left about some IT expert, weren't you? Well, he's turned up.'

'Pete Shannon? Did he get away from his abductor? How is he? Is he alright?'

'No, not him. Ian Pottinger. He went into casualty because he'd got an infected wound in his arm. A nurse got suspicious when she saw it was a knife wound, even though it's been a couple of days since they were alerted. She realised he might be the man we were looking for and that if he'd delayed going to hospital, in that time it could have got infected.'

'He was also limping. Had an enormous bruise on his leg. Told her he'd fallen over a table. She told him it might be fractured and if so, he'd need to have it set. Under the pretence of going to arrange an X-ray, she called the police, and got a couple of security guards to watch the cubicle until they turned up. He's under lock and key now, though the word is that he's not saying anything. So they're none the wiser about what's happened to Shannon.'

'That is interesting. If only we knew if he's still alive and in hiding. If that's the case, I wish we could find some way of letting him know that Pottinger's been arrested. Maybe then he'd feel safe enough to come in and talk to the police.'

'Don't know how. Jordan's kept the press out of the whole Shannon abduction and Pottinger hacking affair. He said he didn't want to alert the thieves to the net closing in on them until he gets names and we turn up on their doorsteps.'

'Too right. Shame though. Shannon was at school with Rach and has done some work for her on the art theft case she's been doing for the insurers. She blamed herself when he disappeared. She's really worried about him.'

'Well, if he's not turned up at a hospital, he's either dead already or he'll survive a few more days until we can get Pottinger to talk. I'll try and get back to you if anything happens. Otherwise, feel free to give me a ring in the morning. Maybe you should try to get some sleep now. You still have to report to Amsterdam in the morning.'

'Yes, good idea. Night, Matt.'

Before Steve headed off to sleep, he thought he'd just take a closer look at the low loader and the motorhome before he turned in, so he went back down to the car deck. He looked in the windows, tried the doors and even felt under the sills, but learnt nothing.

Rach was up above the driver's cab in the sleeping compartment, tucked out of sight, so Steve didn't know how close he'd come to finding her.

Before turning in, he rang Rach's dad and told him the car had been found in Hull, it looked like she was on a case, and he was sure they'd know more at first light.

30

I came to, sometime during the night, hearing a noise like a door rattling. I wondered whether to climb down and take a look, but decided against it. It was probably the driver, checking he'd locked up. Two minutes later, I was more awake and wished I'd not stayed put. If the driver had opened the door, I could have made a break for it, headed for the safety of the public bar and been free.

'Too late now,' I muttered under my breath, and consoled myself with the thought that if I wanted to see where the paintings ended up, to crack the case wide open, I was best staying put until the motorhome reached its final destination. I had to bring the crooks to justice. It might be the only way to find out what had happened to Pete. I wondered if he was still alive. I lay awake for a long time, trying to come up with a plan for when the motorhome arrived wherever it was going, but eventually slipped back into a fitful sleep. I woke to the noise of engines being started all around me. Drivers were returning to their vehicles ready to disembark. I had to get ready for whatever came next.

I slipped to the loo, had a drink of water and a couple of toffees for breakfast, and hid on the floor of the motorhome as I waited for it to leave the ferry. God, I was starving. If I didn't get out soon, I didn't think I'd have the strength to walk down the steps. It wasn't long before I heard the low loader's engine start, and moments later we were on the move, jolting over the exit ramp of the ferry. A mixture of conflicting thoughts competed for my attention. I had to get away and ring Mum as soon as I could. I had to ring Steve. I had to stick in there and follow the painting.

After a short while, we picked up speed and the ride was much smoother, and I risked a look out of the side window. I saw several signs, and worked out we must be leaving Rotterdam on a motorway, autobahn, autoroute or whatever the Dutch called them, and heading for Amsterdam. Steve would be either having breakfast, or have had it and be on the way to the police station by now. I wondered idly where the police station was, then realised it would be in the middle of town, so I could rule out the fantasy rescue that kept invading my mind.

Steve wouldn't even know I was in Holland, never mind that I'd been abducted and couldn't escape. I downgraded that to being a stowaway. After all, any abduction had been done unwittingly on the part of the smugglers. Either way, I was glad that Steve didn't know I was in a somewhat perilous situation. I didn't want him worrying. Time enough for him to know when I managed to find a phone. If I got out quickly, I was hoping Mum and Dad would just assume I got caught up on a case and had forgotten to tell them. Problem solved. I sat down and waited for the car and trailer to stop.

- -

Despite Rach's belief to the contrary, Steve was worried, very worried indeed. He'd managed to get some sleep. The motion of the boat had seen to that. When he woke, his first thought was of her. Where was she and was she safe? Had someone beaten her up, or worse? He put in a call to Matt before he ate breakfast, and was relieved to hear he had some news.

'Good news. I found a link to Hedon Road in Rach's notes. Some old lady reporting noises. It's not a proper paying case. There was a note about this lady, Ida, "being a friend of Gran's" and so Rach seems to have felt she should investigate. Ida Foster wasn't pleased to be disturbed late at night but she told us she'd called Rach just after lunchtime yesterday and had met and spoken to her briefly, before going to a social event at the church. She was expecting Rach to call round again later and tell her what she'd found, and was annoyed she hadn't.'

'Does she know where Rach went?'

'She said the noises were coming from the caravan factory opposite her house. It was all quiet and shut up, so I thought I'd wait and see what you said this morning. I'm on lates, but I can go round if you want?'

'She must have found something. If we go in mob-handed, they'll deny having seen her, and they may be spooked enough to do something silly. Do you think you can commandeer an unmarked car to keep watch, and in the meantime get Barry or Kate to do some digging into the owners and employees of the factory? What's it called?'

'Robinson's. Owned by one Simon Robinson. His father's James Robinson. Has that big building firm. Never heard of any wrong-doing attached to him, but I confess I don't know the son.'

'Neither do I. Robinson rings a bell as being linked to some trouble, but it's a common surname.'

'I'll organise it, Steve, don't worry.'

'Thanks. You don't have to get involved. You've done enough already. You should have been asleep since your shift finished, not running around for me.'

'It's no problem. I'll let the others do the work. They'll ring me only if they find out anything important.'

'Okay then. If you're sure. Or you can get one of them to ring me direct.'

'Don't worry. We won't let you down. We'll do our best to find her. Oh, I nearly forgot - that bloke Wharton you asked about - he runs an import / export business down by the docks. Does a lot of business, so it's no wonder he can afford paintings. Seems legit as far as we know. Anything else you want?'

'Don't think so, thanks, unless you got the owner of that low loader for me.'

'Sorry, I forgot about that. I'll get someone to run it.'

'It's not that important. It could end up anywhere. Talking of which, I best get going. The ferry's docking.'

In no time at all, Steve had grabbed his bag, and was driving down the exit ramp. He hadn't done a lot of driving abroad, so took it slowly until he got used to driving on the right and to the many different signs. Just before he reached the A4 motorway, he passed the low loader with the motorhome, and wondered where it was headed. He'd dearly loved to have followed it, but he couldn't do two things at once, so he gave the driver one last look through his rear view mirror, then he put his foot down, and the eighty or so kilometres to Amsterdam were soon flying by. He needed to get to the main police station as quickly as possible. He'd advised them he would be later than if he'd flown in the previous afternoon, but he didn't want to keep them waiting.

Who was he kidding? As soon as he could get the meeting over, he'd be able to turn his attention to locating Rach. For now, though, he knew the best way to help her was to put her out of his mind and get on with his job.

- -

Once my unwitting driver left the motorway, still heading for Amsterdam according to the signs, I started paying more attention to my surroundings. I'd never been to Holland, and although the landscape was as flat as you might imagine, the view from the window was quite different from the flat East Riding and North Lincolnshire that I was used to. The buildings were mainly of dark brick, even the church towers, although there were some houses and bungalows with white-painted plaster and red tiled roofs.

I'd seen a lot of wind farms as we'd driven down the motorway, and now I saw loads of solar panels. It was obvious Holland was making more effort to be a green country than we were. Maybe they didn't have so many planning rules, or maybe fewer people objected. Either way, they looked to be taking care of their energy needs and leaving the UK lagging behind. I couldn't blame them. After all, pretty views are one thing, but not if you're sitting in the dark and freezing because there's no power.

I passed the time trying to translate the advertising hoardings and wishing I could get out and explore, instead of planning ahead. There seemed no point. I had no idea if we would be stopping in Amsterdam, and even if we were, I didn't know the city. I'd just have to make it up as I went along. The important thing was to escape. I decided that the first opportunity I got, I'd be through the door and running as fast as I could. I'd make for a public place, and then try and get help.

As if thinking about it could make it happen, we slowed down and stopped at traffic lights. If only I could open the door, or even the window, but I couldn't. I knew I'd have to wait until someone opened the door. I was banking on someone removing the painting as soon as we reached our destination.

About ten minutes later we were on an industrial estate, and turning into a yard. We stopped. I knew I had no time to lose. If anyone came in, I wanted to be as near the door as possible. A couple of men in suits came out of an office, and green t-shirt man opened the motorhome door. They came in and stood round the panelling as my driver bent down to his tool bag to open the panel. As quietly as I could, I climbed down from above the cab where I'd hidden temporarily. I was now between them and the door. The steps rattled as I legged it down them and ran for it, out of the yard and into the street.

I heard shouts behind me but didn't turn round. When I reached the corner of the street, I knew where I had to go. I could see an elevated railway line a short distance to my right, and there were people on the platform of a tiny station. They were the only people in sight so it seemed the safest thing to run towards them. I ran as if I was in the Olympics and this was my only chance of a medal. Someone was running after me, but I reckoned I was younger and fitter than any of the three men I'd seen, and I must have had a good head start. I heard a car screech. I presumed it was turning out of the yard to follow me, but still I didn't turn round.

Two minutes later and I knew I had a chance. A train was pulling into the station and I was almost at the station steps. I heard a sound like a car backfiring. I risked a look over my shoulder and wished I hadn't. I was almost out of breath but forced one extra spurt of effort from my lungs and almost collapsed onto the train. I got a few sympathetic looks and the odd curious one. They must have wondered why I'd been so desperate to catch that particular train. As I walked slowly along the carriage, the train doors closed. I heard a shout and a thumping noise, but didn't turn to look. I had my eyes closed, picturing the driver of the car holding what could only have been a gun out of the car window. I wondered how he'd missed. Maybe because he'd been driving at the same time. I held my fingers tightly crossed, praying that Dutch trains prided themselves on their punctuality. Either that, or the driver didn't like his train doors being pummelled, because I was in luck. The doors remained closed and the train set off.

I was so happy to be free. I had no euros for a ticket, but I thought it better to brazen it out behind the façade of an English tourist who didn't understand, rather than hide in the toilet. The train passed into a suburb with shops and stopped again. I thought about getting off, but there was a distinct possibility I might fall into the hands of the smuggling gang, as I'd seen the car following the train on a parallel street. I'd wait to see if they lost sight of the train, or for a busier area. In the meantime, before I forgot, I found a pen and scribbled the Dutch number plate on the back of an envelope.

Before long, we were moving into the city centre and the train track bent away from the ever busier streets. I was sure the car would now be caught up in traffic. We made one other stop. I was terrified the man with the gun would appear but he didn't. All I needed to do was hold my nerve and pray I could avoid a ticket inspector. I'd been watching people as they boarded the train. Some bought tickets at a machine, many punched tickets in a different machine, but not all of them did. Perhaps some had weekly tickets that you didn't punch. No-one seemed to be staring at me so I assumed no-one thought I hadn't paid.

A few moments later we pulled into Amsterdam Central Station. I knew that because it said 'Centraal'. I got off with everyone else and walked down the steps from the platform into an underpass lined with shops, and out to the concourse. I so wanted to stop and look in the shop windows but resisted the temptation. Those men would guess I'd make for the centre, so I ought to make myself scarce and get as far away from the station as possible. I thought my best bet was to make for the police station, but first I needed something to eat and for that I needed some money.

I decided to risk hanging around the station long enough to get some cash. I wasn't sure, but I hoped I'd get euros if I put my debit card in a cash machine. After a short search I found a cash machine by the ticket machines. Thank God for the modern age! No need to queue in a travel agents or bureau de change. I had a bit of trouble understanding what it wanted of me, but a kind lady behind me heard me cursing in English and helped me. I dreaded to think what it had charged me by way of commission and exchange rate, but I didn't care. I smiled when I thought of Clare Brenner's money transfer. For once I was confident I had enough funds. Just as I thought, I was solvent, and the machine handed me my sixty euros.

I risked one more thing before I left the station. I bought a roll filled with cheese from one of the many shops and was rewarded with some coins as well as something to take away my hunger pangs. Then I walked to the front of the station again. There was a huge square outside, which I had to cross to get to anywhere. It was a pedestrian area but it looked very exposed. Although there didn't seem to be a car park, the car following me could have dropped its passenger off to watch the station exits. Was I being paranoid? Maybe it hadn't been a gun that I'd seen - and possibly heard? Might they not have concentrated on moving the painting somewhere else? But it was a multi-million pound smuggling set-up, and they would want to know who I was and if I knew anything about it, or if I was just a stowaway from the ferry. And they were armed.

I wondered if they'd had a good look at me. Probably good enough to spot me emerging from the station. I had to buy something new to wear. Now there was a thought! Oh, joy! A reason to go clothes shopping in Amsterdam! There were no actual clothes shops that I could see in the underpass, but there was the ubiquitous accessory shop and I bought a large blue scarf-cum-shawl to drape around my neck. I'd had my hair tied back in a scrunchie to flee from the motorhome, so I let it down and brushed it loose. Putting on my sunglasses, I glanced in a mirror in the shop and felt I looked different enough to risk stepping out into the open.

I walked briskly across the square and headed for the centre of town. I saw a book shop and bought a small guide book with map, asking the man behind the counter to point out the police station. He said it was not far from the large canal, the Singelgracht, and he kindly marked it on my map with a cross, along with the Dutch word 'POLITIE', so that I could recognise it on signs.

31

Steve had trouble finding the police station, despite having a map he'd downloaded from Google, because there were so many canals going round in circles and one-way systems, but eventually, after several mistakes along the way, he found the modern office block on Nassaukade, right next to the Singelgracht canal. He needn't have worried as Inspector Anna Rijkhart greeted him warmly, and said they had plenty of time, and she'd not actually expected him so soon.

She led him to a bustling office where he was reunited with Dirk, the PC who'd come with her to Hull. Steve hoped he wouldn't want to take them clubbing in Amsterdam as they'd ended up doing with him in Hull. He was too old for all that now. Dirk seemed all efficiency in his home station, and soon presented Steve with coffee and pastries.

He hadn't been there long when he had a call from Barry.

'Morning, Sir. Matt asked me to keep you updated until he's back on duty. I'm afraid there's not a lot to report yet. Kate and I played it cool with Simon Robinson, as requested. We just popped in his yard and said we were investigating a missing person and as her car had been found nearby, could we ask his employees if anyone had seen anything. He was nice as pie, said we were welcome to ask around. He denies all knowledge of Rachel. Said he hasn't spoken to her, seen her, doesn't know her. Or why her car was near his factory. I mentioned that an elderly neighbour had heard noises over the weekend, but he explained them away as being a spot of overtime. A couple of his men were finishing a job that was running late.'

'As expected, I suppose. If Rach was there and found something, he was hardly going to admit it.'

'I know, Sir, but as Matt said, he'd think it odd if the police were asking questions at doors opposite without calling to speak to him and his staff, so we had to ask him, but make it look like we were just covering all the bases. We don't want to spook him, by implying we think he might be involved. We've got a car round the corner, waiting to follow when he leaves the factory. I wish we could get his phone bugged, but it would take too long. There are still a few people in the nearby houses we've not managed to speak to, but so far we've drawn a blank.'

'Thanks for ringing, anyway. I'll be interviewing this Dutch bloke soon, so my phone will be off, but you can always leave a message.'

'There are a couple of other things, Sir. Pete Shannon's turned up, alive and in a better state than Pottinger. He's got a knife wound to his left hand. It was deep and bled a lot, but it had been stitched and it's healing nicely. He's been shacked up with a lady friend we didn't know about. I wish I had his luck with women. He has that many.'

'Stick to the plot, Barry. How did he know Pottinger had been arrested?'

'This lady friend just so happens to be a nurse. Lucky sod has had expert medical care and of course she also heard on the quiet that we'd arrested Pottinger in casualty. Shannon told Jordan how he was trying to find out the kind of computing skills needed to hack into burglar alarms and then targeted various hackers, asking them related questions. Seems a couple replied. God knows why, but hackers are like members of a club, they share new methods and viruses and things. Then he got the list of employees and found a name that matched.'

'Rach didn't have a full list. I wonder how he got it, but carry on.'

'His almost fatal mistake then was to contact Pottinger again. He thought it was another offhand enquiry, designed to get Pottinger to implicate himself, but it drew him out too far. Convinced that Shannon knew too much, he came to disable him and find out how he'd got the information, maybe even see if he wanted in on the deal. Who knows? If not, or maybe in any case, he must have planned to get rid of him. Shannon heard the break-in at the back of his house and lay in wait with a heavy metal candlestick. He floored Pottinger with a blow to the leg, and managed to grab the knife he was carrying, although he sustained the wound to his hand. He stabbed Pottinger when he lunged at Shannon's leg to stop him, and then he made a run for it.'

'I didn't know he had it in him. I'm impressed.'

'He said he was terrified at first that Pottinger would bleed to death, even though it would probably have gone down as self-defence. He went to the nurse's house to have the wound fixed, and she said he could stay. She found out after a couple of days that casualty staff were looking out for a young man with stab wounds, and there'd been no deaths reported, so he presumed Pottinger was still out looking for him. He decided to lay low. Pottinger's been charged now with the hacking, accessory to robbery, breaking and entering and grievous bodily harm. They're trying to get him to give up the person who hired him in return for a lesser sentence, but so far, no joy.'

'I'm sure Rach will be relieved when she hears.' Steve ignored the small voice in his head saying 'IF she hears, more like'. He couldn't allow himself to start thinking Banks had got hold of her and something dreadful had happened.

'The second thing...'

'There's more?'

'The number plate for the low-loader you asked Matt to trace. It's registered to a bloke called Terry Watson, and his wife says it's all legitimate. He bought it from his cousin, Howard Banks.'

'Our Howard Banks?'

'Yes, Sir.'

'Get round to Banks' garage and ask him some questions, like whether this Watson does any work for him and what he's doing driving it in Holland with a spanking new motorhome on it. Let's rattle his cage.'

'But, with respect, Sir, haven't we been told not to harass him? We haven't any evidence of wrong-doing to justify questioning him again.'

'There must be some. But you're right. We better leave it for now. I'll pull in a favour with the Dutch police and ask them to put a call out for the low loader to be stopped and searched. Thanks, Barry. I'd better go now. The inspector's ready to start.'

'Okay, I'll keep you updated.'

When Steve put the phone down he was still very angry about Banks. Anna Rijkhart was surprised until he explained about Rach having gone missing and that he suspected Banks was involved. He told her how he'd spent weeks investigating the theft of expensive cars, and it had led to Banks and his garage and workshop, and how Banks had beaten up Rach when she was tailing him on his wife's behalf, only to get off on a technicality. To add insult to injury, the raid Steve had ordered had only come up with one stolen car, and Banks was trying to pin that on his workshop manager.

Anna set in motion the search for Terry Watson's low loader, before they went to interview Pieter Meerdink. They agreed that it should be tailed to see where it went, rather than pulled over.

'That's great, Anna. Thanks a lot. Now, what have you found out so far from your smuggler?'

'We found the diamonds on him when he went through customs. It was pure chance. He was sweating such a lot. They pulled him over, searched his case and found them. The quantity was about the same as those you found on Jan Petersen, and they were in a similar bag. He also had Cuthbert's address, which is why I suggested you come over. He's not been involved in any previous criminal activity, but he does have drug problems, and we think he may have been talked into carrying the diamonds to pay for his habit.'

'We've interviewed him, Steve, but he won't say anything about who he was working for. That's why I thought we might get further, if you tell him the last courier ended up dead in Hull marina. Maybe his employers haven't told him, and he doesn't have to know it wasn't murder. Then if he doesn't budge, you can tell him that his contact Cuthbert's been murdered and you're searching his accounts and his premises. See if he'll give us more then.'

'I suppose the person supplying the diamonds would assume the last consignment got to Cuthbert before Petersen died in the marina through natural causes, since we never mentioned finding any diamonds. And for the same reason, we think that whoever was waiting for the diamonds in England must still assume Cuthbert stole them and was trying to do a runner abroad, otherwise they wouldn't have entered into a new deal. We think Cuthbert was booked on a ferry to Holland to find out why they hadn't turned up, presumably not having noticed the tiny newspaper report describing the death of a Dutch tourist.'

'I didn't think he'd believe me if I talked about deaths in the UK. That's why I suggested you come over. If we can't get him to name names, then we've got to try to find out what the diamonds were used to pay for, Steve.'

'I'll give it a try. I'm sure he speaks good English like the vast majority of you do in Holland, but could you translate, please, so he can't hide behind pretending he doesn't exactly understand everything I'm saying?'

'No problem.'

Steve followed her down the corridor and into the interview room.

- -

I was desperate to phone Steve but didn't feel safe. I kept feeling I was being followed. Also I needed the loo badly, so I nipped into a coffee shop and ordered a hot chocolate. As was usual for the continent, tea would only come with condensed milk, which I hate almost as much as coffee, so I plumped for chocolate. And I really love chocolate. If it hadn't been for my addiction I'd never have been able to save a girl from the clutches of a serial killer. But I dragged my mind from that other dangerous episode in my life.

I went to the loo and on the way back I asked if I could use the phone as I had lost my mobile. Luckily the waitress agreed. I rang Steve's mobile, amazingly remembering to enter the code for England - 44 - before the number. It went to voicemail. Damn! He must have turned his phone off while he did his interview with the Dutch police inspector. I didn't know the number for the Dutch police station, and doubted if they would take my rambling tale seriously. And what were they going to do? Come out and escort me to safety? I left a message asking him to tell Mum and Dad I was sorry I'd missed Sunday tea but I was on a case. I told him the art thieves were after me, I was in Amsterdam without a passport and on my way to the police station. I thanked the girl. I'd wanted to ring Mum and Dad, but couldn't really ask to use the phone twice. I thought Steve could handle it for me anyway. I paid and set off through the city centre, sticking to busy pedestrianised streets.

- -

Across town, Steve and Anna broke for coffee to regroup, both feeling they were getting nowhere. Steve turned on his mobile. There was a voicemail message for him. He expected to hear Barry with an update, so was stunned to hear Rach's voice instead.

'Steve, it's me. Can you ring Mum and Dad for me please, and say sorry for missing Sunday tea but I'm on a case? I haven't got a passport so I'm coming to see you at the police station. I've found out it's Wharton and Robinson stealing the paintings. Did I say I was in Amsterdam? I'll try to ring again but there were men with guns shooting at the train. See you soon. Love you.'

'Is anything wrong, Steve?' asked a concerned Anna.

'That was my girlfriend, Rachel.'

'Oh, you've found her then. That must be a relief'

'Not exactly. Nothing's ever simple with Rach. She says men have been shooting at her. Here, you listen.' He played the message back again on loudspeaker.

'She's on her way here, that's good. I'll let the front desk know and they can look out for her. You don't by any chance have a photo of her?'

Steve opened his wallet and produced a small bedraggled photo of them both, taken in a booth in Scarborough on a day trip when they were students. 'This is the best I've got, I'm afraid. It's a few years old now, but…' As he handed it over, he told himself it was time he got a more up-to-date picture of Rach. 'It's the only one I have, so I'd be grateful to get it back later, please.'

'I wonder how she got to Holland without a passport? Surely that's not possible?'

'Nothing Rach does ever surprises me. I haven't a clue how she got here, but she must have found something out at Robinson's factory, and she mentioned Wharton too. Do you mind if I make a few calls before we continue?'

'No problem. We can delay the rest of the interview until she gets here. You've got enough on your mind, and she asked you to ring her parents as well.'

Steve listened to the message one more time. It was just like Rach - start out about Sunday tea, then suddenly drop in that she's in Amsterdam without a passport, she knows who's been stealing the paintings, and by the way, men have been shooting at her. He placed a call to Matt.

'Sorry to spoil your beauty sleep, but I can't really dump this on Barry, and I'd rather you liaise with Jordan.' He played the message to Matt, who laughed.

'You've got to hand it to her, Steve. She comes up with the goods, whether by design or not. I'll bring Robinson in, as we've already spoken to him about Rach being missing. Presumably you don't want to mention the paintings until you've spoken to her, but you don't want him doing a runner or burying any evidence?'

'Correct. Talk to him about abducting Rach. And if you could speak to DI Jordan, get him to take Wharton in, please? Rach had her suspicions about him in connection with the art thefts, and that's Mike's case. If Pottinger knows we have Wharton, he might change his mind about telling us what he knows for a lighter sentence. Strictly speaking, if Rach has fingered Robinson for the thefts, Mike's team should arrest him too, but my feeling is we should keep them separate until we find out more from Rach. He may be in charge of robbery division, but we're major crimes, so it shouldn't be a problem. If he kicks up a fuss, ask him to ring me, please.'

'Do you know where Rach is, Steve?'

'Not a clue, and if I know her sense of geography and map-reading, neither does she. I found it hard enough to find the police station myself. Not to mention she may have 'men with guns' following her.'

'I shouldn't worry too much about that. She didn't sound frightened so she must have lost them.'

'I couldn't do anything if I wanted to. I'll just have to cross my fingers as usual.'

There was one more thing he had to do. He dialled Rach's parents' number. 'Hello, it's Steve. Good news. Rachel's on her way to meet me right now. She told me to apologise to you for missing tea, but she got involved in a case which seems to be linked to the one I'm working on, and she's ended up in Holland. Everything else flew out of her head. You know what she's like.'

'That's brilliant news, Steve. What a relief. Thanks for ringing. I know you must be busy. That lass of mine needs her head screwing on sometimes. Good job she's got you to look out for her. Would you please ask her to ring her mum when you see her? I've tried to play it down but she's been really worried.'

Steve said, 'No problem. Bye, now,' and then suggested to Anna that they carry on the interview. If the paintings were linked to Amsterdam, he was beginning to have a shrewd idea that the diamonds were somehow involved. He explained this to Anna and they agreed that Steve should try to draw Meerdink out by mentioning Wharton and Robinson.

'I suppose it can't do any harm, although we don't know how they're involved, do we?'

'No, we don't, but I don't think we'll get anywhere with him otherwise. He wasn't shaken by the death of Petersen. He'd probably not been told his predecessor's name and would in any case think he'd be able to do a better job. Equally, he wasn't bothered by Cuthbert's murder. He's probably feeling safe that there's no-one in England to give him away, and he gets paid by someone in Holland so that's an incentive to keep quiet. Mentioning that the people at the top in England have been arrested might shake his resolve, and make him wonder whether he's going to get dragged into it, whilst the people he reports to get away.'

Anna agreed, and they returned to the interview room, although not before leaving strict instructions with anyone and everyone that Steve be told the minute Rach arrived.

32

I looked at the map for what seemed like the hundredth time, turning it every which way, trying to make sense of it. I'd walked through the shopping area but it was a bit of a maze. Somehow I'd come out the other side and ended up on a street alongside a canal where women were displaying themselves in the windows of the houses. Horrified that I'd clearly stumbled into the red light district, and indignantly thinking it should be clearly signposted to stop innocent girls like me entering it by accident, I rushed along, past more and more women. The place was busy even at ten o'clock in the morning. I wasn't embarrassed but I didn't want anyone to think I was a prostitute. Though to be honest, I thought there were hardly any young ones, and even they looked a bit ropy.

When I'd emerged into quieter streets, I realised I was lost. I wandered on and finally got to the Waterlooplein, a large square, and found it on the map. I found the wide Singelgracht on the map and was about to head off in that direction, but the book shop assistant had marked the police station on the map as being on the opposite side of the town. More confusion. Then I realised that the canals bent right round the very centre of the city, and so did the streets that lined them, without the names changing. So a canal could be in the east, the west and the south. And I was in the south-east instead of the west. If I went straight to the Singelgracht and followed it all the way round, it could take hours, and besides that, the road alongside looked wide and exposed. I couldn't be sure I'd shaken off those men. What I had to do, was to turn my back on the canal and walk in the opposite direction, and just try not to get lost again.

Unfortunately, the smaller streets were lethal for a different reason. I was crossing over to look at a street stall full of beautiful tulips, when I was nearly knocked over by a cyclist. Fortunately she rang her bell at the last minute and I jumped to safety, but she'd showed no signs of slowing down. This proved to be no isolated incident. I found it hard to cope with traffic driving on the right as it was, struggling to look left instead of right, before crossing the road. The silent bikes appearing from all directions at very high speeds just added to my edginess.

It didn't help that there were so many junctions, as roads crossed canals, which themselves had roads on both sides, all over the place. And the bridges were narrow, with tiny pavements. I had to step out into the road often, and kept forgetting which way to look until a bicycle bell reverberated in my ear, making me scurry for whatever bit of pavement I could find.

It wasn't all like that. Besides the tulip stall, I found lots of lovely things to look at. I passed a handbag museum on Herengracht, and bobbed in the open doorway to look around the shop. It was full of pretty things and I was sorely tempted, but I kept my euros in my pocket and after checking where I was on the map, I set off again. I'd felt safe there and it would have been nice to go round the museum, but Steve was expecting me now, and I wanted the adventure to be over.

The smaller canals didn't have the big tourist boats that I'd seen gliding up and down nearer the centre of town, but many had houseboats moored along the sides. I passed a cheese shop. Not a deli but a cheese shop. Really. That's all it sold. Large round cheeses were stacked high on shelves, with smaller pieces laid out in displays beneath. I'm a Wensleydale or Double Gloucester person myself, but Edam's not bad, if a bit rubbery.

Approaching one of the many bridges, I suddenly found myself caught up in a guided tour on bikes. There were about twenty of them, all bright yellow, and what with all the pedals and handlebars, I was lucky to escape with ankles and ribs intact. There were some gorgeous blue and white tiles and other pottery in quite a few of the shop windows, including elaborate vases with lots of openings for popping tulips in.

I was getting nearer to my goal but there were less shops and more pavements filled with bikes chained to railings, which meant I had to step perilously close to the road. As I walked I kept one eye out for the silver Audi that had followed me from the industrial estate. There was always a chance they knew I'd make for the police station, but the walk had taken me so long, my feet were hurting. The men had probably given up long ago. In fact, I needed the loo again.

Salvation loomed, in the shape of a nice-looking café on a corner. I ordered another hot chocolate and asked for the toilet. I was hungry again and added a scrummy looking pastry to my order. It seemed that everyone did understand English, though that maybe wasn't so surprising, as this was still a tourist area. There were a few taking photos of the pretty houses lining the canal. The tops of the tall thin houses had ornate fronts, each a little different in design. I felt happy and safe again. Just one phone call and my worries might all be over.

Unfortunately, the waitress said she was sorry, but there was 'no phone to use'. She did point me in the direction of a public phone and told me it would take my credit card though. I wanted to ring Steve again, tell him what I'd learnt in case it was of use to him in his interviewing. And alright, I admit it, ask if he could come out and meet me.

- -

Meerdink didn't react to the name Wharton, but when Robinson's name was mentioned, Steve picked up on faint tell-tale signs that told him he'd hit a nerve. He pressed the point, stressing that Robinson was sitting in Hull police station at that very moment, and that was enough. Meerdink was already struggling with drug withdrawal symptoms, and now

303

readily gave up the information that Simon Robinson was the name of person who was due to take delivery of the diamonds, in return for the promise of a lighter sentence and some medical assistance. Apparently he'd been expecting to deliver to Cuthbert's jeweller's shop, as he had done previously, but got a call at the last minute to say Robinson would meet him in the foyer of The Deep museum, a quiet place within walking distance of the hotel he'd be staying in.

If Steve was surprised to hear Meerdink had made deliveries in the past, he didn't show it. He'd assumed Jan Petersen had been the only courier until he took a drunken walk and fell in the marina, but he could understand that two couriers visiting Cuthbert's shop would be less conspicuous than the same one at more regular intervals. The important thing was that the link between the diamonds and the paintings was confirmed, if Rach was to be believed. She'd said that it was 'Wharton and Robinson stealing the paintings'.

For some reason Robinson must have thought it so important to make another delivery, that he was prepared to risk collecting the diamonds himself, rather than delay. He'd probably have another jeweller lined up to convert the diamonds to cash, or else the diamonds would be useless to him, but maybe the jeweller wasn't available to collect them from Meerdink, or maybe he wasn't based in or near Hull.

Meerdink denied all knowledge of any other such jeweller and also said he didn't know what the diamonds were to pay for. Steve believed him. He had no reason to lie about it. He steadfastly refused to give up any names for his bosses in Holland. He was obviously still too scared of retribution from that quarter.

Steve and Anna left the room to allow a doctor to visit and an officer to take a written statement from Meerdink. 'Maybe when your girlfriend gets here, she'll be able to describe the men she saw.'

'Hm... I wish she'd left more detail in her message, and I'm beginning to worry that something's happened to her. It's ages since she rang.'

'Maybe, maybe not. If she's on foot, it would take her quite a while even if she knew where she was going. For outsiders, Amsterdam is a city easy to get lost in.'

'I suppose that could be it. If anyone can get lost, Rach can. I just wish she'd phone again.'

'She probably thinks you're still busy, with your phone turned off.'

As if on cue, Steve's mobile rang. He'd kept it on ever since listening to Rach's message, but it was Barry. 'Hi, boss. We've had a bit of a breakthrough, so I thought I'd update you.'

'Thanks, Barry. What's this news?'

'DI Jordan's been on the phone. He brought Wharton in for questioning and let Pottinger catch sight of him being escorted down a corridor. The DI implied Wharton had actually been arrested and charged, and it seems that was enough to loosen

Pottinger's tongue. He said he wasn't going to take the blame, when Wharton had blackmailed him into doing the hacking.'

'Brilliant.'

'Yeah. Apparently, after Pottinger got thrown out of university, he ended up in Hull and faked his references to get himself a job in the IT department of Wharton's import / export business. He didn't know Wharton then. I don't know how, seeing as he's so brilliant at IT, but, according to Pottinger, Wharton caught him fiddling the records and siphoning off cash.'

'Sounds a bit unconvincing,' said Steve.

'Maybe it was one crook recognising another, or maybe Wharton investigates all his employees closely, but apparently he found out Pottinger'd been splashing cash. Either way, when he discovered Pottinger's talents for hacking, Wharton is said to have blackmailed Pottinger into working for him, with a promise of a lot of cash as a bonus.'

'You say "said to have". You're making it sound as if the 'blackmail' angle is not that convincing.'

'True. DI Jordan doubts if Pottinger would've let himself be caught stealing. He thinks it more likely that Pottinger was bragging about what he could hack into, and Wharton took him up on it, but we'll see what comes out, if or when we get Wharton's side of the story.'

'Let's hope we do,' Steve commented.

'Anyway, what does seem true is that Pottinger got a job at the insurers, Thompson and Brenner, specifically to find out the locations of various paintings, and subsequently hacked into the burglar alarm systems. Whether that was at Wharton's command or their joint agreement, doesn't really matter. He's confessed, and named Wharton as the boss.'

'What happens next?'

'DI Jordan's left a car at Wharton's house to ensure no paintings are removed, whether any are stolen or not. Rach's report to the insurers said he had a private vault. The insurers are sending someone up to take a look. DI Jordan's interviewing Wharton as we speak, but he thought you should know what he got from Pottinger, in case the information's useful to you and the Dutch police.'

'Thanks, it might well be.'

Barry continued. 'He also asked me if you've found out anything from Rachel about Robinson and where his factory fits in. Pottinger says he's never heard of him, and denies all knowledge of what Wharton did with the paintings, though he did tell us something else interesting. It seems Wharton has a depot in Amsterdam.'

'Our Dutch smuggler has told us he was due to deliver the diamonds to Robinson, if that helps. I've only just come from interviewing him. I was about to ring Mike Jordan and let him know. I don't know how Robinson links to Wharton and the paintings yet, though. I'm hoping Rach will turn up or ring again soon. In fact, I'd better get off the phone. One last thing, though. Do you have an address for Wharton's Amsterdam depot, please?'

'I knew you were going to ask that. I'm working on it. There's nothing on their website and I can't get through to Wharton's, so Kate's on her way over there.'

'Thanks, Barry.'

Steve filled Anna in on the call, and she asked someone to check if Wharton's depot was in the phone book, but it wasn't. 'Time for some lunch, I think, Steve. It's been a long morning and we can't do anything more at the moment.'

'Good idea.'

Steve was just sitting down to eat when his phone rang yet again. It was Rach.

- -

What joy! There were instructions in English so it wasn't difficult to ring Steve from the public phone booth.

'Hello, it's me.'

'Rach, love. I've been worried. Where are you?'

'Not far from the police station, I don't think. I'm not sure of the road, I keep muddling all the names up, but there's a big antique centre on the corner. Anyway, just listen, first. I saw Wharton leaving Simon Robinson's factory. Gran's friend Ida called me over to see what the noises were.'

'I know that bit. I had people looking for you before I got your message.'

'Oh, really? Did you let Mum and Dad know I was alright?'

'Yes I did. Shall I come and get you?'

'In a minute. I just have to tell you this. Where was I? Yes, I hid in a motorhome to see what was going on, and overheard two men talking about a stolen painting. I reckon Wharton must have just delivered it. Robinson said it was the last one and then they'd have to lie low for a while. I know it was him, because the other bloke called him 'Mr Robinson'. Anyway, he left and the small weasly-faced bloke, Terry, he's called, hid the painting in the side panel of the motorhome. It's the Chagall that's just been stolen from the Keatons in Sewerby. You've got to find it so I can get my reward, Steve.'

'I think I know what happened next. This Terry, let's call him Terry Watson, drives the motorhome on the back of a low loader to the docks and it goes on a ferry to Rotterdam.'

'How on earth did you know that? Have you found it?'

'No. Where is it?'

'It's on an industrial estate just outside Amsterdam. I was trapped in the motorhome. I couldn't get out. It wasn't my fault I ended up in Holland without a passport, honest, Steve. When they opened the door, I got out of the motorhome and ran for it. They came after me but I was lucky, there was a tiny train station for commuters just along the road, elevated so I could see it, and I got on a train before they caught me.'

'Do you know any more?'

'I didn't catch the name of the station but it was a really long one, began with an H. And there were two more stops before we got to the Central station in Amsterdam. Is that enough for your Dutch inspector to find it?'

I heard Steve repeat that information to someone and add, 'Motorhome on low loader. Registration numbers I gave you earlier. Stolen painting in side panel of motorhome.' Then he added, 'Go on, Rach.'

'If the motorhome's still there you might get the painting. But if the men have given up chasing me, then they may have gone back and moved it.'

'What did the men look like, Rach?'

'They wore suits and one had a gun. I don't know if the other did. I ran faster than him but the man in the car caught up. Do you want its number?'

'Why didn't you tell me that first?'

'I wanted to tell you about the painting. The reward'll be huge, Steve.'

'What's the registration number, Rach?'

'I'm looking while we talk. It's a silver Audi. I wrote it on the back of something. Ah, here it is.'

I read it out to him, and then let out a shriek as I caught sight of the silver Audi driving slowly down the street. I legged it. I ran as fast as I could towards the antique centre, leaving the phone dangling from its wire, praying Steve wasn't far away and wishing I'd just asked him to come and get me, or told him the number plate first, or not called at all, but kept moving. I could have been safe in the police station by now.

33

'Rach? Rach? Dammit.' Steve pushed back the chair and stood up. 'Anna, that was Rach. She was in the middle of talking to me when I heard her cry out and then nothing. Something must have happened. Is there a big antique centre nearby? Two men in this car are after her.' He pushed the paper into her hand. 'At least one is armed. It's a silver Audi. Rach was in a phone box and the centre was at the end of the road.'

'I know the one. You can see it from the window. Look. It's only about fifty metres up this road, on the other side of the canal.'

'I'm on my way.'

'I'll be right with you. Willem, mobilise all available units, search the area around the antique centre for this car. Quick as you can.' Anna passed the slip of paper to her second-in-command. 'And, Dirk, have you located the commuter station? Good. Send someone out to locate and secure the motorhome.'

- -

My lungs were bursting but I tore through the doors of the centre before the car caught up with me. A shiny blur flashed past my eyes as I ran past cabinets full of silver, looking for an assistant, a phone, somewhere to hide, anything. I reached the counter. It was unoccupied, with no sign of a phone. I heard the door open as I skidded to a halt round the corner, dropped to my knees and crawled as quietly as I could out of sight behind a display unit. One pair of footsteps entered the building. I guessed the other man had stayed in the car.

Surely there was a human being somewhere to help me?

The noise of footsteps passed by, and receded. I'd be caught if I went back out of the door, so I headed off to one side up an aisle between the cabinets. Luckily I had my trainers on, rather than my glossy red stilettos, and I hardly made a sound. I headed deeper inside. This place was a maze. I heard footsteps again. I hid behind another counter, and they passed. I kept on moving, further from the door, and then I heard voices. Unless my pursuer was talking to someone, I had to assume the voices belonged to people who weren't involved with the gang.

- -

Steve ran down four flights of stairs and along the corridor, searching for the exit. He concentrated on trying to keep his footing, pushing thoughts of Rach from his mind until he could get out on the street. At last he was in the station yard. He could see the antique centre across the canal, further along the street. He wondered if she'd made it there. As his eyes scanned for a gate, he hoped she hadn't been forced into a car, or even run the opposite way, because then he might not get her back.

Anna shouted from the doorway, 'That way. You have to go round. I'll get a car.'

He cursed. He'd have to run further away from where he wanted to be, in order to get out past the railings to the street, and time might be running out.

- -

I crept round one last corner and saw there was a small café inside the antique centre. I was debating what to say when I heard the footsteps getting nearer again, and decided to risk it. I walked into the café and as I did so, I saw an exit into the street fronting onto the canal. Rather than trying to explain, I slipped quietly through the door and walked briskly down the street away from the antique centre. I could hear sirens from the other side of the canal and knew I mustn't be far from the police station.

- -

Steve ran out of the side entrance of the police yard and across the street towards the canal. He could see the antique centre and a figure he knew intimately came out of the side of the building that faced the canal. She was walking away from him. He waited for the sound of the sirens to recede, as police cars set off to search for the Audi, and then he shouted her name.

I heard a shout from behind me. It was Steve. I'd know his voice anywhere. And who else would be shouting, 'Rach' in the middle of Amsterdam? I turned and saw him on the bridge. He was coming to get me.

Sadly, I wasn't the only one who heard him shout. I watched in horror as the Audi raced round the corner. I did the only thing possible. I turned my back on Steve and ran for the next bridge down. The police station had to be across the canal. If I couldn't reach Steve, I'd head there. I heard a screech of brakes and the slam of a door and in that time I almost made it to the bridge. At the last minute a stupid bike came up from behind and rang its bell. I swerved to get out of its way, caught my ankle on a tree trunk, and tripped. I heard a shot and fell into the murky water.

And then it all happened at once. Steve heard a car revving its engine and saw the Audi pull out of a side street and skid to a stop outside the antique centre. A second man came out of the door and jumped in the car. It set off as he was still pulling the door closed. Rach had already set off running. Then Steve heard a

314

horn. It was Anna on the other side of the canal. He pointed to Rach and Anna drove on, heading for the bridge.

Steve heard a shot and then a splash. When Steve looked back towards Rach and the Audi, it was stopped by the canal and a man was shooting down into the water. There was no barrier along the canal. Rach was nowhere to be seen. Steve sprinted down the road. Gun or no gun, he needed to rescue Rach. He couldn't see her. He realised he didn't know if she could swim or not, but even if she could, it had been a while since he'd heard the splash. And there'd been the gunshot.

His heart turned to ice and his muscles struggled to obey as he forced his legs to cover the rest of the distance. As he got near, the man turned and pointed the gun at Steve. He dived into the canal, flinching as a bullet found its target. A horn blared. The man jumped back in the car as it reversed away from the roadblock made by Anna's car. Police sirens sounded as the other roads were blocked and armed police closed in on the car.

Steve sank like a stone. His shoulder felt like it had been hit by a metal bar. He trod water for a second as he got his bearings in the murky water and searched for Rach. After a minute or two, he broke the surface, gasping for breath. Anna was shaking her head. 'I can't see her Steve.' Steve dived again, searching desperately. She had to be down here somewhere. He'd heard of people coming round after five, ten minutes. He didn't know. He was losing it himself. He could feel the strength seeping out of his body. He hadn't been able to do enough. He only had one arm that worked. As he lost consciousness, he felt himself being pulled from the water, and with the last of his breath, he cried out, 'No!'

- -

I thought I heard Steve cry out. I wasn't sure if it was safe to come out, but he sounded in a bad way, and I had to help him. I swam out from behind the canal boat, some thirty metres from where I'd fallen in. I could see people on the edge of the canal, bending over Steve. No-one was looking at me. 'Steve! Steve!' I shouted, but I was a long way off. I swam back down the canal, as quickly as I could. A woman noticed me and pointed. There didn't seem to be any steps, but a lifebelt was thrown down to me. I bobbed up inside it and was hauled up the side. 'What's happened to Steve?' I cried. Someone put a coat round my shoulders as I knelt by him. There was a lot of blood.

'He was shot as he dived in the canal.'

'Oh, Steve, I do love you, but you didn't have to come and rescue me.' He must have heard my voice because he opened his eyes and gave a weak smile. Then they slid shut. He was still breathing but he looked ashen. I was terrified I was losing him.

Two ambulances screeched to a halt. Not like ours, more like estate cars. They wouldn't let me go with Steve. I didn't argue. It was vital he got to the hospital quickly. It was only a short ride. I didn't want to lie down, but they insisted. When we got there I followed Steve along the corridor. They explained they'd started giving him plasma straightaway in the ambulance and I could see colour returning to his face. They'd stopped the bleeding too, and assured me the bullet had gone clean through his shoulder, which apparently was a good thing, as it was "just a flesh wound". That meant that it hadn't hit any organs. He was taken into a treatment room and I sat on a seat outside, drained and exhausted, but overwhelmingly relieved and happy.

The woman from the canal turned up with a cup of tea, and introduced herself as Anna Rijkhart, the police inspector who'd come to Hull. As I've said before, I don't like tea abroad, but this cup had loads of sugar in it and for once I don't think I've ever enjoyed a cup more. I started to tell her about the men in the Audi and the motorhome, but she said it had all been taken care of. She told me I should let myself be examined properly and then rest.

Then the doctor came out and said they'd pumped Steve's stomach, fixed his shoulder and given him a tetanus booster and painkillers. He was weak from loss of blood, and they'd have to keep him in overnight at least, but he was fine. I asked if I could see him, but the doctor insisted on examining me first. He checked my breathing and asked if I'd swallowed any of the canal water. I told him truthfully that it was at most a small mouthful, but he didn't believe me until I told him I was the school underwater swimming champion.

He looked at me quizzically, but then accepted it. I hadn't swum for years but you don't forget how to do it. When I'd tripped on the tree trunk, I'd seen there was no chain or railing, and knew I could escape, so I pushed myself out with my other foot, took a deep breath and landed in the canal rather than on the hard cobbles at the edge. I'd dived down to the bottom to avoid the bullets and swum underwater some thirty yards before surfacing on the far side of a canal boat.

When the doctor had given me a tetanus booster and reluctantly declared me fit, I was taken to the small private ward where Steve was sleeping. I stroked his forehead and then sat by his bedside until he came round. When he opened his eyes, I was eating.

He smiled. 'How did you get out of that canal, Rach? I thought you were dead.'

I told him what I'd told the doctor earlier, finishing, 'there were shots and shouting. I thought I'd better hide and wait for a while. If I'd known you were in there looking for me, I'd have swum back.'

'It doesn't matter now, so long as you're alright. Funny, I didn't even know you could swim. We ought to spend more time together, Rach, and get to know each other better,' he joked.

I was just wondering where the conversation was leading, when there was a knock at the door. It was a nurse. 'I thought I heard voices. How do you feel, Mister Rose?'

'Not too bad, thank you.'

'Good. Police Inspector Rijkhart would like to talk to you, if you feel able.' She showed Anna in. Once we'd exchanged niceties and she'd established that Steve was much better, she agreed to my staying in the room and told us what had happened since we were fished out of the canal.

The Dutch police had blocked the roads and closed in on the Audi, and the men had been arrested at gunpoint. They'd worked out the name of the station where I'd boarded the train and found the motorhome in a nearby yard. They'd found the Chagall and removed it for safekeeping.

'Great! We'll get the reward, love!' I couldn't help but say.

'What about the low loader?' Steve asked.

'Gone. We presume it'll be driven back to England via tonight's ferry from Rotterdam. We're keeping an eye on the docks to be sure, but no doubt you'd rather we let it board, so you can arrest the driver in Hull?'

'Good idea. I'll ring DI Jordan when we've finished talking and give you his number, so you can let him know if the low loader's on the ferry. You said you'd removed the painting. What about the motorhome?'

'We're leaving it on the industrial estate for now. We've replaced the panel and we've set up a camera at the yard entrance to see who comes to collect it. Whoever wants that painting must have already paid, with the diamonds Meerdink was carrying. We're hoping it'll still be collected, even if there's no-one to meet them at the yard. If that's the case, we'll follow it to its destination. I don't know if we'll find any other stolen paintings, Steve. They could be hidden away in private collections right across Europe.'

'Well, now we know Robinson was shipping them in motorhomes, we'll be able to go through his sales records and see if that brings anything to light. Unless he gives us names, though, we're unlikely to find out which motorhomes carried paintings. Even if we did know and if Interpol or local police were to get search warrants for the recipients' homes, I think the paintings will have been squirreled away, never to be found.'

'We're interviewing the men from the Audi. So far they've admitted they worked for Wharton at his Amsterdam depot, but insist they just handled anything he shipped abroad. They deny all knowledge of any paintings. We'll charge them with attempted murder, but it'll be hard to get a conviction for more than owning and discharging guns in a public place, with intent to endanger life. Their excuse for shooting was that they thought Rachel was a thief, and that you were in the same gang, and they thought you were both armed. They said they were only aiming in your general direction to frighten you off. Not much of an excuse but we'll have to see what the jury thinks. Unless Wharton or the buyer of the motorhome gives them up, they'll probably get away with any involvement in the smuggling, but they should still go to prison.'

'Thanks, Anna.'

'I'd better go now. You look tired.'

When she left, Steve was having trouble staying awake. I suggested I rang Mike Jordan instead of Steve, and bring him up-to-date with everything that had happened. Steve wasn't happy about it, but he was too tired to argue. 'Don't forget Terry Watson.'

'The weasly-faced man in the low loader?' Steve nodded. 'Don't worry, I won't. Now get some sleep. I'll be back.'

I went outside and rang Mike Jordan. I filled him in on everything. He was shocked that Steve had been shot, but glad he wasn't seriously hurt. At the end of the conversation, I relayed Steve's request that if Anna rang to confirm the low loader was on the ferry, Humberside Police should be standing by to follow it to its destination, and take appropriate action. He said he'd be in touch.

34

I wasn't quite sure what to do next. I didn't want to leave Steve, but the exertions of the last twenty-four hours were catching up on me. The nurse said that Steve would probably sleep overnight, and if he did wake, they'd let me know. Satisfied, I let her lead me to a cubicle and I soon nodded off.

When I woke up, it was getting dark. I looked at my watch and it was after seven in the evening. I was still in a hospital gown. I went to see what had happened to my clothes, and was handed a carrier with my own clothes and handbag, but also a bag of new things, still with labels, all in my size and a clutch bag containing a new purse with my debit card and euros. The nurse said she'd been told to ring the police station when I woke, and someone would pick me up. She showed me to a shower room and handed me a towel and some soap. Although it was only hospital soap, I felt much better after standing under the hot shower. When I was ready, I found Anna waiting for me.

'You must come to our home and eat. You've had a dreadful day.'

'That's so kind of you. Are you sure? You've had a busy day as well.'

'Not in, how do you say it, the same league as yours.' She smiled and led me to her car. She lived in a pleasant leafy street on the outskirts of the city. Her husband and young daughter met them at the door.

'I'm so lucky Edwin works from home. I couldn't manage otherwise.' She went up and settled her daughter in bed, whilst her husband dished up a casserole. Edwin seemed friendly and over the meal he asked what I thought of Amsterdam. It was hard to answer.

'The city seems lovely, and I hope I get chance to explore before I go home, but not many tourists get shot at, lose their way, get shot at again and then fall in the canal within their first four hours in the city.'

He laughed and then asked after my family. I got a horrible sinking feeling as I realised I'd not rung Mum and it was Gran's birthday and I'd be in so much trouble when I got home. I answered as best as I could, but Edwin could probably tell something was up, as he excused himself shortly afterwards, saying he had some work to do. I helped Anna clear the table and then asked if I might use the phone to call the hospital and ring my mother in England, as I'd only managed to get a message to her via Steve and that was early that morning. I offered to pay, but she wouldn't hear of it. First I rang the hospital and was assured that Steve was sleeping peacefully. Then I rang Mum. It answered almost on the first ring.

'Rachel. What's been going on? I've been so worried. Steve did ring this morning to say you were alright and you were on your way to meet him, but we've heard nothing since. I began to wonder if he was just trying to make us feel better and maybe he hadn't spoken to you at all.'

'I'm really sorry, Mum, honestly I am. This is the first chance I've had to ring. I was at the hospital with Steve...'

'What's happened? Is he alright?'

'There was a bit of a problem catching some crooks, Mum, and he's hurt his arm, but he's going to be alright. Things were so hectic, that everything else went clean out of my head. Is Gran there?'

'Yes. You'd better speak to her. I don't know if she'll forgive you for missing her birthday tea though.'

'Rachel. Is that you? Where are you? What's been going on?'

'Happy Birthday, Gran. Have you had some nice presents? I'll give you mine as soon as I get home.'

'I don't understand why you had to go off gallivanting abroad when you knew it was my birthday.'

'I'll make it up to you, Gran, I promise.'

'How?'

'I'll tell you all the gory details that I won't tell Mum.'

'It's a deal. Whet my appetite now and tell me the rest when you get home and I won't say a word more about you missing my birthday.'

'I went to the factory opposite Ida's and got trapped in a motorhome used to smuggle paintings, and before I knew it I was abroad without a passport. If you promise not to tell Mum, I'll tell you about the red light district and being shot at and chased and falling into the canal, and holding my breath like I used to in swimming club at school.'

'Well, Rachel, now you've apologised, we'll say no more about it and I'll put your mum back on.' She's a trooper, my Gran. She wouldn't let anything slip out while Mum was in earshot.

'When are you coming home, Rachel?' asked Mum.

'I'm not sure. Steve will have to write statements when he's discharged from hospital.' I didn't dare tell Mum I'd got to Holland without a passport, and I needed to sort something out to get home with. 'I'll ring you tomorrow. Enjoy the rest of the evening with Gran. I've got to go now. I'm in the home of one of Steve's Dutch colleagues. I don't want to run up her bill.'

'Alright, Rachel. At least it sounds like you're being taken care of.'

We said our goodbyes and then I asked Anna if Steve had a hotel room booked, which I might use, because I didn't want to put her to any more trouble.

'But you must stay here. We have a spare room. It is no trouble at all.'

'That's very kind of you. And I haven't thanked you for the clothes. I'll repay you tomorrow when I can get to a bank.'

'There is nothing to pay me. I paid out of the police funds. They are suitable for helping a witness and someone who helped solve a major crime, so please think no more of it.'

'Thank you.'

'How is your mother? Did you tell her about your trip?'

'She would be upset, so I didn't tell her much. She was glad that you're taking care of me now.'

'It's nice to meet Steve's girlfriend. He seems a very nice sort of person. You are lucky. I think he loves you very much. When he thought you were in the water he wouldn't give up, even though he could hardly swim. They had to pull him out.'

'I know. I love him very much as well.'

'It's difficult finding time to be together when one of the two is a police officer. Edwin and I have worked hard to be happy. I think you will, too.'

We said our goodnights and I fell asleep in no time.

In the morning, she dropped me at the hospital and I showed off my new clothes to Steve. He was more interested in hearing a detailed account of everything that had happened to me since he'd left the flat on Sunday morning. He wasn't best pleased that I'd decided to climb into the motorhome to investigate, but I think he's finally getting used to me, because he just rolled his eyes.

When I'd finished, he told me how he'd come to be on the ferry, recognised Terry Watson and actually tried the door of the motorhome. 'I can't believe I was so near to you. I could have let you out and none of this would have happened.'

'Ah, but then the Chagall wouldn't have been recovered and I wouldn't be in line for a big reward. I'll have to ring Clare Brenner and claim it.'

'You and your rewards. Have you forgotten you're already getting one for the painting Mills claimed had been stolen?'

'No, but it would be good to have a bit of a nest egg,' I said. What I was really thinking, but didn't like to say, was that maybe we could use it to put down a deposit on a house.

'I nearly forgot, because you didn't ask after him, but Pete's fine. He'd figured out Pottinger was the hacker, but asked one question too many and Pottinger came after him. He wasn't that badly hurt. He'd just been in hiding.'

'That's good.' I changed the subject. 'How do you feel this morning?' I realised I hadn't even given Pete a thought. I'd forgotten he'd gone missing, leaving a pool of blood in his house.

'I feel alright now apart from this shoulder. I'll have to take some time off work until the wound heals properly, but it won't be too long before I'll be able to go back.'

'Will you be able to drive?'

'The doctor said that once the wound's healed, I should get the shoulder back to normal after some physiotherapy.'

I was just going to suggest a holiday might be a good idea, when the doctor arrived to look Steve over. When he left, Steve was all smiles. 'He's given me more painkillers, but said I can leave.'

'That's great. Anna sent some clothes for you as well.'

- -

Before Steve could get changed, the phone rang. It was Matt. 'We've got a result, Steve.'

'I gather Watson caught the ferry last night?'

'Yes, and you'll never guess where he went - only to Banks' workshop.'

'So Banks is involved somehow after all. What happened?'

'Watson stopped in the yard and unloaded some boxes off the back of the low loader, then he lifted the carpet in the cab and removed a flat parcel. He took it into the office. Banks was there. After about a quarter of an hour Watson left and DI Jordan followed him to his home, arrested him and took him to the station. Jordan had rung me when Watson arrived at the workshop, because he knew of our interest in Banks, so Barry called me and we got to the workshop just as Watson was leaving.'

'Have you got Banks?'

'Yes. There were half a dozen left-hand drive modification units on the back of the low loader, so we took him in for questioning. He claimed harassment, said he'd bought them legitimately, which was probably true, but we ignored him. We got a search warrant. There was no wrapping paper in the bin, so we knew he must have hidden the flat parcel somewhere but we couldn't find it. We knew it had to be important, because Watson had hidden it from customs.'

'So he'll get away again?' Steve sighed.

'No. Just wait, there's more. Rach told Jordan she'd heard Watson talking to Robinson about the painting, and then heard him fitting it behind the panel, so we had Watson for smuggling the painting. When we told him that, he obviously didn't see much point in pretending any more that he knew nothing. He said he'd cooperate if we went easy on him. I didn't make any promises but he told me it wasn't really his low loader. He said Banks had signed it over to him, to distance himself and cover his tracks.'

'So is Banks involved in the smuggling of paintings as well? I can't see how.'

'No. Banks stole high-end right-hand drive cars registered in the UK, then changed their identity by fitting them with left-hand drive units bought legitimately, and stolen plates from abroad. He then had Watson take them over on the ferry to sell with forged documents, as legitimate foreign cars, and created a false paper trail to cover how he got them.'

'So Watson was smuggling number plates and documents, and bringing legitimate car parts back to the UK, whenever he delivered a motorhome abroad on the low loader.'

'That's right. He told us where Banks' hiding place was. No wonder we never found anything when we raided the workshop that night Rach was attacked and abducted. He'd built a false wall. Some of the bricks at the bottom weren't fixed as solidly as they looked, and when they were removed, there was a narrow cupboard behind. We found a stash of stuff in there. That's physical evidence, as well as Watson's statement, we've got. Banks is going down for definite this time.'

'That's great news, Matt. Did Banks not know about the paintings?'

'No. He gave Watson the low loader and got him to advertise his services. He told him to accept the first company that wanted him to deliver things abroad.'

'So how come Watson got involved with smuggling the paintings as well, do you know?'

'Greed. Banks was making all the money, while he was taking all the risks. So he grabbed the chance when it was presented to him, to make some more on the side.'

'Watson better hope he doesn't meet up with Banks in prison then. Great work, Matt.'

'There are a couple of last pieces in the jigsaw concerning Robinson and Wharton. Jordan's discovered they've been mates since they went to school together. Wharton's been legitimately doing the paperwork for years to export Robinson's caravans and motorhomes abroad. And they both belonged to the rotary club. It'd be easy for Robinson to slip Wharton an envelope containing his cut of the cash that Cuthbert gave him in exchange for diamonds.'

'You're right, Matt. Then I suppose Wharton went off and bought himself more paintings. I'm sure you can pay cash at auction if you want. And I expect he came into contact with all sorts of foreign collectors at these auctions. He'd suss out any who might want a painting that badly, they wouldn't mind if it was stolen. Then they would pay by way of diamonds, smuggled into the UK to avoid a paper trail.'

'Jordan's had a go at Robinson since the Dutch police found the painting in his motorhome and Rach identified him as being there when the painting was hidden, but so far no joy. But you remember Bob Giggs?'

'The low life that tortured Cuthbert?'

'Yes. I know you linked him with Banks, but he's the sort of thug who's known around Hull as being for hire for anything a bit messy, and it's not unlikely that Robinson hired him when he didn't get his cash from Cuthbert for the diamonds.'

'You're probably right. So you're going to try to use Giggs' name and the torture to loosen Robinson's tongue, and vice versa?'

'Yeah. One of them'll surely talk and name the other, and we'll hopefully get them both.'

'Great work, Matt. Sounds like we might manage to take a whole bunch of villains out of circulation.'

'Don't forget to thank your Rach. She came up with Wharton and Robinson's names in the first place. I don't know how far we'd have got without her.'

'I will, but she's got her mind set on the rewards for the paintings. Praise from the police will just be an extra.'

'What was all that about, Steve?' I asked when he finally finished his call. He filled in the gaps I hadn't picked up from the one side of the conversation I'd heard. 'Fantastic. I'm glad Banks is going to get his comeuppance. You've been after him all along, haven't you? Though you thought he had something to do with the diamonds because of Cuthbert.'

'I did. Their being brothers-in-law led me to believe they were both involved in the diamond smuggling. That'll teach me not to jump to conclusions, but to wait for hard evidence.'

'Who actually stole the paintings?'

'I doubt if we'll ever know. A gang of professional thieves from down south, I expect, brought in by Robinson. They'd do the job, leave the painting at Robinson's factory, get paid in cash and then disappear again.'

Steve eventually finished getting dressed, with a little help from me. I may have actually slowed him down a bit, particularly when it came to fastening his jeans. 'Anyone could come in Rach. Much as I'd like to, we'd better wait till we get to the hotel tonight.'

'So we're stopping?' I couldn't contain my excitement at the thought of actually seeing something of Amsterdam with Steve.

'We'll have to get you some sort of document from the British Embassy, since you left your passport at home, though Anna may be able to sort that out by vouching for you, but I thought we'd have a few days' holiday. Humberside's finest seem to be managing well enough without me.'

'Oh, thanks, Steve. It'll be fantastic.'

'You deserve it, with all these cases you've solved for me. I could get cross with you for getting into trouble when I tell you not to, but I'm beginning to realise you just can't help it. So, we'll just call at the police station and then we'll do whatever you want. Mind you, I'll need a bit of care and attention as well,' he said, pointing to his shoulder. 'I won't be able to drive for a couple of weeks, so I'm afraid you'll have to be brave and drive us back to the ferry when we go home, but we won't need to drive in Amsterdam.'

At the station, everyone was pleased to see Steve up and about. 'I'll just see if Anna needs any statements signing, talk to her about the documents you'll need, and ask her if someone can drop my car off at the hotel. And before I say goodbye, I need to thank her for all her help. She's been great.'

'Yes, she has.' I thought back to her visit to Hull when I'd thought Steve had stayed out all night with her. I couldn't believe now that I'd ever considered either of them would do something like that.

While Steve was in Anna's office, I rang Clare Brenner. She said she'd get a payment to me by the end of the month, to cover the rewards for both the paintings which I'd been responsible for recovering.

333

She named an enormous sum of money. Well it was to me, anyway. It went into five figures. I couldn't take it in.

'What about all the other owners? Are you waiting to see if any other paintings are recovered?'

'No. You finished your investigations, and the Dutch police don't think we'll ever see any of the other paintings again. We're going to pay up. If any of them are recovered in the future, then we'll sell them back to the original owners, if they still wish to have them back. Alternatively, they may prefer to spend the money on another painting or something else. That'll be up to them. Thanks for all your work, Rachel, and I'm sorry you got into trouble.'

'It's okay. Thanks very much for the money. I'll put it to good use. I might even buy a small painting of my own, who knows?'

We said our goodbyes, and whilst Dirk drove Steve's car with Steve and his luggage to the hotel, I signed paperwork with Anna, allowing me to travel back through border control, whenever I wanted. I also thanked her again for all she'd done for us. Steve was back in no time as the hotel was close by, and we set off on foot into Amsterdam to find something to eat.

After lunch we strolled leisurely down the quaint streets that I had raced along the previous day. The city was bathed in sun and the air of menace had gone, although the cyclists were still a nuisance. Steve dragged me out of the way and across the road as one approached, then stopped. It took me a minute to realise we were standing outside a jeweller's shop.

'How can you marry someone who can swim thirty yards underwater, but has never mentioned it?'

'Is that a proposal?'

Steve smiled and kissed me.

THE END